Pointe and Shoot

OTHER BOOKS BY ALISON STONE:

Harlequin Love Inspired Suspense:

Critical Diagnosis
Silver Lake Secrets
High-Risk Homecoming

Amish titles from Harlequin Love Inspired Suspense:

Plain Pursuit
Plain Peril
Plain Threats
Plain Protector
Plain Cover-Up

ALISON STONE

Waterfall
PRESS

Published by Waterfall Press, Grand Haven, Michigan

www.brilliancepublishing.com

Amazon, the Amazon logo, and Waterfall Press are trademarks of Amazon.com, Inc., or its affiliates.

ISBN-13: 9781503937666
ISBN-10: 1503937666

Cover design by Michael Rehder

Printed in the United States of America

To Dad with love

ONE

"Point your toes. Extend your leg." Miss Melinda tapped her fingers on the shelf in time with the music. Her smartphone was connected to the stereo system, allowing the pop tune to crank out from each of the four speakers positioned in the corners of the studio. At the start of class, she had clicked the "Do Not Disturb" feature to stop the relentless texts.

Paige Wentworth, her sixteen-year-old student, lifted her shoulders and let them drop in an exasperated sigh as she moved through the choreography.

"Relax. You've got it." *Positive reinforcement. Always give them positive reinforcement.*

Paige dipped back and extended her arm, then swept it gracefully in front of her as the music wound down, her chest heaving from exertion.

Melinda wanted to tell Paige all sorts of encouraging things, like "Dance isn't everything" or "If you don't enjoy dance, find some other activity to do," but she feared the consequences if Paige's mother ever overheard her. To Mrs. Wentworth, dance *was* everything.

And Mrs. Wentworth tended to hover.

Melinda's gaze moved to the wall clock. Three minutes past Paige's paid hour. Melinda really didn't mind; she sometimes felt like she was stealing money from these moms who were so eager to have their daughters be . . . she wasn't really sure what. The next contestant on one of those TV dance shows? On Broadway? *Really?* Or a dance teacher someday? *Where's the glory in that?*

Melinda always thought it was a shame that parents pushed their kids to reach the apex—whatever they defined that to be—without considering all the positive aspects of dance in and of itself: confidence, good posture, and exercise, which was key for this couch-potato generation.

Without waiting to be dismissed, Paige ran to the corner and grabbed her water bottle.

"Nice job this week, Paige." Melinda silenced the music, which had been set on repeat. But she wasn't ready to check her messages. Not yet.

"How's she doing?" Mrs. Wentworth stepped into the studio, a huge smile on her face and an expensive bag on her arm. It always startled Melinda how Paige's mother seemed to appear out of nowhere.

"Great." If Melinda had learned one thing in her short teaching career, it was that parents rarely wanted to hear anything other than "Great." But the only parents she ever opened up to were the ones she trusted not to go all *Mommie Dearest* on her.

Or on their daughters.

Instinctively, Melinda curled her fingers into fists and dug her nails into her palms, remembering how she'd had to bite her tongue last week when Mrs. Wentworth questioned the level of difficulty of her daughter's choreography.

"She needs to push herself to win the competition," Mrs. Wentworth had said in a haughty tone. "Is this routine difficult enough?"

Why did parents with zero dance background feel they had the right to question her? Oh, yes: they paid her. That—in their world—gave them every right. Melinda blinked slowly, feeling her cheeks heat at the memory.

"Would you like to see her progress?" Melinda asked now, struggling to loosen the tight set of her jaw, when all she really wanted to do was usher them out of the studio, lock up, and go home.

Check that. She had plans to meet a few of her friends out. Inwardly she groaned. *Why did I agree to go out with them?* She'd rather go home, decompress, and stream the next episode of that vampire show on Netflix.

"I would *lov*—"

The word *love* died on Mrs. Wentworth's lips as Paige grabbed her mother's arm and pulled her toward the door near the waiting area, an extended foyer in a converted Victorian home just outside of Tranquility's town center. Paige let go of her mother's arm, put on her fleece jacket, then stuffed her feet into tall, fuzzy boots even though it was only early October. Fashion never went out of season, Melinda supposed.

"I'm meeting Cindy and Emma," Paige said. "And I'm already late. Come on, Mom." She stretched out the word *Mom* as if it had two very long syllables. Normally the whining of any student would grate on Melinda's nerves, but she had to chalk one up for Paige tonight—she knew how to work her mom. The girl came by it honestly enough. When her mother wasn't pushing Paige to be on the top of the dance heap, she was pushing her to be one of the popular girls. Cindy and Emma were the pinnacle of popular, and everyone at Tranquility High School knew that. Including Paige's mother.

No way would *Mom* make Paige run through the dance again if it meant keeping Cindy and Emma waiting.

But even Melinda knew Paige wasn't friends with those girls. Though they all danced together, their mothers' competitiveness had rubbed off and forced them to have a falling-out. Or maybe that was last week.

Melinda decided to keep her mouth shut. Nothing good would come from questioning Paige's friendships. The girls needed someone they could confide in. Sometimes that someone was Melinda.

Eight months . . .

Eight months until Melinda graduated from college. Eight months until she moved to New York City. Eight months until she broke her mother's heart. Her mom claimed to support the dreams of her only daughter, but Melinda suspected her mom really wanted her to stay in small-town Tranquility on the shores of Lake Erie, where snow bands threatened to bury residents under seven feet of snow. And drive housebound residents crazy once they'd consumed all the milk, bread, and toilet paper that they'd cleared from the shelves in preparation for the storm.

What her mother didn't say could be gleaned from her tone of voice and posture. Melinda refused to succumb to the guilt, though. She and her mother had always been exceptionally close; it had been only the two of them for so long, until her stepdad came along and adopted her. However, the small window to succeed as a professional dancer would soon slam shut. Of course, New York City held no guarantees. But Melinda had to try.

And it wouldn't hurt to get away from her suffocating ex-boyfriend. Nothing like a few hundred miles' separation to finally convince him she meant it when she said it was over. Even tonight he had constantly texted her, to the point where she stopped answering.

Why can't this guy take a hint the size of a construction sign flashing, "I Don't Want to See You Anymore—Exit Next Right"?

"Tomorrow at three?" Mrs. Wentworth's lilting voice cut into Melinda's rambling thoughts, and she couldn't help but wonder if the woman had asked the question more than once.

"Sure. Three's fine." Melinda had wanted to tell Paige that she didn't need so many private lessons, but that wasn't what a parent like Mrs.

Wentworth wanted to hear. If a person had a checkbook linked to Harrison Wentworth's bank accounts, they could afford to pay for the advantage.

Who was Melinda to argue? Mrs. Wentworth had promised her a bonus if her daughter won the competition in Buffalo in early January. Money Melinda could ill afford to lose.

Money no one else had to know about.

A pang of guilt fisted her stomach. Money that the studio was entitled to—in part, at least. Money the studio could certainly use to do some maintenance on the aging house. Mentally she gave herself a hard shake. She wasn't hurting anybody, and a win would look good for the studio.

And New York City would be all that much closer come January.

If it hadn't been for Melinda's father, she would never have been able to pay for college. She was grateful, but she wanted to do New York City on her own. Mostly, anyway.

The knot between Melinda's shoulder blades began to ease. She loved working with the dancers at Murphy's Dance Academy—most of the time—but the parents were often another story.

Melinda finally checked her phone—*ugh, more messages from Kyle*—as she waited for the Wentworths to pull out of the gravel parking lot. She brought it out of "Do Not Disturb" mode, just in case her friends had to contact her about tonight, then she went into the cozy empty office off the foyer. The studio was generally closed on Friday nights, except for private lessons. Every other day of the week, Miss Natalie, the owner of Murphy's Dance Academy, was in the office—or her daughter, Miss Jayne, was. Miss Natalie was spending less time there of late and Miss Jayne was picking up the slack. Jayne wasn't a dancer herself, but had taken on the day-to-day running of the studio now that her mom was growing forgetful. In doing so, Miss Jayne had given up her dreams of becoming a cop like her dad and older brothers.

Melinda refused to do that. A person shouldn't have to give up their dreams. But deep in her heart, Melinda knew Miss Jayne was doing the right thing. Miss Jayne always did the right thing.

That's why Melinda couldn't delay New York City any longer. If she did, anything could be waiting around the corner: a meniscus tear in the knee, a rotator-cuff injury, or an aging parent who suddenly needed her undivided attention.

A subtle sound pricked the hairs on the back of Melinda's neck. She looked up, expecting Paige or her mother to appear in the doorway claiming they'd forgotten something. When neither did, a ball of fear knotted in her gut.

She should have left when the Wentworths had. This big house made for a wonderful dance studio, but empty, it freaked her out. Too many places for a creeper to hide. She blamed her vivid imagination on all the true-crime shows she liked to watch. And she blamed that addiction on Jayne Murphy.

Sitting at the desk chair, Melinda stuffed her bare feet into her sneakers and fumbled with the laces. She tried to quiet her rioting emotions by rationalizing that the noise could have been anything. The furnace kicking in. The sump pump in the basement. The hundred-year-old house settling.

Had she imagined the footprints in the mud outside her bedroom window last week?

Maybe.

Melinda had mentioned the footprints to Jayne, who suggested that it sounded a lot like an episode of *Forensic Files* that had aired the week before. Melinda had had to search her memory. One episode blended into another, but she suspected Jayne was referring to the episode where the single mom had a neighbor who finagled his way into her home by offering to help with odd jobs. They arrested him after finding an imprint of his size-eight work boot—freakishly small for a man—in the dirt outside her first-floor bedroom window.

When Melinda tried to show Jayne the footprints, they had already disappeared, destroyed by the recent rains. Jayne had offered to have one of her cop brothers stop by, but by then Melinda had begun to think she *had* imagined the whole thing.

So Melinda had gone for the less dramatic solution. She made sure to keep her bedroom window locked and her shade drawn, but she didn't tell her parents. How would they allow her to move to New York City if she was too afraid to sleep in her bedroom in quiet little Tranquility?

Another rustling sound raked cold fingers of unease across her scalp. An overwhelming urge to vacate the studio rolled over her. In an adrenaline-soaked panic, she grabbed her Vera Bradley bag, a generous Christmas gift from Lily—or was it Lila?—and stuffed her hand inside, groping for her car keys. Her fingers brushed against the hard plastic of the key fob.

Thank you, Lord.

Key fob in fist, Melinda darted through the first floor of the Victorian, securing all the doors and windows, turning off lights and straightening chairs. Her mouth grew dry as her eagerness to be done, already, pulsed through her.

Standing in the doorway of the studio that ran the length of the back of the house, Melinda noticed a dark shadow sweep across the smoked glass of the emergency-exit door.

She froze, her hand hovering over the light switch as her pulse clamored loudly in her ears. Thank God she had already closed and locked that door after having cracked it open earlier for fresh air. *I did lock it, didn't I?* She flipped off the lights and pressed herself flat against the wall, trying very hard to be invisible. And trying very hard to convince herself it was an animal or a tree branch, anything other than what her wild imagination had generated: an axe murderer come to hack her body into little pieces.

You're imagining things, just like the footprints.

Melinda pulled her cell phone out of her bag, ignoring the texts from Kyle and texting Jayne instead. That way, if she went missing, they'd know when to start the forty-eight-hour clock. As in, if the police didn't find the kidnapped victim in the first forty-eight hours, they were more likely going to find a body than a traumatized victim.

By the time Melinda reached the front door, she had worked herself up into a frenzy. She stared out into the empty parking lot, wishing she could twitch her nose like Tabitha in those old *Bewitched* episodes and already be locked safely inside her car. Stalling, she glanced down and realized she hadn't actually sent the text to Jayne.

She held her thumb over the button on the bottom of the phone, and all the apps came to life. She reread the text before hitting "Send":

Melinda: Leaving studio. Locking up. See you in am.

Jayne: K.

Jayne's response was immediate. Melinda's boss mustn't have had anything better to do on a Friday night.

She shouldn't talk.

Melinda laughed at herself and reached for the door handle when her phone dinged.

Jayne: Netflix Night? ☺

Melinda: I wish. Meeting Bailey at Burgers and Buns. Wish I could just go home and veg. ☹

Jayne: You'll have fun. <Confetti horn emoji> Drive safe.

Melinda tapped out a quick THX. She then slipped the phone into her bag and held her keys at the ready. She'd often wondered if she could truly gouge someone's eyes out with them. The thought made her shudder as she pushed open the heavy wooden door with its glass inserts at the top. Adrenaline making her dizzy, she spun around and slid the key into the slot, and the deadbolt drove home. She jiggled the door handle, then spun back around and tore down the steps, nearly missing the last one.

With her key fob aimed at her rusty VW Jetta, Melinda sprinted across the parking lot, her bag banging against her hip. She jabbed the "Unlock" button and sucked in a breath when it didn't make the familiar chirping noise.

"Come on," she muttered. Aiming the fob at the door, she stabbed the button repeatedly, finally releasing the locks. *Thank You, God.*

Melinda yanked open the door and threw her bag on the passenger seat. She slammed the door, flipped the locks, and vowed to cut back on caffeine and crime TV.

Melinda pressed the keyless ignition button and the engine hummed to life. "That's my baby." She patted the dash much like she did her beloved Trinket when the fluffy bichon frise remembered to do her business outside. What Melinda wouldn't do just to go home and cuddle up with her on the couch.

A nervous laugh escaped her lips as she jammed the gear into drive. *Scaredy-cat. How are you ever going to survive in New York City?*

The beams of her headlights illuminated the front of the dance studio. She'd miss this place. She had been dancing here since she was three years old. Miss Natalie had been her first teacher.

Climbing up the ladder in the professional world of dance would be difficult, but it'd be worth it. And no matter what happened, at least when she woke up as an old lady someday, she'd know she had given it her all.

Melinda pulled out onto the road and flicked on the wipers against some raindrops. At least it was only rain. In a few short months, this would be snow.

Her phone dinged on the seat next to hers. Her mother's constant warning rang in her ears: *"Text messages can wait. Never use your phone when you're driving."*

Maybe her friends had cancelled. Hope swelled in her chest. *If only.* The thought of soaking in the bathtub with a good book came to mind. Then curling up with Trinket and watching Netflix . . .

Ignoring her mother's rule, Melinda picked up the phone and quickly scanned the message.

```
716-555-2436: Hey. Change in plans! Meet
us @ Henry's Waterfront Cafe.—B
```

Whose phone number is that?

B. *Bailey.* Melinda's friend was forever letting her phone battery run dead. Maybe she borrowed some guy's phone at the bar to send Melinda a quick message. Typical Bailey move. Spacey and flirty.

Melinda groaned. Henry's was all the way in the other direction. Down by the lake. Maybe she could pretend she hadn't seen the message and tell her friends she had gone to the original place, and when they weren't there, she went home.

A very tempting plan.

Melinda turned the wipers on high, pulled alongside the curb, and parked. Needing to vent, she shot off a quick text to Jayne.

```
Melinda: Ugh. Bailey just texted. Girls
night now at Henry's Waterfront Cafe. Hate
last minute changes <crazy face emoji>

Jayne: Go have fun. Be safe.
```

Melinda was tempted to plead sick and bail out for the night. But the group of them had been friends since kindergarten, and they'd know for sure that she was lying.

She turned on her signal and pulled away from the curb.

Eight months. New York City. Huge. Glorious. Anonymous. New York City.

Melinda made a U-turn and headed toward Henry's.

She'd stay for exactly one drink. Her stomach rumbled. Okay, maybe a few hot wings, *then* she'd leave.

By the time Melinda reached Lake Road, the rain was coming down in huge sheets. Even on high, her wipers struggled to keep up. A bead of sweat trickled down her back as she white-knuckled the steering wheel.

Her phone dinged again.

Instinctively, she glanced down and saw the thin line of light from the screen, facedown on the passenger seat. She should have silenced it and put it in her bag like she normally did. Like her mother had taught her to do. But she was secretly hoping she'd receive another text announcing *another* change of plans, like *Cancelled. Go home! Read that book!*

A strange light made Melinda look up. The blinding headlights of an oncoming car sliced across her line of vision. The car was in her lane! She cranked her steering wheel to the right—no left, left, *left*. She should have gone left. She'd forgotten about the curve in the road.

Brake, brake, brake!

Her tires hydroplaned on the wet pavement.

Cold dread pulsed through her veins.

Her car slammed through the guardrail with a horrible screech of metal on metal.

Her old, reliable beater became airborne and landed with a horrendous splash into the lake. Her body slammed back against the car seat, and a searing pain shot up her back into her neck.

No, no, no . . .

Cold water rushed in and licked at her toes. All those crime shows she watched. What was she supposed to do?

Think. Think. *Think.*

The icy water gurgled up to her waist already.

Frantically, she patted the seat next to her for her cell phone. It was gone.

Tears blurred her vision.

Panic crippled her mind.

Dear God, no. Help me.

Melinda unsnapped her seat belt as a lurching motion pulled her car down faster, nose first.

The black of night and murky water consumed her vehicle. She wrenched the door release. It wouldn't budge.

You idiot! She hadn't remembered to buy one of those sharp-tool thingies to smash the window in exactly this situation. She had planned to. Someday. But her someday was here.

Fear seized her brain.

She gulped in a breath from a pocket of air.

The cold water crept up to her neck . . . her chin . . .

Mommy! Mommy! Mommy!

She choked on a mouthful of water.

Trinket would be waiting for her by the back door. *Oh, sweetie . . .*

She wrenched on the door release.

"Come on, come on, come on . . ." A sob ripped from her throat.

The pulse in her head ticked out the final moments of her life. *No!*

Tilting her head as water filled her ears, she stretched . . . stretched . . . searching for precious air.

Water poured into her mouth. Her nose.

Her lungs roared for air.

Eight months. New York City.

Eight months . . .

TWO

*B*zzzz. *Bzzzz. Bzzzz.*
The vibration of Jayne's cell phone set on silent mode crept into her dream without waking her up.

Bzzzz. Bzzzz. Bzzzz.

The angry face of yet another dance mom dissolves into a long black tube that appears to be the attachment on a vacuum cleaner. A younger version of her mother, dressed in a black leotard, with her hair pulled into a severe bun, gets right up into Jayne's face and whispers, "Are you going to answer that?"

Bzzzz. Bzzzz. Bzzzz.

"Mmmm . . ." Jayne tries to pry her lips apart to speak but she can't because, for some strange reason, she has duct tape over her mouth.

Bzzzz. Bzzzz. Bzzzz.

Panic washes over Jayne as she tries to figure out where she is and why she has duct tape over her mouth. Okay, think, *she commands her dreaming self,* you've watched plenty of crime shows. Think! *The only news segment that comes to mind is one that gave detailed instructions on how to free duct-taped hands, not a mouth.* "Hold your arms up over your head and—"

"Stupid, girl. You think you'd make a good cop?" A disembodied voice mocks her. *One of her brothers? All of her brothers? Her subconscious?* "Use *your hands! Use your—"*

The shrill ring of a landline ripped into her dream, and finally, Jayne Murphy startled awake. She bolted upright, and the Kindle she had put down so she could close her eyes for just a minute slid off her chest and thudded to the carpeted floor. The kaleidoscope of funky images from her warped dream vanished, leaving her in the black of night with only narrow slits of moonlight filtering through the partially open louvers.

Brrrinngg . . .

Jayne jumped up from the family-room couch and lunged for the wall phone in the kitchen before it rang again. She didn't want the noise to wake her mother.

I'm twenty-six and I still live at home with my mother.

She squinted at the clock on the stove. *11:11*. She made a quick wish that the call wouldn't be bad news. Yet no good news came at this late hour.

"Hello." Her voice came out raspy, sleepy, slightly panicked.

"Jayne?" The controlled, quiet tremble of the familiar voice she couldn't quite place sent Jayne's nerves on edge.

"Yes?"

Sobbing sounded across the line as if the woman had been holding back until this very moment.

"What's wrong?" Jayne asked, still unsure of who was on the line. The old phone lacked caller ID.

"Melinda. She . . . she was in a car accident." Jayne finally placed the voice: Victoria Green, Melinda's mother. The Greens had lived right behind the Murphys for twenty years, starting back when Victoria was a new widow with an infant daughter. Back then it had just been Miss Victoria and Melinda, but that all changed when David Green welcomed a new wife and daughter some thirteen years ago.

A cold band of dread squeezed Jayne's lungs, making it difficult to breathe. She tucked the phone between her ear and shoulder, grabbed the plaid blanket from the arm of the couch, and draped it around her.

Has something terrible happened to their much-loved daughter?

Jayne's mind scrambled to get her head around what exactly had happened. "Melinda texted me around nine when she left the studio." She had no idea how or why that might be relevant, but she shared the information all the same. Guilt swirled with nauseating fear. Had working late put Melinda in the path of a drunk driver? "Where was the accident?" Jayne hated the high-pitched tone of her voice.

"Her car . . . her car went into the lake."

A throbbing started behind Jayne's eyes. The last-minute text had changed the location of Melinda's girls' night out to Henry's on the waterfront.

"What hospital? I'll meet you there."

Silence crackled over the line.

Jayne's heart beat wildly in her chest.

"Melinda . . . She's . . ."

"Oh, no . . ." Jayne's vision narrowed and tiny dots danced in her eyes. "She's going to be okay, right?"

"Melinda's g-gone." Victoria broke down into loud sobs that could only be described as keening. "My baby's gone. She's gone."

Pressing the phone to her ear, Jayne slowly pulled out a kitchen chair and dropped down into it, tethered to the wall by the stupid coiled landline cord. She really needed to replace this phone with a cordless one, but her mother maintained the current one was perfectly fine.

Perfectly fine. How would anything ever be fine again? A swell of nausea almost had her bolting for the bathroom, but she got ahold of herself.

"What do you need? I can do whatever you need. *Anything.*" For the third time in her young life—and three was certainly not a charm—Jayne felt completely helpless. The only difference? This time she knew what to expect in the days, weeks, months ahead.

The excruciating grief.

The endless questions.

The guilt.

The hollow feeling.

Thirteen months ago, her closest brother, only one year older, had been killed in the line of duty.

Jayne blinked and ignored the tears trailing down her cheeks. "Want me to come over? Is David home?"

"No, it's . . ." Victoria's voice grew more distant, as if she were checking a clock. "It's after eleven. David's traveling, but . . ."

Jayne stood and stretched the cord so she could peer out the window over the sink. From there she could see the police car parked in the Greens' driveway. The Greens had lived there for as long as Jayne could remember. Jayne was only five years older than Melinda, a perfect age back then to keep a young girl company so her single mother could go out for Saturday-night dinner, especially since Jayne's parents were right across the yard. Eventually Victoria had met David Green, and then Melinda once again had two doting parents, especially after David adopted the seven-year-old.

Thank goodness Melinda's mom had someone . . .

Jayne pressed her lips together, fighting to control her emotions.

Poor, sweet Melinda, with a smile that drew everyone to her. She was likable and had a certain quality—a certain stage presence—that you either had or you didn't.

Now she's gone.

"Melinda was supposed to teach . . ." Victoria's voice grew quiet. "She has classes tomorrow."

Jayne gasped. *Oh, no . . .* "You're kind to think of us, but that won't be a priority. Not now."

"It's important to the little girls. Can you find a substitute teacher?"

The little crystal angel tchotchkes her mother had lined up on the windowsill came into focus. Even the holes on the window screen seemed well defined. Jayne blinked rapidly and braced her hands on the sink's edge as she pressed the phone between her ear and shoulder. No one would be taking dance classes on Saturday. Not after their favorite dance teacher, second only to Jayne's own mother, had been killed in a car accident.

Jayne stood and moved toward the base of the phone, anxious to do something. "I'll be right over. You shouldn't be alone." Before her neighbor had a chance to protest, Jayne had hung up the phone, grabbed her hoodie sweatshirt from where it hung by the side door, and threw it on over her PJs. She shoved on her flip-flops and was about to slip out the back door when she remembered her mother sleeping upstairs. Holding her breath, Jayne listened for any creaks or sounds overhead that indicated her mother had gotten out of bed.

Silence, save for her own ragged breathing.

Thank you, Lord.

Jayne said a quick prayer that her mother would stay in bed for now. The last thing Jayne needed was for her mother to wake up and decide to wander. Alzheimer's was a cruel disease. And life wasn't fair and all that.

But Jayne had to have faith that God would spare her any more evidence of it.

At least tonight, anyway.

THREE

Parking three blocks away from Melinda's house is far enough, right? I open the car door and press it closed with a silent click. A rush of adrenaline and an I-can't-believe-I-actually-went-through-with-it vibrates through my body.

I did it.

I did it.

I actually did it.

I ran Melinda off the road. I ran *her* off the road.

I killed her.

Well, I *think* I did.

Doubt twists my gut. I had only planned to run her off the road. Ruin her dancing career. Kill her dreams. Not her.

But maybe it was fate.

An unexpected zing vibrates through my body at the memory of watching Melinda's car plow through the guardrail and into the lake. It was nothing short of spectacular. My view was limited to the rearview mirror. I slowed down only momentarily, because I couldn't risk stopping. Couldn't risk getting caught. But I captured the glorious image of the back end of her car disappearing over the edge.

A secret thrill races through me.

I zip my jacket and flip up my hood despite the fact that the rain has stopped. I walk toward her house, trying to avoid the ring of light from the street lamps dotting the road. Reality is working its tentacles into my brain. Now what?

What have you done?

Unease tries to knot my stomach, but I fight it.

I did what I had to do.

After I caught a documentary on late-night TV of the 1994 Olympic-figure-skater soap opera that was Nancy Kerrigan versus Tonya Harding, an idea blossomed. The sweet, prissy skater dressed in a lacy white number had folded over and clutched her leg, wailing, "Why? Why? Why? Why?" in a cacophony of high-pitched moaning and sobs. A sound that even now scrapes across my brain. But I couldn't be so bold as to approach Melinda with a baseball bat. Not directly. She'd scream before I even got within two feet of her. And to hire someone would be to reveal my plan.

No one could be trusted.

I had to take matters into my own hands.

Prove that I'm more than people give me credit for.

I had to provide the kneecap blow myself. End her dreams. Fulfill my own.

But now I've killed her.

Feverish excitement burrows into my very soul. Who knew I had it in me? Squaring my shoulders, I plod forward. I have to see if she's really dead. I couldn't park by the lake and wait to see if the rescue crews pulled out a live person or the coroner zippered her into a body bag. There would be questions. Lots of questions. I'd be a witness.

No one can know I'm a witness. It would be far too coincidental that I happened to be there. Far more than a witness.

I ran Melinda off the road.

I'm a murderer.

Is she really dead?

Renewed glee races through my body. What a refreshing change from the anger and rage that have been my constant companions.

Melinda's gone.

She'll no longer be a thorn in my side.

Would anyone suspect I had it in me? I'm beginning to understand why adrenaline junkies jump off the sides of cliffs, or race cars at breathtaking speeds, or run people they detest off the side of the road.

It's exhilarating.

"Reach out and take what you want. It's yours for the taking," the self-help guru's raspy voice whispers in my ear. Bud Byrdie made his fortune by encouraging humans to be go-getters. To create the future they imagined. To rid their lives of those who stand in the way. Even I realize Mr. Byrdie meant that metaphorically, but the end result is the same.

Remove the roadblocks. Put your life into high gear.

An image of my father mocking me when he found my first self-help book on my bedside table fills me with rage, as it did that day, back when hormones and high schoolers were the bane of my existence. How was I supposed to succeed if the only man in my life tore me down at every turn? A late-night infomercial had sparked my interest in the words of Bud Byrdie. Everything I needed to succeed was already in me.

What do you think of me now, Father?

I'm only a few houses away and my nerves practically vibrate. The quiet is unsettling. Soon, the news will reveal that a young woman has driven into the lake. Blame it on the weather or texting. Maybe both. If they check Melinda's cell phone, they'll discover that a text came in at that exact moment.

Inattention. That'll make a good headline. *She's not so perfect now, is she?*

That stretch of Lake Road is fairly deserted. Mostly businesses closed for the night. What are the odds someone saw me cut into Melinda's lane, sending her into a panic and over the edge? Unlikely.

And the police will be quick to close the case. Rainy weather, a curve in the road, and driver inattentiveness. A recipe for disaster.

I couldn't have planned it better.

Is she really dead?

I thought she'd drive into a tree. Break a leg. Sustain a head injury. A back injury, maybe. Anything to stall or end her career. Who knew she'd swerve into the lake?

A rustling noise sounds from the nearby bushes and a cold chill slithers up my spine. I can't help but laugh. I'm actually a bit skittish.

Silly, silly, silly.

"Don't let fear stop you from embracing what you want." More self-help mumbo jumbo. But it's not. The constant replaying of the digital recordings has given me the backbone to take action.

Finally.

And action has led to results beyond my wildest dreams.

The sound of tires crunching on gravel sends my heartbeat jack-hammering in my chest. I slink under the shadow of a tree. It's too late to pretend I'm out jogging, so I hold my breath until the car passes. Probably some poor chump who works the midnight shift at the local factory.

After the red taillights disappear, I continue my way toward Melinda's place. A few houses away, I hear a dog barking frantically at the window.

Just great. That's all I need. Some nosy neighbor saying they saw someone fitting my description lurking around the neighborhood.

How would they describe me, anyway?

Or maybe the tired homeowners will suspect their dumb mutt is yapping at a deer or a raccoon, something that *should* be lurking in the quiet neighborhood. Not me.

My curiosity propels me forward. Not far from my destination, I slip behind the nondescript houses. It would be easier to stay in the shadows if I skirt around and cut through the backyards.

My emotions shift from excitement to apprehension.

Courage is action in the face of fear.

One yard away from Melinda's, I stop in my tracks and hold my breath. My lungs are about to explode, but I can't make a sound. Someone is out there. In the yard.

I can sense them.

I've come too far to stop now.

I dip under the neighbor's awning—an awning that will probably come down next week in anticipation of inclement weather. The *drip-drip-drip* from the earlier rain chips away at my good humor.

The dark shadows are a perfect hiding place.

I squint toward the moving form, the muffled shuffling of feet through grass in need of mowing, when recognition dawns. Jayne Murphy is rushing between the yards, her body slumped with grief. I'm conflicted between my hatred for this woman and my glee that she seems defeated.

Of course Jayne would be running to the rescue. Or to console.

Can it be true? Is Melinda dead, or is the way Jayne carries her body indicative of a young woman who's worried about her longtime friend?

Now that I've convinced myself that Melinda's dead, injured isn't permanent enough for my liking. Death will finally end my obsession with her. Allow me to rise and be who I am meant to be.

A phoenix on the eve of my rebirth.

Despite the interloper, curiosity lures me to the backyard of Melinda's house. A long-abandoned play set hunkers in the shadows. I peer around the corner. A police car sits in the driveway and my pulse spikes.

A police car could mean anything. Missing? Injured? Dead?

What do you want? A black van with the word Coroner *splashed across it?* I smile to myself. That would be convenient.

I swat at an annoying insect buzzing around my head. What am I doing here? What do I hope to prove? I can't knock on the door, ask for Melinda, and feign surprise when she's not home.

No sane—no innocent—person would do that at this hour.

No, this was a very, very stupid idea born out of impatience.

Patience has never been my strong suit.

I must get out of here before I'm discovered. I'll have to wait for news of Melinda. Act surprised, distraught, heartbroken when I hear about the horrible accident along with everyone else.

I have to bide my time.

I've been burned before by playing games. I'm not that chump anymore.

I turn around and head back to my car, parked on another street. Staying low, I skulk through the yards.

Because getting caught is never part of the game.

FOUR

Officer Danny Nolan slammed the faucet off and set the glass of cold water on the counter, its contents spilling over the edge. Bracing his hands on the sink, he stared out over a familiar yard. One he had known in happier times. Turning his back to it, he glanced into the living room at a grieving Mrs. Victoria Green, mother of the deceased Melinda Green. He kept repeating those facts over and over in his head, trying to make them seem cold, impersonal, part of the job.

Danny didn't deal well with grief. But that was a cop-out. Who did? It was his job to notify the next of kin, and now it was his job to remain with the woman until such time as he could convince her to identify the body.

The body.

A young woman who hadn't yet graduated from college.

Danny drew in a breath through his nose and wondered what he had done wrong in his life to have landed this assignment. Pausing in the archway to the living room, he braced himself against Mrs. Green's sobs. The gut-wrenching sound immediately took Danny back to another time, another place. A little over a year ago. The family room of the Murphy home, where everyone had gathered after his partner's funeral.

A slow breath hissed between tight lips.

Get a grip.

Patrick Murphy—his lifelong best friend turned partner on the force—had been killed in the line of duty while waiting for his sandwich at a local sub shop. Danny and Patrick had pulled into the gravel parking lot during their lunch break. A game of rock-paper-scissors determined whose turn it was to grab lunch at Ted's Big Subs. Patrick had picked scissors to Danny's rock. Danny's last words to his best friend were "You lose, sucker."

If only he had known.

If only he could turn back time.

"Do you think she was texting?" Mrs. Green asked, her gravelly voice snapping Danny out of the loop that had been relentlessly playing in his head for the past year. A person wasn't likely to forget the day his partner died. Nor was a person likely to gloss over the fact he'd taken a teen's life, even if the punk deserved it.

"It's too early to tell, ma'am," he said.

A horrible groan-sob ripped from her throat. The little dog by her side lifted its head, startled, then settled back in, resting its chin on its master's thigh. "I told her a million times never to text and drive." She pressed her lips into a thin line, then looked up at Danny pointedly. "Arrive alive. Isn't that the campaign?" She held her trembling fingers to her lips, as if trying to quell her rioting emotions. "I should have never let her have a cell phone." As if she had much control over what a twenty-one-year-old adult daughter could or couldn't do.

"I'm very sorry, ma'am."

"Is that my water?" she asked abruptly.

"Yes, sorry." Danny blinked a few times and crossed into the stuffy living room. Mrs. Green took the glass of water with a shaky hand, and he was reluctant to let go for fear the glass would tumble down onto her legs and then onto the pristine white carpet.

"Can I get you anything else?" He placed his hands on his hips before realizing this probably wasn't the most sympathetic gesture, so he dropped his arms to his sides, where they hung like weights.

Once again, he doubted his ability to do this job, an uncertainty that had haunted him since the day he had held Patrick's head and screamed into his shoulder radio, "Officer down, officer down! We need an ambulance here!"

Help hadn't arrived in time, but the news stations had. Danny's life had never been the same.

He ran a hand across his mouth. "How long before your husband gets home?" he asked, determined to focus on the here and now.

"David's secretary tracked him down. He's in Korea on business. He travels a lot. He's a very successful businessman." Her voice had a faraway quality to it, as if she had detached herself from the situation. She absentmindedly stroked the dog's head.

"Is there someone you'd like me to call for you? Someone who can come sit with you?" Someone who could accompany her to identify the body.

First things first.

"Mrs. Green," he repeated, "is there another family member I can call to come sit with you?" Danny lowered himself onto the edge of the couch and studied Mrs. Green's profile until she shifted on the cushion and met his gaze. Confusion creased the corners of her watery blue eyes as if she didn't understand a word he was saying.

The sound of the screen door scraping across the concrete drew his attention. Mrs. Green, deep in a world of grief and hurt, didn't indicate that she'd noticed. Nor did her well-loved pet. *Some watchdog.*

Danny got up, walked toward the sound, and came up short. There in the kitchen stood Jayne Murphy, Patrick's little sister. "Hello?"

As if she'd read his mind, she said, "Victoria called me."

His eyebrow twitched. Earlier, he had given Mrs. Green privacy to make a few calls, but she hadn't mentioned that anyone was coming over.

"Victoria Green," Jayne said with an edge of annoyance, like, *Duh, you know that.* "I live right behind her." He did know that, he just couldn't get his thoughts together upon seeing Jayne. The sight of her had unleashed a fury of feelings that he chose to stuff down. Tough cops were good at hiding feelings.

When Danny didn't say anything, Jayne added, "Melinda works . . . worked . . . for my mom's dance studio. We're good family friends. I used to babysit for her when she was little." All the small ways people's lives overlapped seemed more powerful—more poignant—when a person ceased to exist in this world.

Danny nodded and stepped aside. "Mrs. Green's sitting on the couch in the living room."

Jayne rushed past him, dressed in gray PJ bottoms and an oversized T-shirt, her zip-up sweatshirt fluttering open. The last time he had seen Jayne close up, he was a pallbearer at her brother's funeral. He had also caught sight of her a few times on the local news stations while her brother's death was still ratings-worthy. She had tearfully questioned Danny's incompetent response to the 911 call that a shooter was in the sub shop. How could he explain, without sounding like he was making excuses, that her big brother had entered the sub shop *before* the call went out? That Patrick hadn't rushed to the scene first; he was only in the shop because he wanted a sub that day. That the killer had pulled out his gun *because* her brother was there. A classic case of wrong place, wrong time. And by the time Danny responded to the 911 call from a witness in the shop, the shooter was holding Patrick at gunpoint. As Danny yelled to the young punk to drop his gun, the kid fired. Then Danny fired.

Two dead at the scene.

There was nothing more Danny could have done. That's what the police shrink told him. It didn't matter. None of it did.

Patrick Murphy was dead.

Danny rubbed the back of his neck and turned to watch Jayne on the couch with Melinda's mother. Holding the older woman's hands in her own, she repeated, "I'm so sorry. I'm *so* sorry."

For the first time, the little white dog left Mrs. Green's side, jumping off the couch, curling up under the end table, and placing its head on its front paws as if sensing the tragedy that had befallen its human family.

Danny's gut twisted. Jayne had lost yet another person close to her, and the grief rolling off of her was palpable. As palpable as it had been when her brother had died.

Danny suspected Jayne believed what most of Tranquility had come to conclude: that Danny Nolan had gotten a pass because his father was the chief of police. Maybe it was Danny's guilty conscience that had prohibited him from trying to clear the air in an interview. The news stations would have eaten it up. *Chief's son murders teen. Partner dead.* Instead, Danny had allowed the police department's official statement to speak for itself. He wouldn't permit the TV vultures to capitalize on his best friend's death any more than they already had.

"I can't deal with this. She can't be gone." Mrs. Green's voice shook.

"I know it's hard," Jayne said, studying the carpet in front of her. "When's David expected home?"

A fresh wave of sobbing started. Between the mournful sounds, Danny deciphered a "late tomorrow," a "Korea," and a "Why would this happen to my baby?"

Danny flicked a gaze to the grandfather clock in the corner. He had been there for an hour. He needed Mrs. Green to identify her daughter's body.

"Excuse me."

Jayne looked up at him as if she had forgotten he was there.

"I . . . um . . . Someone needs to identify the body." Clenching his jaw, he hated how he struggled to separate his emotions from his job.

Melinda's mother clutched Jayne's hands as if she were a life raft in the middle of an ocean during a storm. "Could you go with the officer to the morgue? I can't."

Danny drummed his fingers against his thigh. "Ma'am, I think—"

"Please, Jayne, do this for me?"

Jayne pushed to her feet, her hands still bound by Mrs. Green's tight grip. "I'll go with you," she said to the grieving woman, her voice filled with compassion. Jayne Murphy seemed better at this than he had been. Or maybe that was because she had a personal relationship with the victim's mother.

The older woman slumped in the soft cushions of the couch. "I can't. I just can't."

Jayne swallowed hard. An "okay" squeaked out of her throat. "I'll go with . . . the officer. First, let me run home and throw on some clothes." She glanced down, as if for the first time realizing she still had on her PJs. She held up her finger. "Give me a minute."

Jayne stepped outside the hospital, which housed a morgue in its basement, and braced her hands on her thighs and gulped in the fresh air, allowing it to fill her lungs. Behind her, Danny paced outside the automatic door, talking on his cell phone and intermittently setting off the doors.

Open . . . close . . . open . . . close . . .

Jayne ran her hand under her nose. Twice. The smell of disinfectant that lingered must have been created by her imagination, because she had never set foot in the same room as the body.

The body.

No—Melinda. My dear, sweet friend, Melinda.

Jayne had had to identify her dear friend's body via photographs in a small room near the morgue. Yet even with the forced distance, she'd never clear her mind of the images of poor, *poor,* sweet Melinda. The girl's lips had turned blue and her face was ashen. Her beautiful hair was wet and flattened against her head.

Melinda had drowned when her car went into the lake. Jayne squeezed her knees and filled her lungs. What a horrible, horrible way to die.

"You okay?" Danny placed his warm hand on the small of her back.

She straightened, stepped away from his touch, and crossed her arms tightly over her chest. "Could have been worse. I thought I was going to have to be in the same room."

"Photographs are hard enough." The way Danny studied her made her stomach flutter.

"Yeah, but images seem less . . . real, I guess." Inhaling deeply, she smelled wet soil and grass. *Wet soil and grass. Wet soil and grass. Focus on that.*

Danny reached out as if he were going to touch her arm, then suddenly pulled his hand back and dragged it across his face. "This has to be hard for you. I mean with—"

"Patrick?" She resented the way he hemmed and hawed about her brother's death. As if she might have forgotten that she had lost her closest brother, if only Danny was careful enough not to mention his name. Turning her back to him, she dug in her purse for her phone. "I have to call Victoria. Tell her it's Melinda."

"A formality."

She spun back around. "A formality?" Anger bit at the edges of her words. "Her daughter died."

Danny lifted his hands in an apologetic gesture. "I didn't mean . . . It's just . . . in this job, I've had to learn to distance myself. She knows her daughter's gone. You're confirming what she already knows."

"I'm dashing any hopes, however irrational, that her daughter isn't really dead." Jayne remembered that horrible feeling. *No matter what anyone tells you, when you receive catastrophic news, you hope and pray that the person is wrong.* Once Jayne talked to Victoria, all false hope would be shattered.

"Now starts the process of planning the funeral," Danny said.

"One nightmare followed by another." As Jayne strolled over to Danny's patrol car, her mind flashed back to the time she had held her mom's trembling hand while Natalie struggled to remain standing as the mortician—correct that, funeral director—stood stiffly with his hands clasped in front of him and an oily smile plastered on his lips. He could have been selling used cars as easily as caskets in mahogany, cherry, oak, or, for the cost-conscious consumer, pine.

The whole experience had irked Jayne. Picking out a casket had seemed too practical at a time when she'd wanted to curl up in bed and forget the world.

But her mother—her family—needed her, and Jayne always did what was expected of her.

Absentmindedly, Jayne pulled the seat belt across her lap and buckled in. Under other circumstances, she might have played around with all the gadgets that lit up the inside of Danny's patrol car. She might have keyed in a few of her friends' license-plate numbers to see if they had any violations. Fun stuff like that. But not today.

"What you did here tonight was a good thing." Danny's deep voice rolled over her in the dark confines of the car, like aloe to a burn.

"Yeah," Jayne said noncommittally. "I can't stop thinking about what Victoria has ahead of her, and"—she shrugged—"I can't stop thinking about when I had to help my mom plan Patrick's funeral."

As Danny pulled out of the parking lot, he muttered, "I can't imagine."

She shook her head, staring straight ahead at the yellow lines illuminated on the deserted road. The blue lights on the dash read

2:15. Only three hours had passed since she had received that horrible phone call.

Jayne tapped her fingers on the armrest. "The worst part was watching my mom. No parent should outlive their kid." She traced the outline of the automatic window switch. "At the funeral home, my mom looked up at me with those eyes. So confused. Little did we know then that the strong, independent Miss Natalie was beginning to show signs of dementia."

"That's tough."

"Yeah." Jayne tried not to show her annoyance at Danny's one- and two-syllable answers. "You know who had to pick out Patrick's casket? *Me,*" she said without waiting for an answer. "Finn and Sean, my tough-cop brothers, were useless. If they opened their mouths, their stoic expressions might crack. And heaven knew they couldn't show anyone how much they cared." Voice hitching, she turned away from him. The subtle blue glow from Danny's open laptop cast a soft light inside the vehicle, allowing her to see her reflection in the passenger window. She appeared almost ethereal, and her mind snapped back to the ghostly image of her friend's bloodless face in the photographs.

She ran her finger along her bottom lip, trying to conjure up the steely backbone that had kept her moving through the long, dark days following her brother's murder.

Surprisingly, Jayne had become the rock of her family during that time. But was it really surprising? Jayne always did whatever she was supposed to.

"You don't mind, do you, Jayne?"

"Good girl, Jayne."

"Thank you, Jayne." (If she was lucky.)

Even as Jayne listened to herself ramble on in the confines of Danny's dark patrol car, a little voice warned her to shut up already. Maybe it was because she was talking to someone who had known Patrick better than even she had. Someone who had been there when he died.

A familiar ache pressed on her lungs.

"In the end, I had to pick out the casket," Jayne repeated, unable to stop herself. Was she subconsciously punishing Danny for his role in her brother's death? "I picked oak. I figured Patrick"—her voice cracked on her big brother's name—"would have liked it. He once made a coffee table out of oak."

"I remember that table."

Jayne shifted in her seat to face him. "Do you?" She hadn't intended to sound so darned eager, but anyone who remembered a piece of her brother's life would be another person who wouldn't allow him to be forgotten.

"It's in the basement, right?"

She nodded, taking a moment to find her voice. "How do you remember that?"

"One time Patrick and I went out and got drunk. Stupid drunk. We were seniors in high school."

Jayne found herself holding her breath, clinging to each precious word—each precious moment—of what was once her brother's life.

"We got home really late. I didn't dare go to my house, because, you know, *the chief*. So I went to your house and decided to crash in the basement. You guys had a couple of old couches down there."

"Still do," Jayne whispered.

"Well, your idiot brother"—Jayne could hear the smile in Danny's voice—"he decides to sit on a corner of the table."

"The glass top?"

"Exactly." Danny shook his head. "He's lucky we didn't have to rush him to the emergency room to have glass removed from his *but-tocks*." He pronounced *buttocks* in the silly way she and Patrick had as kids, enunciating each syllable. *But-tocks, but-tocks, but-tocks.* Jayne smiled at the memory. Their mother used to yell at them to stop, with empty threats of a bar of soap in the mouth.

"The glass broke cleanly and he landed on the concrete without further injury," Danny continued. "The next morning—when we were sober—we put the glass in the garbage and no one knew any better."

Jayne covered her mouth. "That's what happened to the glass." A giggle erupted from her lips as she imagined her brother's surprised reaction when his makeshift seat broke out from under him, knocking his drunk butt on the floor. Served him right, she supposed.

"Thanks for sharing that story," Jayne whispered, trying not to break down into a blubbering fool. She cleared her throat before she continued. "My family doesn't talk about Patrick too much. And when we do, it's always with such reverence." *Patrick would hate it.* "I miss talking about the way Patrick really was. The smart yet goofy guy, who could build a beautiful coffee table, then forget the glass is too fragile to support his weight." She paused, reflecting. "Miss Natalie talks about him more now. I think because she forgets he's gone." She sighed heavily. A little part of her was mad she had let down her guard in front of Danny.

"I miss him, too," Danny said, not taking his eyes from the road.

A long silence stretched between them. After a while, he said, rather glumly, "We're almost back in your neighborhood. You ready to face Mrs. Green?"

Jayne cut him a quick glance but didn't say anything. She didn't have to. She'd never be ready.

FIVE

Parked alongside the curb, Danny rested his forearm on the steering wheel and stared up through the windshield, no doubt taking in the gorgeous night sky after the storm clouds had parted. Jayne couldn't help but admire his strong profile. When had her brother's childhood best friend grown into such a handsome man? Her cheeks flushed and she glanced away for fear of getting caught staring. She was *not* up for that humiliation. Not after everything else.

Without facing her, Danny asked, "Do you need a few more minutes before we talk to Mrs. Green?"

No amount of time would make this any easier. The chirp of her cell phone startled her. She fumbled around in her purse, wondering why her phone always found its way to the very bottom. Her blood ran cold when she noticed the caller ID.

"It's her."

The phone rang again.

"What should I say?" Panic rendered her unable to think clearly.

"Just say hello. The rest will come."

Jayne met Danny's eyes, then glanced down at her phone. Her clumsy finger slid across the "Accept" button. *Twice* before she was successful. Then she clicked the speakerphone icon.

"Hello." Jayne swallowed hard, feeling the time stretching yet also slipping through her fingers.

"My Melinda's really gone, isn't she?" Victoria Green's surprisingly strong voice filled the inside of the vehicle.

"I'm almost at your house. I'll talk to you in person." She avoided Danny's eyes for fear she'd lose it.

"Tell me now," Victoria demanded. "I can't bear it another minute."

Jayne glanced up at the roof of the car and said a silent prayer. *Dear Lord, please provide the right words of comfort for this woman.* Then the words poured out in a rush. "Yes, I'm sorry. Melinda's gone."

A strangled sob sounded over the phone. "She's with Jesus. She's with Jesus."

A prickly heat washed over Jayne. She remembered how much she had relied on her faith when her brother was killed, but had she *really* been faithful? Jayne had gone through some very dark days where she questioned everything. But that was part of the grieving process, right?

"I'm on my way over," Jayne whispered, uncertain of everything.

Victoria's sobs grew louder, followed by a muffled rustling in the background.

"Jayne?" A different voice came across the line.

"Yes?" Jayne frowned at Danny as she tried to place the voice.

"It's Carol Anne," Melinda's stepsister said. She and Jayne had graduated the same year from Tranquility High School.

"Oh, Carol Anne, I'm so sorry. I'll be right there, okay?"

"You've already done so much. You must be tired."

"No, don't worry about me. Can I bring you anything?" The desire was strong to do something—anything—to comfort the grieving.

"I'm afraid we need time." Carol Anne sounded oddly composed, but Jayne understood that. Through her own family tragedies, Jayne had found a strength she didn't know she had. "I'm here for Vicky now. Perhaps we'll see you later this afternoon. After you've had some time to rest."

"Oh, Carol Anne, are you sure I can't do anything for you?"

"We'll be fine."

"Okay . . . You know where to find me if you need anything. *Anything.*" Wasn't that the most cliché thing to say to someone at a time like this? But what else was she supposed to say?

Jayne pinched the bridge of her nose. "I'm really sorry."

"Thank you."

"Night." Jayne tapped the screen of the phone and turned to Danny. "I guess they don't need me." Jayne suddenly realized that she didn't want to go home to a quiet house. Her mother tended to sleep in to nine or ten o'clock, and the idea of the long hours stretching ahead of her filled her with loneliness. Jayne crossed her arms over her seat belt, unable to quell the quiet trembling.

"Are you okay?" Danny asked.

"No. You?" She hated the edge to her voice, but she couldn't help herself.

"I didn't . . ."

Jayne waved him off, suddenly feeling silly. Embarrassed. "You don't owe me an apology. I shouldn't have snapped."

"You lost a good friend."

"It hasn't sunk in. It won't until Melinda's not at dance class." Her brain started to hurt as she considered all the practical things that had to be done in light of the tragedy. "I'm going to have to e-mail all the students at the dance studio. Cancel her classes." She bit her lower lip. "How am I supposed to handle this? I can't very well send news like this through an e-mail blast, can I?" Bending forward, she dragged a hand through her hair, then sat up straight again. "Is the accident already on the news?"

"The accident might be, but the identity of the victim won't be released until the family has had time to notify other relatives and close friends."

"Okay," she said, running that over in her mind.

"Why don't you e-mail all her students and their parents that you're having an impromptu meeting. What time is the first class?"

"Ten a.m."

"Make it for then. I'll go with you to answer any questions. Hopefully news won't have leaked before then."

"You'd do that for me?"

Danny shrugged, and a smile transformed his handsome face. "Why not?" The warmth and sincerity in his voice touched her heart. She'd missed him, even if she'd always had to compete with him for Patrick's attention when they'd been kids. Danny was like the brother she already had.

Once, Patrick had agreed to play Monopoly with her. Jayne had run to the front closet, climbed on the step stool, and grabbed the game box from the top shelf. The moment she had finished setting up the bank and selected their game pieces—Patrick was always the race car, and that day Jayne had selected the iron—her big brother announced that he was going to ride bikes around the neighborhood with Danny. And out her brother ran, without so much as a glance at his sister sitting at the dining-room table with no one to play with.

The memory made her feel both nostalgic and pathetic.

Jayne traced the stitching on the center console. "You're really nicer to me than you should be," she whispered, "everything considered."

The smile slid from his face. Danny checked the traffic and pulled away from the curb, apparently tired of the conversation.

"How's your mom?"

Following Danny's lead, she let it drop. "In a way, her dementia has been a blessing. She doesn't always remember Patrick's gone." Turning away from him, she studied the homes of her sleeping neighbors.

Soon, the tragic death of one of their own would be the topic over the backyard fences. And for others, it would be the subject of their latest Facebook posts.

How tragic.

So sorry.

{{{Hugs}}}

And for the more spiritually minded: *Thoughts and prayers. <Praying hands emoji>*

Then, at the slightest suggestion that Melinda may have been using her phone, the posts would digress into:

Kids today need to pay attention to the road.

Followed by:

Hey, let's be respectful. The family might be reading these comments.

To which someone would reply:

I doubt the family is on Facebook right now.

Jayne closed her eyes, trying to rein in her spiraling emotions.

"Miss Natalie has gotten worse? I hadn't realized."

"It's pretty much progressing like the doctors told us it would." Jayne smoothed a hand across her wet cheek. "Sometimes we sit back and talk about Patrick. My mom's able to do that without the reserve so many people have when they've lost someone. So, hey," Jayne said with forced cheeriness, "there's that. I try to look on the bright side."

Danny made a sound with his lips that she couldn't decipher. The car slowed and he flipped on his directional to turn into her driveway.

Jayne glanced toward her house, then at Danny. "Will you take me to the scene of the accident? I won't be able to sleep if I go home now."

He tightened his grip on the steering wheel. "I'm not sure that's a good idea."

"Oh wait, you've been working way past the end of your shift. I'm sorry. I shouldn't have asked." She reached for the door release on his patrol car, and the dome light popped on.

Danny sighed and his shoulders sagged. "I will, but do *not* tell your brothers."

"Why not?" She raised a skeptical eyebrow and pulled the door closed again, plunging them back into darkness save for the lights on the dash.

"Oh, don't give me that. You know what I mean. All your brothers are super protective of you. They'll want to know why I had you out there."

Jayne did know. All too well.

Despite that, Danny did as she requested. When he turned onto Lake Road, she swore she could hear each beat of her heart as if it were amplified on one of those ultrasound things, like when she'd taken her pregnant sister-in-law to the doctor's. That had been such a happy time.

Stop thinking so much.

Pushing against the seat belt, Jayne needed to get out. Get active. Burn some of this stress. "Are we almost there?"

"Yeah, right here." Danny pointed to a narrow berm along a curve. The gravel crunched under the tires as he pulled up. The tail of the caution tape tied to the guardrail flapped in the wind.

A subtle buzz started in Jayne's head. Without waiting for Danny, she pushed open the door and climbed out. Beyond the jagged edge and twisted metal of the guardrail, the pull of the water was magnetic. Leaning forward, she stared at the boulders below, heavily shadowed under the distant streetlamps. A shudder coursed down her spine as a vivid image of Melinda being swallowed by the frigid water overwhelmed her. Clamping her hands over her mouth, she swallowed a sob.

She heard Danny approach from behind, muttering something about getting back into the car. "Be careful." He touched her arm.

"I will." Jayne held her jacket tight against her and swayed as the world seemed to close in around her. A stiff breeze cooled her warm cheeks.

Jayne looked up at Danny, a muscle working in his square jaw. "It was raining," he said. "And the curve here . . ."

She swallowed hard, trying not to think of the panic that must have been surging through Melinda when her car plunged into the lake below.

"The traffic investigator already took measurements. She skidded but couldn't stop before the guardrail."

"Will they request her phone records to see if she was texting?" Jayne asked, her voice barely above a whisper. Her throat ached with unfathomable grief.

"Unless there's evidence of foul play, there won't be a criminal investigation." He cleared his throat. "The traffic investigator has already been out here. With the weather and the curve of the road, there's no reason not to rule it an accident." He touched her arm and encouraged her to take a step back. "Her vehicle has already been recovered. There's no sign of contact with another vehicle."

"That was quick," she whispered. "Is that who you were talking to outside the morgue? The traffic investigator?"

"I got the report through the chief." He sighed heavily. "I'm sorry, Jayne. I know this is hard."

"Did they recover her phone?"

"No. If it's not at the bottom of the lake, they might eventually recover it from her vehicle, but it's not going to be worth much. The phone's probably destroyed."

"So, we may never know if she was texting?" Holding her arms close to her sides, Jayne gripped her elbows.

"Does it matter?"

Danny was right. It wouldn't bring her back. But Jayne wasn't a fan of unanswered questions.

Had a quick look cost Melinda her life?

Jayne drew in a deep breath through her nose. *One stupid decision.*

She hated that this could be Melinda's legacy. Mothers and fathers who didn't even know her would use her as a cautionary tale.

"Don't be like Miss Melinda. She glanced down for a second and drowned in the lake. Don't let that happen to you. It only takes one second of inattentiveness."

Inexplicably, anger bubbled in her gut. Anger regarding Melinda's death. Anger for the unfairness of it all. One. Stupid. Mistake.

"So that's it? She missed the curve and now she's dead?"

Compassion radiated from Danny's brown eyes. "I know this is very hard on you," he said once more. "You went through the police academy. If you were investigating this accident, what would you do?"

"Fat lot of good the academy did me." Jayne ran a shaky hand across her forehead.

"But if you were a cop, what would you do?"

Jayne noticed an elderly man sitting across the street on a shadowed porch illuminated by a lonely lamp. "I'd look for witnesses."

Cursing under his breath, Danny chased after Jayne as she strode across the street, nearly getting herself in his pile of accidents-to-investigate folders. And it wouldn't have been pretty. Car-pedestrian accidents never were.

Unlike Jayne, Danny glanced both ways, making sure the traffic was clear before hustling to catch up to her. Her long red hair was pulled back in a ponytail and her hips swayed in her jeans. He couldn't believe how much Jayne had changed from her awkward-teenager years.

Now wasn't the time to think about that. Her brother would have punched him in the throat just for venturing in that territory. He smiled at the memory of Patrick once noticing Danny check out his little sister. "Off-limits, man. Off-limits."

"What's so funny?" Jayne must have caught him smiling.

"Something your brother once said." Man, it felt good to think of Patrick and smile in the same moment. Danny realized he'd done that a couple of times now, all with Jayne.

She slowed and tilted her head in curiosity. "What did he say about me?" A light danced in her eyes.

"Told me you'd make a fine cop some day."

Jayne tucked a wayward strand of hair behind her ear, and her eyes immediately reddened.

Oh, man, why did I have to go there?

"I didn't mean to upset you," he said.

"Funny thing about when someone dies. No one wants to talk about him for fear that they'll upset me. But not a day, an hour, a minute goes by that I don't think of my brother. So your words didn't suddenly make me sad. I'll always be sad about missing my brother. Your comment just brought a nice memory to the surface and"—she shrugged—"sometimes those memories come with tears. But it would be a shame if we stopped talking about him, right?" She tapped his arm. "Come on." With renewed determination, she strode up the driveway.

Danny stared after Jayne in awe. He'd been avoiding her entire family. For obvious reasons.

Maybe he had been going about this all wrong.

Maybe she no longer blamed him for her brother's death. Had she had a change of heart?

What does it really matter?

Regardless of what anyone else thought, Danny blamed himself. He always would.

All the news coverage—*the first police officer killed in the line of duty in Tranquility, New York, in twenty-five years*—had done nothing to ease his conscience. All the armchair sleuths had their own theories as to what had happened that dark day . . .

A rumbling semi drove past and turned into a nearby industrial park. Danny snapped out of it and called to Jayne when she was halfway up the driveway. She slowed and turned around.

"The chief has already spoken to this gentleman. Said he didn't see anything out of the ordinary. Besides, it's the middle of the night."

"We're here. I saw a light and a person on the porch. What can it hurt to talk to him again?" With her hands in her jacket pockets, she jogged the last little bit toward the door. Danny ran a hand across the back of his neck. He had brought Jayne out here because she had asked, but he hadn't expected her to go all Richard Castle on him. He hustled to catch up.

An elderly man stepped out onto the porch stoop from an adjacent sunroom. He must have seen them approaching. The man gripped the metal railing and carefully navigated the crumbling cement steps. The house was probably seventy years old and one of the last remaining residences now on a street dotted with businesses and light industry.

Danny held out his hand, and the elderly gentleman gave him a surprisingly firm grip in greeting. "Hello, I'm Officer Nolan."

"Ah . . ." The elderly man lifted his chin to study him through his bifocals. "You any relation to Chief Nolan who was out here earlier?" Deep breaths punctuated his words as if descending the steps had exerted him.

"My father."

"Ah . . ." Something else, a trace of recognition, seemed to flit in the depths of his eyes. He opened his mouth to say something, but Danny jumped in before the man had a chance. It wasn't unusual for people to recognize him from the news and comment on the unfortunate death of his partner.

"I didn't catch your name, sir."

"George King. Lived out here since I got married. All alone now. Lived here for fifty years. My kids are always trying to get me to move into an apartment." He held out a shaky hand, palm up. "But why would I want to move away from this?"

Danny turned and stared over the water, mostly dark now, but the view in the light of day must have been worth a lot. Mr. King did have a nice setup there, despite the generic commercial buildings that had popped up around his small Craftsman-style home.

"Did they find the other car?" Mr. King asked between ragged breaths.

"The other car?" Danny jerked his head back, then immediately reined in his surprise. His father hadn't said anything about another car. As far as he knew, the report made no mention of that.

"I told Chief Nolan that I saw another car braking right after I heard the sound of metal crunching metal." The older man winced. "Nothing on the TV worth watching much, so I come out to the sun patio here and read. I use it through the year until winter comes. I'm out here a lot, considering I don't sleep much." He glanced down at his watch, then gestured to the glass enclosure off the front of the porch. "Anyway, I'm into a new novel. The one that's on the bestseller list." He tapped the pads of his fingers together. "You know the one I'm talking about?"

"No, sir," Danny answered. A lot of the people he came across in his line of work were lonely. Wanted to chat. Maybe that was why the chief hadn't mentioned all the details of his conversation with this gentleman. "I haven't read much fiction since school."

Jayne grumbled next to him.

"Can you describe the car?" Danny surveyed the street from his current vantage point.

The older gentleman twisted his lips. "Not so much. The car slowed right after the loud noise, then went about his business. Seems mighty cold if you ask me."

"The car was headed east?"

"Yes, beyond the curve." He pointed in that direction.

"And by all accounts, the victim's car was headed west. The car you witnessed slowing down was already beyond the point where the victim's car entered the water." Danny squinted toward the streetlights lining the road.

"Her name was Melinda Green," Jayne said through gritted teeth.

Danny nodded, acknowledging her. "The other car may not have seen what happened. Might have tapped his brakes for any number of reasons. Maybe he heard the noise. Maybe it had to do with the weather. It was raining hard when the call came in." Danny realized he probably shouldn't have been running through all the scenarios out loud, but perhaps he wanted the elderly gentleman to come to the same conclusion the chief had. Or else why hadn't his father mentioned the car to him? Or maybe he hadn't yet had an opportunity.

"I don't know," Mr. King said, rubbing his hand over the scruffy white whiskers on his jaw. "The noise was . . ."

"Did the chief say he was going to follow up on this car?" Jayne asked, shifting her feet.

In the brightness of her eyes, Danny could see her brain churning out all sorts of nefarious reasons for Melinda's accident.

Just like she had done after Patrick died.

Danny pulled out his notepad and pen, determined to focus on the case at hand. "Do you have a description of the car that slowed down, Mr. King?"

"Can't say that I do. Four-door maybe. A sedan, for sure. Not a truck or anything."

"You saw the other car go through the guardrail?" Jayne asked.

"The noise had me look up from my book. The car was already through the guardrail. Saw the taillights in the water. I called 911." He shook his head. "Thought maybe they'd get there in time to save them." He raised his eyebrows. "Anyone survive? No one seemed to know earlier."

"Afraid not," Danny said.

Mr. King shook his head in disbelief. "Aw, too bad." His gray brows arched over bright-blue eyes. "A kid?"

Danny tipped his head, as if to say, *Sort of.* He frowned. "College student."

The elderly man shook his head again and made a *tsk* noise. "Shame."

Danny slid his notepad back into his breast pocket, then he dug a business card out of his wallet. "If you think of anything else, call me."

The old man seemed pleased. "Hmm . . . Every time I call about the late-night deliveries at the business a few doors down, the police seem annoyed. The trucks are loud. They beep to enter the property and then again when they leave." He held his open palm toward the sunroom. "No wonder I'm up all night reading."

"Sorry about that," Danny said. "If you remember anything about the accident, anything that strikes you later, let me know."

The old man slipped the business card into his trouser pocket and jangled his change. "Will do."

Mr. King smiled at Jayne. "I don't think we've met before." Jayne held up her hands apologetically. "I'm not a police officer. My friend was killed in the car accident." Her voice hitched on the word *killed.*

"That's a shame," he repeated. "Really thought the police would get here in time to save her." A faraway look descended into his eyes as if he were replaying the horrible scene. "Afraid I wouldn't have been any help, myself. Can barely make it down to my mailbox on a good day."

Jayne touched his arm. "You called the police. That was important. Because of you, she at least had a chance."

Mr. King ran a hand over his mouth. "Yeah, well . . . Sorry to hear your friend didn't make it."

"You have my number if you think of anything." The long night had drained Danny of any patience, and his emotions hovered close to the surface.

The older man jingled his change in his front pants pocket again. "I do." Mr. King seemed somewhat pleased with himself.

When Danny and Jayne reached his car, she said, "Do you think there's anything to this other car?"

He opened the car door for her. "Get in."

A spark of anger flitted in Jayne's eyes as if she didn't like to be dismissed. He strode around to his side of the patrol car and climbed in. "I'll talk to the chief. Rule anything out. But don't—"

"Start coming up with conspiracy theories?"

Danny gave her a wry grin, then started up his vehicle.

"I don't do that anymore." The defensive edge to her tone was unmistakable. "I learned my lesson after the flower-delivery guy."

"I'm sure you did." Danny rolled his eyes at the memory. "That was classic."

Once, in elementary school, she had called the police on a white van parked in her neighborhood. Despite the 1-800 number advertising flowers plastered on the side of the truck, Jayne was convinced the driver was trolling for young girls. Three squad cars came into the neighborhood, and the elderly deliveryman, who'd happened to stop for lunch at his daughter's house, didn't know what hit him. Danny and Patrick had had a good laugh over that one.

"You guys egged me on."

"That's your side of the story."

Jayne let out a long sigh. "Thanks for bringing me here. I needed to see this spot for myself."

"Ready to go home?"

"Yeah." She sounded weary. "I need to check on my mom. Catch a couple hours' sleep. Then get to the studio."

"Okay. How much time do you need to get ready? I'll drop off the patrol car, get a little rest, then pick you up." Despite the gritty feel of his contacts, he wasn't going to have Jayne face the young dancers alone.

"You don't have to. You must be tired."

"I don't mind." Being around Jayne had reminded him of hanging around Patrick, and he didn't want that feeling to end. Not yet.

As they neared her street, Jayne bowed her head and scratched her eyebrow. "Don't let it out of the bag to my girls that you don't read books. I'm trying to stress the importance of dance *and* academics." The playful tone of her voice lifted his mood. He had suspected she wasn't going to let him live down his slip back there, when Mr. King asked him about the bestselling novel.

"I don't have time to read." *This might be fun.*

"You don't have time to read?" Jayne rolled her eyes dramatically. "We all have the same twenty-four hours, buddy."

"Whatever." He turned up her driveway, parked, and reached for the door handle.

Jayne held out her hand to stop him. "I can see myself in." She unbelted herself and climbed out. Pausing, she spun back around and leaned in through the open passenger door. "I don't know how I would have gotten through this night without you."

His heart constricted, and he wasn't sure what she'd want him to say. So he said nothing.

"Thank you," she said, her voice barely above a whisper. With a sad smile, she slammed the door shut. She jogged toward the side door and disappeared without so much as a wave.

SIX

"**W**hy is *he* here?" Jayne's mother glanced suspiciously over at Danny as they negotiated the front steps of Murphy's Dance Academy.

"Danny's going to help me with something this morning." Jayne released her mother's elbow and unlocked the front door of the Victorian home. She pushed open the heavy oak door, allowing Miss Natalie—*everyone* called her mother Miss Natalie, including her family—to enter the studio. With Danny's help, Jayne had informed her mom of the horrible news of Melinda's death. She took it as expected, but by the time she had changed into her leotard and flowing skirt and wrapped her long hair into a tight bun, Miss Natalie acted as if this were any other day.

One of the only benefits of dementia.

Jayne had sent out an e-mail blast to the dance community to meet at the studio at ten. She had left several voice mails for Miss Quinn, another dance teacher, to call as soon as possible. The last thing she wanted was for her to learn of Melinda's death on the news.

Miss Natalie set her purple tote on the corner chair in the office, then changed from her outdoor shoes into her well-worn jazz shoes.

Dementia had slowly eroded her short-term memory, but two things—dance and her faith—had been so deeply ingrained that she still remembered she had to teach dance class on Saturday mornings plus a couple of evenings, and she never forgot the prayers learned in childhood. However, it was hit or miss if she remembered which day was Saturday, so more days than not, Jayne's mother awoke and dressed in her leotard and wound her hair in a meticulous bun.

"Danny . . ." Her mother seemed to notice Danny for the first time (again) when she glanced toward the doorway of the office. Her face grew bright. "Danny. Danny Nolan?"

"Yes, ma'am," he said. "How are you?"

"Never been better." A slow smile tipped the corners of Miss Natalie's mouth. Recognition lit her eyes as she pointed at him with enthusiasm. "You're friends with my Patrick."

Jayne cut him a cautionary gaze. *Don't mention Patrick's death. She doesn't always remember.* She prayed her words reached him telepathically.

"Yes, I am."

Danny's face flushed a deep red. Suddenly, a ribbon of shame wound its way around Jayne's lungs and made it difficult to breathe. She had been so hurt by Patrick's death, she had lashed out and intentionally hurt Danny in turn. He had brushed off her attempts at an apology earlier that morning, but she owed him more than mere words.

Miss Natalie reached out and patted Danny's cheek. "My, you've grown. Why don't you come around anymore? I'm sure Patrick would love to see you." At the mention of her youngest son's name, her shoulders rounded and she seemed to turn in to herself. An emotion Jayne couldn't quite pinpoint flickered across her mother's face. "I haven't seen Patrick in a long time, have I?" She clutched the fabric of her skirt around her thighs. "Is he okay? I'm worried about him. All your brothers wanted to be just like your dad. Had me worried from the day each of them were born. But your father assured me there was no better place to be a police officer than in Tranquility, New York. He was always so proud of his hometown."

Jayne wanted to jump in. Save Danny from having to answer her mother's confused questions. Emotion grew thick in Jayne's throat. *Dear Lord, please help me say the right thing.*

What had the counselors told her when her mom was first diagnosed? *"Don't correct. Don't scold. Be patient . . ."*

So many things Natalie struggled to do each day. Jayne loved her mom dearly, but on a day like today, she sorely needed the mom she used to have. The fiercely strong, intelligent, independent woman who would know what to do.

"Everything's okay, Mom." The lie tasted bitter on her tongue, yet she had faith that Patrick was in heaven and they'd all be reunited one day. He *was* okay. More than okay. But Jayne's heart hurt. For the brother who would never grow old. For her mother's confusion and longing to see her son. And for herself. She missed her big brother.

Leaning over, Jayne gave her mother a hug. The back of her throat ached. "We better get ready for the day, okay? The dancers will be here soon."

Her mother stood with a regal air and smiled. If there was one place where her mother was almost her old self, it was at her dance studio. For this reason, Jayne worked hard to keep it running smoothly. Jayne couldn't lose her mom, too, after losing her dad at age fifteen and her brother last year.

She forced herself to return her mother's smile.

Danny gave her an encouraging nod. Smiling, she flicked her fingers in a quick wave. *Thank God he's here with me.* In less than ten minutes, she had to face thirty-five dancers who were about to learn that their beloved Miss Melinda had died in a car accident.

Yet another horrific loss.

Keeping the floor-to-ceiling mirror at her back, Jayne stood in front of Studio A, the classroom that had once been a sitting room with an adjacent dining room. Jayne didn't want to see her own reflection as she struggled to keep it together. There was something to be said for the body's natural response of feeling numb after shocking news.

Before she'd left the office, she had tried Miss Quinn's number one more time with no luck. Once her dancers had the news, there'd be no keeping it under wraps.

"Have a seat on the floor," Jayne repeated as each dancer arrived, mostly with their mothers, but an occasional father strolled in looking like he'd rather be doing yard cleanup, office work—*anything* else. Jayne smiled politely when parents approached her, assuring them she'd fill them in as soon as everyone was here and asking them to please be patient.

The dancers cozied up with their closest friends and scattered in groups across the floor, while their parents chatted quietly among themselves around the perimeter of the room.

Jayne studied their faces, wishing she didn't have to share her knowledge. Soon, the fathers' primary concern would be comforting their daughters and finding a way to escape. Whereas the mothers would press Jayne for every last detail, where few were available. The wives who had sent their husbands on this Saturday-morning errand would regret it, because they'd have no answers to their burning questions. Questions *they* would have asked. Questions that would never cross their husbands' minds.

"Was Melinda drinking?"

"What was she doing on Lake Road?"

And, of course, *"Who's going to teach her dance classes now?"*

"I'll start when everyone gets here." She shot Danny an it-shouldn't-be-too-much-longer smile, praying that Miss Quinn would arrive soon.

Jayne crossed the room to the window and adjusted the horizontal shade. It didn't need adjusting, but she couldn't stand there anymore under the intense scrutiny of the dancers and their parents.

She also couldn't stop thinking about the bit of information Mr. King had given them about seeing another car passing at the same time Melinda had gone through the guardrail.

Was there something more to this than an accident?

She was about to step away from the window when she saw Miss Quinn hopping out of the passenger side of a car she didn't recognize. *Thank goodness.* Now she could inform the entire dance community at once.

Jayne turned around and smiled tightly, wishing she could freeze this moment. The *before*. Miss Natalie worked the room, greeting "her girls" and chatting with their parents.

The girls were a blessing to Jayne's mother. They understood that she was getting "forgetful," and, since most of them regarded her as a grandmother figure, they treated her as such, with love and respect.

The parents valued Miss Natalie's reputation—and with that, the reputation of Murphy's Dance Academy. There was a certain pride when you walked into the dressing rooms of a dance-competition venue wearing a purple-and-white Murphy's Dance Academy jacket. Automatically, other dancers knew you were being trained at one of the top studios in all of Western New York. And because of that, the dance families respectfully kept Miss Natalie's "forgetfulness" under wraps. For now, anyway.

And now Jayne had another prayer to add to her bedtime routine, that the studio could maintain its reputation after losing a bright star like Melinda.

Hard, icy dread pooled in her gut. How could she be so cold as to worry about the dance studio when her good friend had lost her life?

Miss Quinn appeared in the doorway, looking frantic and disheveled. Upon making eye contact with Jayne, she crossed the room to her. "What is it?" Her tone was breathy and panicked.

Pulling Miss Quinn into a fierce embrace, she whispered into her ear, "I'm sorry I couldn't reach you earlier. I have bad news . . . *really* bad news."

Quinn pulled back, horror ablaze in her eyes. "What is it?"

Jayne blinked slowly a few times and grabbed Quinn's hand and squeezed. The din of chattering girls grew louder. She glanced at Danny, then the clock, figuring it would be disrespectful to everyone if she didn't start shortly. Just then, Mrs. Smythe breezed into the room with her daughter, Emma, and made a direct line for Jayne, a determined look on her face. Emma joined her friends seated on the floor. The daughter cupped her hand to her mouth and whispered in Cindy's ear while sneaking furtive glances at Jayne.

They knew. *But how?*

"Is it true?" Mrs. Smythe asked, her tone suggesting she was about to spread a juicy bit of gossip. Rage swept in and overtook Jayne's grief.

"Is *what* true?" Quinn's lower lip quivered.

"I'd like to talk to everyone as a group." Jayne held out her hand to Mrs. Smythe. "Please join the other parents."

Dark anger raced through Mrs. Smythe's eyes, and she sniffed her indignation and tugged on her form-fitting cropped jacket as she strode over to the other moms in high heels, her tight jeans a testament to the hours she obviously spent at the gym.

"Girls, girls . . ." Jayne raised her voice, but still the dancers and their parents kept talking. "It'll be okay, Quinn," she whispered, still holding her trembling hand.

Danny whistled and the girls went silent. A few of them, eyes trained on Danny, each leaned toward their closest friend and whispered. Jayne cast a quick glance at Danny to see him through the eyes of the preteens through high-school seniors. Nice-fitting jeans. Golf shirt stretched across a broad chest. Yeah, she understood the giggles and whispers. Dangers of working with teenagers. However, Jayne was about to burst their teenage dreams and give them a big dose of stark reality.

With all the girls staring at her, Jayne slid her arm behind Quinn's back and pulled her close. Jayne made eye contact with Paige and smiled. The poor girl sat apart from her friends and watched Jayne with a certain knowing.

Silence hummed in Jayne's ears and the room suddenly felt stuffy. "Hooo . . . it's hot in here."

"What's going on?" Mrs. Smythe stood with her hip cocked and her smartphone in the palm of her hand, as if Jayne was interrupting something important. Perhaps a game of Words with Friends. No, Candy Crush. Definitely Candy Crush.

Jayne memorized the moment. Bottles of water, dance bags, and light jackets littered the floor next to the girls as they contorted themselves in various positions that flagged them as dancers or perhaps yogis. Jayne's knees ached just looking at them.

Danny came around Jayne's other side and gently touched her elbow, giving her silent support.

"Girls, I have some horrible news."

"It's true!" Emma had an awkward smile on her face. Her eyes glowed bright as if she had guessed the answer to a trivia question and had just won a trip to Disney World.

Jayne's hand flew up, shushing her. "Please, this is very difficult to say." She swallowed hard. "Miss Melinda was in a car accident last night."

"Oh, no . . ." Quinn slumped against her.

"Are you okay?" Jayne gripped her waist tighter, trying to keep her on her feet.

"Is she . . . ?"

"I'm afraid she's gone," Jayne whispered so only Quinn could hear. "I'm sorry." This was not how she wanted to tell her.

Quinn nodded, water and fear filling her eyes. "I can't believe it. I need to sit. I'll be okay." Lifting a trembling hand to her mouth, Quinn slid down the wall, sat cross-legged on the floor, and absentmindedly picked at a piece of masking tape there.

The girls started to chatter, and their high-pitched voices grew louder. Their parents chatted behind them; some were tapping away on their phones. No news traveled faster than the news of someone else's misfortune.

"Girls!" Jayne's voice cracked. She hated raising her voice, but the chaos in the room unnerved her. If she couldn't get these dancers under control, how did she ever think she'd be effective as a cop?

"Is Melinda okay?"

Jayne had to do a quick scan of the room to finally realize it was Paige speaking. *God bless Paige for focusing on the relevant information.*

"This will be hard to hear, and that's why your parents were invited today." Jayne blinked as her face grew hotter and hotter and the droning in her ears grew louder and louder. She was starting to have that disconnected, out-of-body experience. A panic attack. The only other time she'd had one was when she had seen her mother nearly pass out after Finn told her about Patrick.

This day—like each of the times she'd lost someone she loved—would be imprinted in her mind. Jayne would never again be able to walk into Studio A without thinking how she had failed to effectively impart the worst possible news these girls would hear in their young lives.

Miss Melinda, their favorite teacher, was dead.

Jayne stared at a point above their heads, a trick she had learned in a public-speaking class in college.

I regret to inform you . . .

No, no, no . . .

Rip it off like a bandage.

The entire room was staring at her, but it was Danny's eyes she sought. "Our beloved friend and dance instructor, Miss Melinda, was in a car accident. I'm afraid she passed away."

A horrible shriek broke the tense silence. A few girls clung to their friends in weepy embraces. Others cried silently in their mothers' or fathers' arms. Cindy, one of the teen dancers, moved next to Miss Quinn and rested her head on her shoulder. That's when Jayne let down her guard and allowed Danny to pull her into an embrace.

For the first time since the phone had woken her from her jumbled dreams some eleven hours ago, she allowed herself to take comfort in something. Someone.

Jayne wasn't sure how long she had been standing there with Danny's strong arms wrapped around her when she tuned in to the sound of a woman's voice. She pulled away and swiped at her tears.

Mrs. Peters, Cindy's mom, stood there, her cheeks blotchy. "Miss Melinda was working with Paige on a dance for competition. Do you think . . . well . . . do you think that since Paige no longer has a teacher that maybe she won't be ready for competition? My daughter's been working with Miss Quinn." She gestured with her open palm toward Miss Quinn and her daughter, comforting one another on the floor. "Perhaps Cindy should take Paige's place at the competition?"

Instant anger heated Jayne's face. She bit her tongue hard. Now was not the time to lash out.

"We'll discuss that later, Mrs. Peters."

Mrs. Peters had the good sense to blush, but not enough sense to shut up. "Miss Melinda loved dance, and I think she'd want us to celebrate her life by continuing to do what she loved."

Jayne's mother appeared, as if out of nowhere. "Mrs. Peters, perhaps we can discuss this in the office." Natalie gave Jayne a knowing smile.

Jayne loved her mother. Loved her even more when she knew exactly what to say. Her years of training had taught her to tactfully handle obnoxious parents even as her dementia claimed many of her short-term memories.

Jayne leaned over and planted a kiss on her mother's cheek. "Are you okay?"

Miss Natalie stepped back and smiled broadly. "Don't forget, sweetheart, I've been doing this for longer than you've been alive."

"I know, Mom."

Mrs. Peters followed Jayne's mom to the office, seemingly deflated. Mrs. Smythe stood aside, watching the situation unfold with more interest than was warranted.

How would Miss Melinda's death benefit them? That's what some of these mothers were thinking as, even now, they jockeyed for their daughters' hierarchy in the studio's food chain.

Jayne's shoulders tensed and a headache throbbed behind her eyes. Her pale complexion in the floor-to-ceiling mirror startled her. Circles darkened the skin under her eyes. A bleak thought swept across her mind. She tried to dismiss it as paranoia, but was it *that* irrational to consider that Mrs. Peters could have tried to run Miss Melinda off the road so that Cindy could benefit?

The elderly gentleman on Lake Road had seen another car. Jayne's mouth grew dry as her suspicions cranked up with her racing pulse.

She ran a hand down her long ponytail. She hadn't slept much. She was delirious. Reverting to her old paranoid ways. No, these moms were ruthless, competitive, but murderers? Over dance?

Never.

SEVEN

Jayne pulled a stack of dinner plates from the cabinet while Miss Natalie hummed a familiar tune and mixed her Irish stew in the large pot on the stove. Nothing much had changed about Jayne's childhood home, including the kitchen. When Jayne was a toddler, her father had added a mirrored backsplash above the counters to give the room a more spacious feel. All these years later, it only gave the small kitchen a dated feel.

Jayne carried the plates to the dining-room table and set them down with a clack. As she placed the dishes on her mother's white linen tablecloth, she wondered if it was possible to feel nostalgic for something even while experiencing it. Although Melinda was not technically family, her death reminded Jayne how fleeting time was. Like trying to hold water in cupped hands as it leaked between the fingers.

Jayne's dad used to sit at the head of the table; now her oldest brother, Finn, had taken his spot. Patrick's place had been quietly filled by Jayne when she shifted one seat to the right. Her seat was alternately vacant or filled by Patrick's three-year-old daughter, little Miss Ava, whenever Patrick's widow saw fit to drop her by and then quickly slip away, as if seeing the Murphy family was too much to bear without him.

Jayne had considered canceling this Sunday's dinner, but Finn had insisted that Mom needed consistency.

More like Finn needed a home-cooked meal.

Besides, it was easy for Finn to make such dictates. He showed up and ate dinner. Jayne and her mom did all the preparations and cleanup.

The sexist division of labor in her family would have miffed her more if she hadn't long ago come to the conclusion that it was easier to roll with it. The Murphys had apparently been a patriarchal family for generations, and Jayne certainly wasn't in a position to change that.

At least she never had to cut the lawn or take out the garbage. She tended to look on the bright side.

Jayne strode back into the kitchen to grab the silverware.

"The boys should be here soon," her mother said, not for the first time.

Jayne glanced at the clock. Twelve thirty. "About thirty minutes, Mom." Her brothers usually showed up before one so they could park themselves in front of the TV for the football game. Even though the last thing Jayne wanted to do was have company, she was grateful for the distraction.

Yesterday at the studio, Jayne had hung around for as long as it took to field questions from the dancers and their parents. Miss Quinn had pulled herself together and was a major help with the grieving students. She'd even offered to fill in for Miss Melinda's classes, but Jayne decided to close the studio for a week. Give the families time to grieve. Give herself time to decide how to best move forward.

With a stack of silverware in her hands, Jayne leaned her backside on the laminate countertop, watching her mother alternately stir the stew and add a pinch of something. "We might need a new teacher at the studio. Do you have anyone in mind?" Miss Quinn was good with the young dancers, but she lacked experience with the older teams. Murphy's had allowed her to work with one or two older dancers on solos to gain experience. But could the studio hand over its top competition team to someone who lacked experience?

A pang of guilt twisted her insides. Here she was worried about her mother's studio and replacing Melinda, while poor Victoria was planning her daughter's funeral.

Miss Natalie set the spoon down on the ceramic stovetop. Jayne resisted the urge to slip in behind her and place a small saucer under the spoon. "We're hiring a new teacher? Do we need another one?"

Jayne reached out and brushed her hand gently across the smooth skin of her mother's arm. "Let me ask this. If a teacher took a leave of absence, who would you recommend filling in?"

"Is someone sick?" Miss Natalie glanced around the kitchen as if the answer might lie somewhere between the stack of mail on the counter and the coffee mugs on the rack.

"Don't worry, Mom. Everything's fine." Jayne hoped God wasn't keeping track of her lies. She squinted out the back window to the house behind hers. The Greens' short brick ranch seemed innocuous enough on that gray October day. But Jayne knew better.

She turned away from the window. Hosting Sunday dinner for her brothers *was* a good idea. It would get her out of her head for a few hours. *Maybe.*

"How many are we having for dinner?" Miss Natalie's voice floated in from the dining room, where Jayne had partially set the table.

"Should be the five of us today." Finn was bringing his fiancée, Melissa, and though Jayne's niece wasn't going to make it, her brother Sean never missed Sunday dinner.

Jayne poked her head around the corner to find her mom staring at a plate. "Is this my china?"

"I thought we'd use the everyday dishes." Her mother had always insisted her china be hand washed, and Jayne wasn't interested in any more work than necessary today.

Well, Jayne was *never* interested in more work than was necessary.

"This will be fine. Do we have some colored napkins? For a pop of color."

Jayne smiled at the hint of her old mom. "Of course."

"Did we set enough places?" There was that look of bewilderment again.

"Finn's bringing Melissa."

"Melissa . . ." Her mother repeated the name as if it might jog her memory.

"His fiancée."

"Do I like Melissa?"

Her mother's comment stopped Jayne in her tracks. Finn had been dating Melissa for over five years and had only recently set a wedding date. Next spring. But prior to their getting serious, her mother would tell Finn that Melissa wasn't good for him. Jayne wanted to believe acceptance had since silenced her mother's protest, but in reality, she feared her mom had only forgotten that she didn't like the woman.

Not interested in any more conflict this weekend, she changed the subject. "Dinner smells good, Mom." Jayne smiled. For as long as she could remember, she and her mother had stood side by side on Sunday afternoons chopping onions, carrots, and celery for the stew.

Her mother returned her smile. "Gram gave me the recipe. She had me making her Irish stew when I was eight years old." She lifted a shaky hand to her forehead, then peeked out from under it. "Gram's been gone for a long time now, right?"

Jayne nodded, trying to be gentle. The counselor had warned her that for Alzheimer's patients, any mention of the loss of a loved one could be like hearing it for the first time.

She placed her hand on her mother's cool arm. "Gram's in heaven." She decided that was the more tactful answer. "Her stew was the best."

A fleeting expression of sadness crossed her mother's face, just before the doorbell sounded. Jayne furrowed her brow. Her brothers didn't ring the doorbell.

She patted her mom on the back. "I'll get it."

Jayne touched her hair and then her shirt, then decided it didn't matter. It was probably some kid selling popcorn for twenty-five bucks a shot. She passed the front-hall mirror and was startled at the halo of frizz around her head from the humidity outside—and her face was whiter than white.

She grabbed the door handle and pulled it open. Danny Nolan stood there in a thin blue sweater that stretched across his broad chest. She immediately felt like she was seventeen again. And she wondered if a person could actually die of embarrassment.

Feeling shy, she dipped her head and studied her pink toes from her pedicure a few days ago. Well, at least she had that going for her.

As soon as Jayne opened the door in her apron and wild curls that framed her pretty face, Danny Nolan realized coming here had been a big mistake. Maybe. "You seem surprised. Weren't you expecting me?"

"Um . . ." Pink colored her cheeks. She glanced behind her toward the kitchen and ran her hand across her hair. "No, please, come in."

"Did I get here too early?"

Jayne opened the door wider. "No, not at all. Come in."

Danny held out the bouquet of flowers and a bottle of wine. She smiled and their eyes met briefly. "What a nice guest. My brothers show up late and with nothing but their appetites."

He stepped into the foyer, and she squeezed past him to close the door. "I brought that, too." He tilted his head. "Your brothers aren't here yet?"

"No. They should be here soon."

He drew in a deep breath. "Something smells good. Miss Natalie's Irish stew?"

"Every Sunday."

Nostalgia swept through Danny. The Murphys' house on Treehaven was as familiar—maybe more so—than his own childhood home. He had practically grown up here. He was the younger of two boys from a broken home. His mother had never wanted to be a cop's wife and had bolted when her sons were young. So Miss Natalie had practically adopted him, not that the Murphys could afford another mouth to feed on the salary of a cop and a homemaker.

"Miss Natalie invited me when I was at the dance studio yesterday."

Jayne lifted her head as if to say, *Now it all makes sense*, but she was evidently too polite to actually say it out loud.

Danny gently touched Jayne's arm and she paused, her hair brushing against his cheek. The clean scent of her shampoo mingled with the wonderful aroma of a home-cooked meal. "I'm sorry. I guess I'm still getting used to the idea that your mom gets forgetful. I should have run the idea by you."

Jayne smiled and patted his hand with genuine warmth. "No, this is my mother's house. She can invite whomever she pleases."

"Thanks for not making this awkward." Danny gently tugged on a strand of her hair and winked. He strode toward the kitchen, where Miss Natalie greeted him with open arms. He wasn't expecting the strength of her embrace, and he smiled despite the flood of emotions washing over him.

"Hey, stranger. Why haven't you been around?" Miss Natalie held him at arm's length, then she patted his chest with her open palm. "You've been working out."

Danny puffed out his chest and laughed. "I have."

She stared at him and then suddenly tears formed in the corners of her eyes. She opened her mouth to say something when a commotion sounded at the front door, followed by the clack of dogs' claws on the tile floor, charging in their direction.

Danny met Jayne's eyes, feeling a brief connection before everyone's attention was demanded by the two Goldendoodles jumping around their legs.

"Finn and Melissa are here." Jayne gave each of the dogs a little scratch on the head before greeting her brother.

Finn swooped into the kitchen and grabbed hold of one dog's collar and then the other's. "Sorry about that." He had a sheepish grin on his face. All the Murphy brothers shared a strong resemblance. Now it was like seeing a slightly older, more thin-faced Patrick walk into the room. A heaviness pressed on Danny's chest as the room grew close.

"You're happy to see me. Aren't you? Aren't you happy to see Aunt Jayne?" Jayne had crouched down in front of her brother's dogs. Their tails wagged wildly in greeting.

She straightened and held out her hand. "Melissa, you remember Danny, right? Melissa and Finn finally got engaged." She added the last bit of information with a pretentious tone as if to say, *La-tee-da*.

Melissa instinctively held out her hand to show off her diamond ring, something Danny had noticed most newly engaged women did.

"Congratulations?" Danny cringed when the word seemed to end on a question. That hadn't been his intention, but he had fallen behind Jayne's lead.

"Thank you." Melissa smiled tightly then leaned over and grabbed the dogs' collars from Finn. "I'll take them outside."

This house had always been abuzz in what Danny could only describe as friendly chaos.

Finn yanked open the refrigerator, the beer bottles rattling in the door. He grabbed two, twisted the caps off, then handed one to Danny. "Come on. Guys retreat to the family room."

"Go for it," Jayne said as she opened the fridge and pulled out a few condiments.

In the family room, Finn said, "Have a seat. Take a load off." He tossed a decorative pillow onto the floor. "Here, or grab the recliner." Finn's welcoming attitude took Danny off guard.

Danny gave him a thin-lipped smile and sat on the opposite end of the couch, hoping he could avoid the inevitable small talk with one of his senior officers on the Tranquility PD.

What did I expect by coming here?

Jayne strolled into the dining room with an easy sway of her hips.

Turning his attention back to Finn, Danny dragged a hand through his hair. Finn leaned forward, bracing his elbows on his knees. "Heard you got the call this past weekend."

There was no mistaking what "the call" was. It wasn't often someone drove their car off the side of the road into the lake.

"Yeah. I'm sorry about Melinda. I know your families are close."

"Well, mostly Jayne. She used to babysit for Melinda. Poor kid." He took a long pull of his beer, then glanced over his shoulder to make sure no one would overhear. "Any word on what happened? I heard the chief even went out on this call."

Danny set his beer down on the coaster on the table next to him and ran a hand along his stubble. "Traffic investigator figures she missed the curve during heavy rain."

"The news had reports of distracted driving."

"Texting while driving makes for higher ratings, I suppose." Danny shrugged, thinking about how there was no proof whether Melinda had been texting at the wheel or not. How her mother had warned her against it. But people were human. Despite their best efforts, they made mistakes.

Danny had made his share.

"Jayne can ask a lot of questions," Finn said. "Just do me a favor and don't let her get caught up in this. It's not good for her."

Danny rubbed a hand across the back of his neck, afraid if he didn't speak up, he'd get caught in a lie of omission. "I stopped by the accident scene after the fact with Jayne."

"You took her out there?" Finn's authoritative tone made Danny pause.

A hot flush of regret washed over Danny in the cozy family room. The same room where he and Patrick had spent hours creating grooves in the old shag rug with Matchbox cars. "She wanted to see the accident scene."

"Not a good idea. You know Jayne, right? She likes to imagine all sorts of scenarios. If you want to close this case, don't get her involved." Finn raised his eyebrows. "Bad weather. Unfamiliar road. Possible texting. Case closed."

A sense of defensiveness cut through Danny. "Jayne's not involved."

"Did I hear my name?" Jayne appeared with a glass of wine in her hand. At some point when Danny hadn't been looking, she'd taken off the apron, combed her hair, and pinned it up, exposing the pale skin of her neck. He quickly glanced away, as if he had been staring too long.

"Danny told me he took you out to the accident scene," Finn said.

A flash of annoyance pinched the corners of her mouth. "I wanted to see where Melinda died."

"You get fixated on that stuff. It's not healthy," Finn said.

"Then someone needs to do their job." Jayne bit out the words, and her gaze ping-ponged from Danny to her brother and back.

Finn leaned back in his chair. "The investigators will do their jobs. It's not your place to get involved." He softened his tone, as if that might help. "Let the police do their job, Jayne. I know it's hard to accept your friend's tragic death."

Jayne took a long drink of her wine, watching her brother over the rim. Then she lowered the glass. "I wouldn't dream of getting involved." Her tone was even. "I suppose I should go make dinner." She spun on her heel and returned to the kitchen. Despite her cool smile, her anger rolled off her in waves. If Finn had noticed it, he didn't react. His full attention was on the opening kickoff of the football game.

EIGHT

Nothing's sexier than a man who does dishes." Jayne handed Danny the last pot to dry.

"If I had known that . . ." He dried it and placed it in the rack.

"Never you mind." She yanked the dishrag from his hands and playfully snapped him with it, barely catching his thigh.

"I can't believe your brothers *never* help."

Jayne raised her eyebrows. "You've met my brothers, right?"

Danny threw up his hands in surrender. "You couldn't have reminded me about that thirty minutes ago?"

Jayne laughed. "I never look a gift horse in the mouth."

She was enjoying Danny's company, probably too much, and she wasn't ready for the evening to end. Was it weird that she suddenly found herself drawn to this man she had known for most of her life? Or were they simply bonding over their connection to Patrick?

Her mother was dozing in her recliner while the late football game played on the TV. Her brothers had left as soon as the Buffalo Bills lost—yet again.

Danny rested a hip against the counter, apparently not ready for the day to end yet, either. Or maybe that was a little bit of wishful thinking on her part. "I enjoyed hanging out here today. It was like old times."

Jayne took his hand. "Come here." She led him toward the front hallway. Releasing his hand, she grabbed her coat out of the front closet. "Let's sit outside where we won't disturb Miss Natalie. I could use some fresh air."

Danny helped her with her coat. The scent of his aloe aftershave, mixed with a touch of Palmolive, reached her nose. It was a heady combination. All the men in her life had been averse to housework, unless it involved a power tool, the lawn, or four wheels.

Danny stepped out behind her onto the porch and closed the door. He stuffed his hands into his jeans pockets and drew in a deep breath. Until now, she hadn't realized how tired he looked.

Patrick's death had taken its toll on him, too.

Holding on to the metal railing, Jayne lowered herself to the top step, the cold from the cement seeping through her jeans. She patted the concrete next to her. "Have a seat."

As Danny settled in, his solid thigh brushed against hers.

"I didn't realize how cold it was." A puff of white air escaped from her mouth as she tucked her hands under her armpits. "Are you okay out here?"

Danny sniffed. "I'm fine. October's my favorite month."

Jayne shot him a you've-got-to-be-kidding-me stare. "October? With winter approaching? Don't you miss the sun? The beach? Afternoons by the pool?"

He laughed. "I don't exactly tan. And I'm not a fan of the beach. Sand getting into all sorts of places. And I can't remember the last time I had time to lounge by the pool."

Jayne mirrored his laugh. "I don't exactly tan, either, but October, really?"

"Sure—Halloween, candy. What's not to like?"

"Cold weather. Snow."

"How often does it snow in October?"

"Um, October storm a few years ago?"

"How about cooler nights and the leaves change? Sometimes I think I'd like to take up photography. Capture the images."

"You're a regular Renaissance man."

Their easy banter reminded Jayne of the days when she used to join in while Danny hung out with Patrick. Before Patrick told her to get lost and find her own friends. In a way, she'd had a love-hate relationship with Danny. He'd often come between her and Patrick, the closest brother to her age. Finn and Sean were born in quick succession, so when Patrick came along four years later, Jayne's parents decided he needed a playmate.

No one had counted on Jayne.

But her mom was thrilled to finally have a baby girl. Patrick, not so much.

That's how Patrick had ended up with a tomboy sister for a playmate, until he met Danny in kindergarten. The Nolans lived in the same neighborhood, a few streets over. Close enough for a kid to hop on his bike and leave his little sister kicking up the dirt because her brother bailed on her.

"I often resented you."

Surprise flickered in Danny's expression.

Without thinking, she reached over and touched his knee. "I didn't mean . . . I meant when we were little. Patrick was supposed to be my playmate. Before you came along, he used to play all sorts of board games with me for hours. Our older brothers never gave either of us the time of day." She playfully nudged his shoulder with hers. "But I guess I'm over it. I haven't played a board game in eons."

He covered her hand on his knee. It felt strong, reassuring. "Patrick was an awesome best friend. We had so much fun," he said, a hint of nostalgia in his voice. "I'm just sorry that meant leaving you in the dust—because, boy, did we hear about it." He rolled his eyes in feigned annoyance. "You cried and complained about me taking Patrick away all the time."

"Maybe when I was four."

He turned to study her, his face only inches from hers. "I'm not so sure about that. You certainly had a flair for the dramatic."

"I did *not*." Two could play the I'm-not-really-annoyed-but-I'll-pretend-I-am game. She pulled her hand out from under his, but he quickly recaptured it and pressed it between his strong hands.

Danny grew serious and ran his thumb across the back of her hand. Tingles of awareness raced up her arm. "I'm sorry I took Patrick away."

She longed to remove the hurt evident in the depths of his eyes. But the weight of his words held more meaning than she dared to explore. She slid her hand out from between his and grabbed the railing to pull herself to her feet. She rubbed her palms together, and little specks of chipped paint fell to the ground.

Danny stood, rolled up on the balls of his feet, and let out a heavy sigh. Their gazes lingered for a moment before he stepped back and crossed his arms tightly over his chest. "I wish it had been me."

"Don't say that." How many times had she wished the same thing? Well, not exactly that it had been Danny, but that it had been someone other than her brother. Selfishly, she'd wished her grief and suffering on someone else.

"I don't know how a guy ever gets over losing his partner." He plowed his hand through his hair. "It's a nightmare."

"I don't think you'll ever get over it, but it's times like this where your faith comes into play. Pray for comfort and peace."

Danny gave her a rueful smile. "I'm afraid I left my faith at the exit to the Saint Al's graduation. Nine years of Catholic education. Poof." He made an exploding gesture with his fingers.

She furrowed her brow. "Really?" She couldn't imagine dealing with all of life's tragedies without having God to rely on.

"Yeah, well, I haven't exactly led the most charmed life."

Jayne knew Danny's mom had bailed when he was a little kid and his dad was a heavy-handed enforcer, but still . . .

"I'm sorry my family shut you out after Patrick died." She stuffed her hands in her back pockets. "I'm sorry I—"

Danny held up his hands. "I think I've had enough touchy-feely stuff for today."

Jayne froze for a second, then smiled. "Sorry. I get carried away sometimes. Say what I'm thinking without a filter."

Danny took a step closer and his deep voice washed over her, making her nerve endings hum. "I appreciate what you're saying. I do."

"Well"—she laughed awkwardly—"now that I got that off my chest . . ." She stammered, "You'll have to come again for Sunday dinner."

"I'd like that."

"Oh, and I hate to bug you about this, but before you go, did you talk to your dad about that other car on Lake Road at the same time as Melinda's accident?"

"Yes." Danny rolled his shoulders up, then let them drop as if the mere mention of his father was unpleasant. "He talked to Mr. King himself that night. He doesn't think his statement is reliable."

Jayne's heart raced in her ears.

"Claims he could smell alcohol on his breath."

"Mr. King seemed fine when we talked to him. And that doesn't mean he didn't see something. The chief's not going to follow up on it?"

"The traffic investigators will probably wrap up the case in a few days. I don't think they have reason to pursue it further."

"I guess it's easier to accept something if we have someone to blame."

Danny placed his hand on the small of her back. The subtle back and forth of his thumb sent an awareness, a warmth, coursing through her. She fought the urge to lean into him. To take comfort in his touch.

"Jayne?" Her mother stood behind them at the screen door.

She straightened and Danny pulled his hand away, like two teenagers caught in a compromising position.

"Thanks for dinner, Miss Natalie." He touched Jayne's arm and mouthed *I have to go*.

"You're welcome," her mother said.

Jayne pulled open the screen door and smiled at her mom. "Everything okay?"

"Yes, dear." Her mother tracked Danny's movements down the driveway. "Who is that young man? He looks familiar."

"Danny Nolan. A friend of ours."

"He's a handsome man."

"*And* he does dishes." Jayne smiled brightly as she hooked her mom's arm and led her back inside.

Jayne's mom had settled in to watch the news that came on after the football game. The quiet evening made Jayne feel ill at ease. Helpless. Maybe she could bring some of her mother's stew over to the Greens' house. It's what people did. An assortment of casseroles, breads, and desserts had lined the Murphys' counters after Patrick's death. Food that mostly went uneaten by a family who was too distraught to care.

But it was the thought that counted, right?

It took Jayne a few minutes to find a container and its matching lid. But once she did, she was even more sure that stopping by to check on the Greens was a good idea.

"Mom, I'll be right back. I'm going over to the Greens' house. Okay? I won't be long."

"Yes, dear," her mother said without much emotion.

Jayne watched her mother take a sip of tea, then she slipped out the slider door to the back deck and across the yard to Melinda's house.

If she wasn't mistaken, a car had just pulled away from the curb out front. The entire house was dark except for a few lights in the kitchen.

Through the screen door, she heard David talking. She knocked and called out at the same time. "Hello, it's Jayne. I have some of my mom's stew."

Trinket's claws clacked across the floor. Melinda's beautiful white dog yipped at the top of the small flight of stairs. Footsteps sounded— of the human variety—and David appeared at the door. "Hi, Jayne."

She held up the warm container. "I brought stew."

"That's nice of you. Come in." David shooed away Trinket, and the little dog disappeared from the top of the stairs.

"Oh, I don't want to intrude. I'll drop this off and go."

"Don't be silly. Victoria will be happy to see you."

He pushed open the screen door, and Jayne slipped past him. Flowers, casserole dishes, and sympathy cards lined the counter. The image was so familiar it was like a punch to the solar plexus.

"Do you have room in the fridge?" She forced the words out from a too-tight throat.

David took the container from her. "I'll find room."

Victoria sat at the kitchen table with a bottle of wine. "Join me." Before Jayne could refuse, Melinda's mother grabbed a large wine goblet from the cabinet and filled it to the rim.

Jayne slipped into a chair across from Victoria and took a few sips. "This is good." She held the glass away from her and gently swirled the dark liquid, careful not to spill it. "How are you?"

David tapped the back of his wife's chair. "I'll let you two visit."

Jayne watched him walk away, a shadow of the man she had known.

Victoria took a long drink of her wine. "Does it ever get better?"

Jayne breathed in and out slowly, praying for the right words. "You'll never stop missing Melinda, but it won't be as painful as it is now."

Victoria shook her head. "I don't know how I'll go on."

Alarm pulsed through Jayne's veins. "You have so many people who love you." She glanced around at all the expressions of condolences. She took a few more long gulps of wine, hoping to dull her ever-present despair.

Victoria laughed, a strangled sound void of any mirth. "Do you know how many people stopped over today?" She took another sip of her wine, her voice echoing in the large glass. "I saw people from the dance studio." She pointed at Jayne with the hand wrapped around the stem of the glass, the liquid nearly sloshing over the edge. "Miss Gigi even stopped by. I don't think Melinda ever told you this"—her words had the soft edges of someone who had passed pleasantly buzzed two drinks ago—"but Miss Gigi was relentless in trying to get Melinda to teach at her studio."

"That's pretty nervy." Miss Gigi had left Murphy's Dance Academy to open the only other studio in Tranquility. Now she was trying to poach the other teachers.

But it doesn't matter now, does it?

Victoria looked up, the light over the table reflecting in her shining eyes. She started counting on her other hand. "Barbara from church stopped by . . ." She sighed. "She makes the best banana bread. And that strange girl who moved in next door brought something." Her forehead creased as if she was trying to remember what the neighbor had brought. "Oh, and Quinn, and Kyle . . ." She studied her fingers. "The poor kid. He and Melinda had been going through a rough patch. I guess he was still hoping they'd get back together." She tossed back the rest of her drink.

Jayne did the same and then set down her glass and blinked slowly. *Whoa.* She'd polished off the large goblet of wine way too quickly. She covered Victoria's hand before the older woman could refill her glass. "Melinda was loved by a lot of people."

Victoria sniffed and nodded.

Jayne squeezed her hand. The buzz from the wine felt good. "It will get better. It will."

The look in Victoria's eyes lacked conviction.

The two women reminisced a little longer before Jayne blinked at the clock on the oven. It was getting late.

"I should go." Miss Natalie would be eager to get to bed. She stood and the room swayed. "I think I had a little too much wine."

"No such thing." A slow smile spread across Victoria's face and stopped short of her grief-stricken eyes.

David appeared from the back hallway, as if he had been listening to the conversation wrap up. "I'll see you home."

Jayne giggled. "I think I can make it across the yard."

He gave her a funny look. "I need some air."

Jayne swept a kiss across Victoria's cheek. "Why don't you get some sleep?"

Victoria stared at her blankly, as if the suggestion was ridiculous. "Night." She flicked her hand as she reached for the wine bottle with the other.

David and Jayne stepped out onto the driveway, the cool air a balm on Jayne's fiery cheeks. Cigarette smoke wafted from somewhere nearby. "Night, David. Please let me know if there's anything I can do."

Jayne was growing tired of the cliché expression. She imagined the stew would end up in the trash along with everyone else's good intentions.

"You've already done so much for us."

Jayne paused at his tone.

"Thank you for identifying Melinda's body." He dragged a hand through his hair. "This whole thing has wrecked Victoria, but if she had to do that . . . I just don't know."

Jayne shrugged as if to say, *It was no big deal.*

"Did the police say anything about details of the accident?" he asked.

Jayne studied David, the moonlight glistening in his eyes. She was grateful for the shadows. As close as she had been to Melinda and Victoria, David had always been somewhat distant, spending most of his time working and, when he was home, behind his laptop.

"What do you mean?"

"You went with the police officer to identify . . . Did he say anything about the cause of the accident?"

Jayne stuffed her hands into her jacket pockets. Did she dare tell him about the other car? Could she be responsible for adding to the man's palpable grief? "It was raining. There was a curve—"

"I know all that!" He barked at her, then bowed his head, covering his eyes with one hand and waving an apology with the other. He pulled himself together and said, "Is life really this random? This unfair?"

"It's hard." Her pulse thrummed in her ears.

"Your brothers are cops. Can you please see what they know?" He glanced anxiously toward the screen door. "You were like a sister to Melinda. You're part of our family." He placed his hand on her shoulder. "I need to know. I just need . . ." He bowed his head and sobbed quietly.

"I understand. But . . ."

David straightened and pulled himself together. "Thank you."

Jayne nodded, turning to walk away, the buzz from the wine making her pulse pound in her head.

"And Jayne?"

The gravel crunched under her sneakers as she spun back around.

"If you learn anything, tell me. Not Victoria. She's too frail."

"I'll see what I can find out," Jayne said. She strode across the yard, stumbled up the deck steps, and caught herself from taking a face-plant with outstretched arms.

Icy dread pooled in her stomach. Nothing good could come from this.

NINE

G uilt has me stalking Melinda's house.

Is it really guilt? Or curiosity? Or fear that I'll be found out?

"Feel the fear. Move past it. Seize the opportunity." Another one of Bud Byrdie's mantras taps across my brain as I wait.

You won't get away with it if you keep lurking around here. How would you ever explain what you're doing?

Voices sound from the driveway. The prickly evergreen scrapes my arms as I step closer to see. To hear. Panic explodes in my head, sending tiny lights dancing in my eyes when I realize it's Jayne and the doting dad.

I quiet my breath so I can hear the conversation. Hear his concern. Jayne's promise to see what she can uncover.

Tracking her movement across the yard, past the play set, I shift to remain hidden. So Jayne thinks she's going to find out everything she can about the accident? What's there to discover? Did someone see something?

The fool stumbles up the back deck. Serves her right. She's still chummy with her neighbors. Anger roils my gut. *Poor, poor Victoria.* That woman is as weak as they come. She pushed Melinda to offset her own weaknesses. Maybe things would have been different if Victoria hadn't been so hyperfocused on her daughter. Pushing her to be what she'd never be.

Maybe Melinda would have made other choices if her mother wasn't pulling all the strings. Directing her path.

Settling back in, I wait. Patience thus far has been my friend. The lights in Jayne's house go out, one by one. The last light out must be her bedroom. Where I can find her.

Where she sleeps.

I wait a little longer.

Finally, my time has come. Holding my breath, I cross to Jayne's house. Climb the deck. The wood creaks under my weight and I pause. I search beyond my reflection into the Murphys' dark, empty kitchen.

Seize the opportunity.

I reach out and grab the handle to the slider and tug. The door rumbles in its track.

A rush of excitement washes over me. *It's open. No alarm. That's what you get for getting sloshed, oh, stupid Jayne.*

Heartbeat pounding in my ears, I step into the kitchen. My eyes have already adjusted to the darkness. The room is familiar. I remember the three-tiered birthday cake sitting on the island. Nothing but the best for Melinda's surprise sixteenth birthday party. The Murphys and the Greens had been one big freakish happy family.

Pulling my hood over my head, I make my way to the stairs and stare up the dark passageway. Something compels me to climb the stairs. I pause when a step creaks under my weight. But I continue to the top and turn right on the second floor. *The last light extinguished.* I peek into the first bedroom. Based on the furniture, I suspect it's Miss Natalie's.

I turn, and in the next room I see Jayne lying in her bed, her arms flailed out by her sides. Her heavy breathing indicates she's sleeping. Sound asleep. Too much wine.

Emboldened, I step into the room and creep to her bedside.

How easily I can hurt her now. More than I already have. Stop her from looking into the accident.

But I left no traces when I ran Melinda off the road.

No evidence.

To smother Jayne would be a futile exercise. I'd only draw unnecessary attention to myself.

Be patient.

Jayne snores abruptly and I freeze in place. Adrenaline surges through my veins. She settles again into a deep slumber. I back out of the room, realizing I've been foolish.

Trust that you made no mistakes in your initial execution.

Trust that you'll make no more.

Trust no one.

TEN

A few days later, Jayne found herself sitting in the last pew of the church, trying to hold her emotions at bay. This church had been the site of her father's funeral, then her brother's, and now Melinda's. Her chest grew tight with unspent emotion. How much loss would she see before she turned thirty? Fate had been unkind.

No, not fate; she had to continue trusting God to get her through this.

With calming breaths, Jayne tried to clear her mind. When that didn't work she busied herself by studying the church bulletin from last Sunday. Boy Scout pancake breakfast in the school hall after Mass. Bingo on Wednesday in the cafeteria. And parents who wanted a tour of the school were welcome to call the school office.

Reading the bulletin kept her from making eye contact with Melinda's friends, family, and dance students. One quivering lip or hug might send Jayne over the edge and she wouldn't be able to pull herself together.

She prided herself on holding things together.

Next to her, her mother grasped the rosary beads and her lips moved with the familiar prayers. *Thank heaven for ingrained traditions.*

The air around her grew still, charged with expectation. Jayne stole a glance toward the front of the church. Above the sea of black clothing, on the left of the altar, she noticed the statue of the Virgin Mary holding baby Jesus. The statue dated back to World War II. How many times had she stared at it? Sister Donna, her third-grade teacher, had told her class that if they prayed with Mary, she could intercede on their behalf because Jesus would never say no to a request from his mother. It seemed like such a quaint concept, one Jayne clung to even now. It brought her peace and comfort.

As Jayne stared at the beautiful statue, she couldn't help but wonder why the Blessed Mother hadn't asked Jesus to spare her father. Her brother.

And now Melinda.

Had Jayne not prayed hard enough to keep her friends and family safe?

"God gave people free will," the priest had told Jayne when he'd met the family at the hospital. And because of that free will, bad things happened.

Jayne quickly looked down and swiped at a tear rolling down her cheek as her composure cracked. She clung to her faith, but some of her childish notions clung to *her* like a tight-fitting wool coat. Perhaps Sister Donna had been telling the class fairy tales.

Miss Natalie leaned toward her. "Is it Sunday?" Her whisper carried across at least seven to ten pews in the hushed church.

Jayne patted her mom's arm. "No, Mom. It's Wednesday."

"A holy day of obligation?" Her mother glanced down at the missalette, as if that might give her a clue as to why they were at church on a Wednesday morning, of all days.

Dear Lord, give me strength and the right thing to say.

"Mom"—she reached over and took her mom's hand in hers, sensitive that this information might come as a shock to her—"we're at a funeral."

Her mother's mouth formed a perfect O as deep wrinkles lined the corners of her eyes. Worry aged her instantly. "Who died?"

The two young women in the pew in front of them turned and gave them a quick glance, not of annoyance, but of curiosity.

Jayne squeezed her mom's hand. "It's okay." She fingered her mother's rosary. "Why don't you finish your prayers?"

Her mom looked at the beads as if she hadn't been holding them all along.

Jayne flinched when the deep hum of an organ sounded from the balcony. The congregation, as if one, rose to its feet. Jayne touched her mother's elbow, and they joined the rest in standing.

The altar servers, two young girls and one young boy dressed in white vestments, carried a cross and led the procession, followed by eight young men serving as pallbearers. Jayne's world tunneled to a single image when she saw Danny escorting the casket.

How did that come about?

Their eyes connected as he passed. He wore his grief like a shield of armor. For a fleeting moment, she wondered if her sidetracked law-enforcement career hadn't been a blessing instead of a curse. Could she deal with the ugly side of humanity that police officers witnessed day in and day out? Hide her emotions like Danny?

Jayne's father had been the only one to encourage her to pursue her dreams. He'd had every confidence in her. She blinked rapidly. Her father's casket. Her brother's casket. Now Melinda's. All pushed solemnly down the center aisle of Saint Aloysius Church.

Keep it together.

Jayne found herself unable to recite the prayers during the funeral as a knot of emotion clogged her throat. The image of Melinda's mom unfolding the pall and spreading it across the casket would forever be etched in her memory. Victoria had patted the fabric like she was tucking her daughter in for the night and not covering her casket.

At the end of the funeral, Jayne stood in the pew with her mother, respectfully allowing the procession to file out of the church. As Victoria passed, she made eye contact with Jayne, who gave her a subtle nod.

Her heart shattered for this woman; her only daughter was gone. So that was it. Melinda's short life wrapped up in a little bow.

Just as Jayne was about to escort Miss Natalie out of the pew, Melinda's friend Bailey stopped and wrapped Jayne in a tight embrace.

Bailey had straight blonde hair, a short black leather coat, and tall boots on. She looked respectable, and far more fashionable than Jayne would ever be, or could afford to be.

"I can't believe she's gone," Bailey said, her lower lip trembling.

"I know."

"Hi, Miss Natalie." Bailey leaned over and kissed the woman's cheek. Once upon a time, most young ladies had taken a dance class or two under Miss Natalie's instruction.

Jayne's mother gave Bailey an overly cheerful hello, her defense mechanism to overcompensate when she didn't recognize someone.

"You guys were all such good friends," Jayne said.

Bailey's eyes grew red. "She was supposed to meet us out that night."

"I know. She worked and then left to meet you guys down by the lake. You can't blame yourself."

"That's what I don't understand." Bailey shook her head, her shiny blonde hair falling over her shoulders. "We were waiting for her at Burgers and Buns in town. Not by the lake." She lifted her shoulders to her ears, then let them drop. "We can't figure out where she was going."

Jayne turned to her mother and handed her a bulletin. "Mom, can you sit here a minute? I need to talk to Bailey."

Miss Natalie sat and studied the paper.

Jayne pulled Bailey off to the back corner of the church. "What do you mean?" Jayne struggled to keep her tone even. "She texted me when she was leaving the studio. She said you texted her and changed the location."

"We didn't . . . I didn't." Bailey twirled a strand of hair around her finger. "She said I did?" Her voice grew high pitched.

"Can I see your cell phone?"

Bailey dug her phone out of the side pocket of her purse. "Here." She handed it over, then took it back to unlock it. "Here."

Jayne found the text stream between Bailey and Melinda from Friday afternoon. It was heartbreaking in its ordinariness.

```
Bailey: Hey chickie, what time do u get
out of work?

Melinda: Private lesson. 9?

Bailey: ☹

Melinda: Go on and I'll meet you guys
when I'm done. Burgers and Buns?

Bailey: Yep. Already dreaming of hot
wings!!! <Fire emoji>
```

Jayne held out the phone to Bailey. "That was it? No other texts? A group message?" Her stomach bottomed out. "Nothing?" All these messages had been exchanged prior to the start of Melinda's private lesson.

Bailey shook her head, her hair swinging freely over her shoulders. "It doesn't make sense."

Bailey's eyes lit up. "Check Melinda's phone."

"I don't have it." She dug out her own phone, though, to at least show Bailey the text from Melinda.

"What does this mean? Someone claiming to be me sent her to a different location? Why?"

Jayne covered Bailey's warm hand with her own. "I don't know. But I'll look into it." She ran a hand down her long ponytail, then glanced over her shoulder for her mother. "Did you see Miss Natalie?"

Bailey raised her pale eyebrows and shrugged. "I think she followed the procession outside."

"I have to find her. But we need to talk more." Jayne had to find out if Melinda's closest friends knew who else she might have been hanging out with.

Who had texted her to meet at Henry's?

By the time Jayne arrived home with her mother, she was obsessed with finding out who had texted Melinda to change the location of the girls' night out. She already knew from Danny that requesting records from the phone companies involved subpoenas and red tape that could take weeks—and that was *if* someone in law enforcement was willing to investigate.

And there was no indication they would.

She helped her mom out of her light jacket and tossed it over the banister. "Are you tired? Want some tea?"

Miss Natalie nodded. "Yes. Some tea and cookies sounds nice." She paused by the front door and took in the yard. "Your brothers need to rake."

Jayne rested her hands on her mom's shoulders and looked outside. Their neighbor Ricky Rhymes was already accumulating a large pile of leaves. The kind of pile she and Melinda would have jumped in as kids, only to become the target of much groaning by one of her brothers who was responsible for clearing the yard. Ricky's efficient movements suggested he wanted to be done with the job at hand and get back to his computer.

His computer. Ricky was a tech genius. Excitement bubbled in her chest. He might know how to access Melinda's texts. Somehow.

Maybe.

"Is my show on?" Miss Natalie asked, snapping Jayne out of her wandering thoughts.

"Um . . . I'm sure there's something on."

Once Miss Natalie had her tea and cookies and was settled comfortably in her chair, Jayne gave her a quick kiss. "I have to check on something for a minute, but I'll swing back in before we go over to the Greens'. Are you up for going out again this afternoon?"

Miss Natalie took a sip of her tea. "I'd like to rest, if that's okay. Did you have something in mind?"

Jayne pushed the plate of cookies away from the edge of the side table. "You rest. I'll be back shortly."

Anticipation vibrating through her nerve endings, Jayne jogged toward the front door and was relieved to see Ricky still raking the leaves. It would be so much easier to approach him casually if he was outside. Putting her jacket on, she ran across the street.

Richard—or Ricky, as most people called him—was attacking the random twigs and leaves scattered across his meticulously maintained lawn. The *twang, twang, twang* of the prongs on the metal rake seemed to be in time to whatever beat was pulsing through his head. Ricky and his wife had moved in across the street about three years ago.

"Ricky," Jayne called as she approached him from behind. "Ricky." When he didn't answer, she reached out and touched his shoulder. Poor Ricky jumped like one of those cats in the cucumber videos.

Ricky tossed the rake down and flipped his over-the-ear headphones off his head. "You scared the tar out of me."

Jayne stuffed down her smile. "Sorry. I called your name."

Muffled, tinny sounds still beat from the headphones draped around his neck. Ricky held up his finger, reached into his jacket pocket, and turned off the sound. Then, as if suddenly realizing who she was, he lowered his head. "Sorry to hear about Melinda," he mumbled. "Peggy mentioned it. I don't watch much TV. I missed the local news." His leg twitched as he spoke.

"Thank you." Jayne's voice cracked. "Quick question." Shoving her hands in her jacket pockets, she tried to figure out how best to broach this. Ricky was no more than thirty, and one of those really smart guys who lacked a few social graces. He worked with computers all day, so it came as no surprise that he always seemed squirrelly around people.

"Yeah?" Ricky picked up the rake and leaned against the handle for support.

"I'm trying to see if Melinda sent or received any text messages before her accident."

Red splotches of color bloomed on Ricky's face. "It's against the law to text and drive." His eyes grew wide. "If the police pull you over, you can get a ticket and then insurance rates skyrocket. I keep reminding Peggy about that." In the few years that Jayne had come to know Ricky, she'd seen that he viewed life in black and white, with his bubbly wife Peggy being the one exception. If she were a color, she'd be orange with yellow and purple polka dots.

"I know it's illegal to text and drive." Jayne forced a cheery smile. "And I believe Melinda would *never* break the law. I just need to see something for my own peace of mind. It doesn't make sense that she ended up in the lake."

"I can't imagine drowning." Ricky tapped his fingers on the handle of the rake in time with his bouncing foot, as if the notion of being trapped in a car, water slowly filling the interior, was too much to contemplate. "And her phone was in the car? Of course it was," he said in answer to his own question.

"Yes."

Ricky's eyes brightened and Jayne could almost smell the smoke.

Yet a sinking feeling twisted in the pit of her stomach. Ricky was smart, but Jayne feared the answers rested in either Melinda's lost phone or within documents only the police would be authorized to request.

Ricky dragged his hand through his mussed hair. Jayne imagined him planted in front of his computer most days until his cheery wife shooed him outdoors to rake. However, Jayne suspected Ricky enjoyed a meticulous yard as much as his wife. "Are the police working with the phone companies?"

Smiling shyly, Jayne did a little flirty thing with her lashes, feeling ridiculous. She wasn't the flirting type. "I heard phone companies are notoriously difficult to work with. And this is really just for my own curiosity. Is there another way?" She coaxed him, thinking there had to be a way a guy as smart as Ricky could hack into the phone records. But would he risk doing something illegal for her? She quickly added, "Something legal? Like maybe if Victoria logs me into Melinda's online wireless account?" Jayne had been looking at her own wireless account, though, and was doubtful that it would provide the needed information.

Ricky's eyes lit up. "Sometimes people have their smartphones connected to their tablets. Did she have a tablet? If she did, you might be able to see her last text message and the time it came in." The number of words he strung together exceeded all their previous conversations. Apparently, a jazzed Ricky was chatty.

Hope surged through Jayne. "Great idea." She patted his biceps in triumph. "Really great idea."

Pleased with himself, he smiled brightly and held up the rake. "I need to finish here."

"Thanks," Jayne said. "Thanks a lot."

Ricky returned to his twitchy raking motions. *Twang-twang-twang.*

"Hey, Ricky?"

The young man arched his eyebrows, waiting.

"Keep this between you and me, okay?"

"No problem." He gave her a quick shrug before putting his headphones back on.

As Jayne walked back across the street, she said a little prayer that Melinda's tablet hadn't also been lost in the lake.

Jayne checked on her mother, exchanged her heels for flats, then jogged across the yard to the Greens' house for the after-funeral reception. But she was distracted with the idea of finding Melinda's tablet.

Jayne pulled open the screen door at the Greens' house and winced as it scraped across the concrete. The cacophony of chatter from inside the house made her nerves hum. She had exceeded her capacity for crowds today, but she had to pay her respects and find the tablet.

Melinda's little white dog found its way to her in the kitchen. Jayne crouched down, gathering the fabric of her long skirt, and scratched the dog's head. "Hey there, Trinket." She leaned closer and whispered, "I know you miss Mellie. I do, too." She reached into her pocket and slipped a bacon treat to the dog. She kept a box at her house for her brother's dogs and Trinket.

Jayne lingered for a moment, petting the dog. "Okay, Trinket, I guess I can't delay the inevitable." The dog pranced around Jayne's feet as she straightened. If she wasn't careful, Trinket would take her legs out from under her.

"A dog fan?"

"Isn't everyone?" Jayne spun around. Danny stood in the doorway. She couldn't help but admire how handsome he was in his Sunday best—that is, *if* he actually got dressed in his best on Sunday.

"I'm partial to big dogs. Not these little ankle biters. You know, a dog a man can walk."

"Like my brother's two big dogs?" Jayne rolled her eyes and laughed, grateful for the familiar face. "You're not looking to slip a little dog in your man-purse while you shop?"

"Ha ha," Danny said, never taking his eyes off her. "I missed you after the funeral."

"I had my mom," she said as an excuse for having returned home instead of attending the family's private burial, which had followed the Mass. "How is it you ended up being one of the pallbearers?" Jayne glanced around to be sure she wouldn't be overheard.

"The funeral home reached out to me last night. They said Victoria gave them my name. Perhaps since I was the one who told her about her daughter? Maybe because she knows you and I are friends. Accepting was the right thing to do."

"It was." She tried to focus on the conversation while Trinket lifted her paws and scratched at Jayne's bare legs.

Danny climbed the two steps into the kitchen, closing the distance between them. "I enjoyed dinner at your mom's the other night. Thanks for having me. It felt good to . . ." He shrugged again, suddenly looking younger than his twenty-seven years. "It felt good to be around your family. You're very lucky."

"I am." Even after everything . . .

The corners of his mouth curved into a soft smile, transforming the sadness around his eyes.

"You know, you're welcome anytime." She placed her hand on Danny's solid chest—before she pulled it away as if she had been burned.

"I'd like that."

Jayne turned away and dragged her fingers through her ponytail, trying to play down her fiery red cheeks. This was Danny Nolan, her brother's best friend since kindergarten. The little string bean of a teenager who hadn't bulked up until he'd made weight lifting a part of his daily regime.

"I had an interesting conversation with Bailey Stevenson at church," she said, keeping her voice low. "She claims Melinda was supposed to meet them in town. Not down by the lake."

"Maybe she had errands to run," Danny suggested.

Jayne slowly shook her head. "Not that late at night. Plus, Melinda texted me herself that they were meeting at Henry's Waterfront Café. That her friends had switched it from Burgers and Buns."

"Come here." Danny guided her outside with a gentle hand to the small of her back. As he leaned in close to talk quietly, she tried to ignore the hint of aloe and, if she were a betting woman, Dove soap.

"What is it?" She studied his eyes, tiny flecks of yellow accenting the brown. An awareness she didn't dare acknowledge awakened within her.

"I checked with one of the officers who investigated the accident. There's no sign of Melinda's phone. The divers pried open the door while the vehicle was still submerged. We can only surmise that it's on the bottom of the lake."

"But—"

"You have to stop this." Reaching out, he brushed the back of his knuckles across her cheek, leaving her acutely aware of him in a way she didn't want to be. Not now. Was he trying to manipulate her into compliance?

She backed away from his touch. "*You* stop. I need to—"

"Sometimes people die in freak accidents. *Sometimes* bad stuff just happens." Frustration laced his clipped tone.

"Aren't you a ray of sunshine?" She glared back at him.

Danny sighed heavily.

"Come on, you know I can't drop it. Not until I find out who sent that text. That night, Melinda told me Bailey changed the location. Today after church, Bailey told me she didn't. I checked Bailey's phone, and now I need to check Melinda's."

"Her phone is in the lake."

She tilted her head and raised her eyebrows as if to say, *It's not over till it's over.*

"You're not going to let this drop?"

"I need the truth. Someone texted Melinda. They *wanted* her on Lake Road."

"Maybe she was going to meet other friends first. It could have been a wrong number. It was probably nothing."

Jayne tipped her chin in defiance. "What if it wasn't? What if it was *something*?"

"You watch too many cop shows."

Pushing past him, she yanked open the screen door and said in a harsh whisper, "That may be true, but *that* doesn't mean I'm wrong."

ELEVEN

Danny stood in the crowded living room of the Greens' home, politely smiling and nodding at a bunch of people he didn't know. Jayne pitched in and cleared empty serving trays, replacing them with fresh trays of food. She seemed to have a great relationship with Victoria Green. David Green seemed more aloof, resting his shoulder against the fridge and absentmindedly moving every time someone had to get something out of it.

People coped in their own ways.

Danny's cell phone vibrated in the interior pocket of his suit coat. He pulled it out and glanced at it. *The chief.* His father was the last person he wanted to talk to. But no one ignored Danny's father.

Or kept him waiting.

He swiped his finger across the screen. "Hello."

"Good. Are you at the Greens'?"

"Yes, let me step outside so I don't have to talk above the noise." He lowered the phone and wove through the crowd, breathing a sigh of relief when he stepped outside and the cool autumn air hit his face. He shrugged out of his suit coat and draped it over his arm. "What's going on?"

"Is Kyle Duggan at the reception?"

Danny searched his brain. *Kyle Duggan.* "Mayor Duggan's kid?"

"Yeah."

"I'm not sure what Kyle looks like." Danny had a mental imagine of a nerdy kid in pants that were a tad too short and glasses that were a tad too big, standing at his father's swearing-in ceremony for his first term in office. Some six, seven years ago. "I can ask around."

"No, no, don't ask." The chief paused. "Keep this under the radar. The mayor called in a favor."

Danny glanced toward the door, as if someone nearby would be able to hear his father on the other end of the line.

"Why, what's going on?"

"This stays between you and me." Danny envisioned his father leaning back in his oversized office chair, gesturing with his index finger as if his son were standing right in front of him. "The kid's trouble. Always has been. Tranquility PD has already had to bury a few things."

"Like what?" Danny clenched his jaw. That kind of stuff got under his skin.

"A DUI, minor drug infraction, and a few other minor items."

"You gotta be kidding me." Danny draped his suit coat over a lawn chair and pinched the bridge of his nose.

"Have you ever known me to kid?"

Unlikely.

"What do you need, Chief?" he asked, eager for his father to get to the point. Taking his chances by pressing him. But today felt like one of those days he was willing to push the limits.

"The mayor's worried about Kyle. He left the house this morning distraught because his girlfriend died."

"Wait, back up. Melinda Green was dating the mayor's son?" Jayne hadn't mentioned anything about that. He supposed she had no reason to.

"Yeah, this is what I'm trying to tell you. Go find the kid and make sure he gets home safely. Make sure he doesn't do anything stupid like get behind the wheel of a car after throwing a few back." He heard his father sniff, and it grated on his nerves like it always did. "You know how that works. Not all guys are tough."

The sucker punch slammed its intended target. Danny had tossed back his share of drinks after Patrick's death, and his father's only advice had been, "Move on. Bad stuff happens. Deal with it."

Danny gave himself a hard mental shake. Going head to head with his dad never solved anything and only left him more enraged.

"You think he's been drinking? Is he of age?" Not that age would stop a kid determined to get drunk.

"Kyle's twenty-two. Plenty old to drink, but apparently not smart enough to stay out of trouble. I'm leaving it up to you to find him and escort him home. If the kid gets picked up for a DUI, the mayor will have a hard time getting out from under it. Election's next month."

Not to mention the disservice to any other person Kyle might encounter on the road.

A long silence stretched across the line, followed by a phone ringing in the background.

"I have to go," the chief said. "Update me later."

Danny ended the call without saying good-bye, then braced himself to return to the reception. He wanted nothing more than to go home, relax a bit before heading into work. But the chief had given him a job.

Drawing a deep breath, Danny pulled open the screen door and entered the Greens' house, stepping up the few stairs to the kitchen. He recognized Jayne's backside as she leaned into the refrigerator, and he would have playfully given her a catcall if they weren't at a funeral reception.

"Hey there," he said.

"You're still here."

"You disappointed?"

She twisted her mouth and shrugged as if it made no difference.

"Can we talk?" He leaned in close so as not to be overheard.

Jayne looked at him and lowered her chin. "Now? Here?"

"Which one is Kyle?"

Her right brow dipped.

"I haven't . . ." She glanced around. "Oh, wait, yeah, he's stand-ing over there getting a little chummy with one of my dancers. Too chummy. Paige's only sixteen." With a hard set to her mouth, she lifted a hold-on-a-minute finger and wove her way over to Kyle. Jayne said something to the girl, who then joined her friends across the room. Kyle disinterestedly watched Jayne walk away while he took another swig of his beer.

"Great," Danny muttered under his breath. The kid *was* drinking. He'd have to babysit him or risk the wrath of both the chief and the mayor.

Danny caught Kyle's eye and gestured to him. The mayor's son set his drink on the table and strolled over. "Yeah," he said.

"Let me drive you home."

Kyle ran a hand under his nose and teetered back. "Do I know you?"

"Let's just say I work indirectly for your dad."

"Whoa." Kyle held up his hands. "What if I said I'm not ready to go?"

"Listen," Danny said, trying to contain his anger, "I have specific instructions to see you home."

Kyle rolled his eyes as if to say, *Or what?*—and really, he was right. If Kyle got pulled over for driving under the influence, his daddy would get him off. Like he had before.

But Daddy was being a little more cautious this close to Election Day.

Danny decided to take his chances, and he grabbed Kyle's arm firmly and shoved him toward the door. "We're going."

❖

A subtle commotion drew Jayne's attention toward the door. Had Danny just taken Kyle outside? Before she had a chance to investigate, Paige sidled up next to her. "We were just talking. That's all. I know Kyle was dating Melinda. It would be tacky if I . . . I mean, we were just talking." Paige touched her arm and whispered in her ear. "But if you ask me, I think Quinn has a thing for him."

"Why would you say that?" Jayne scanned the room and found Quinn talking to Carol Anne by a platter of food. "A lot of people are coming and going. You shouldn't gossip."

"Just saying." Paige's cheeks grew pink.

Jayne wrapped her arm around Paige's shoulders. "It's okay. This has been hard for everyone. How are you doing?"

Paige lifted her shoulders, then dropped them in a heavy shrug. "I'll survive."

Wanting to lighten the mood, Jayne forced a smile and stroked Paige's arm. "Promise me you won't date college guys until you're in college." At the very least, Jayne could impart some practical advice to the young women who chose to study at Murphy's Dance Academy. That was the part of the job she was growing to love.

"How about when I'm a senior in high school?"

"How about we talk about that when you're a senior?"

Paige gave Jayne a quick hug, then pulled back and smiled. She did a little pirouette-thingy and joined her friends sitting in the corner of the living room.

Jayne smiled, but for some reason, a subtle unease crept up her spine. Perhaps because it was past time that she run home and check on her mom. She glanced around, realizing that people were starting to filter out, but she didn't want to leave without helping the Greens clean up. Victoria had had the food catered, but she'd be on her own for cleanup.

As if reading her mind, Victoria came up behind Jayne and gave her a hug. "I don't know how we would have managed today—this week—without you."

Jayne reached back and patted the woman's hand on her shoulder. "How are you holding up?" It seemed so trite, but what else could she say?

People tended to say the dumbest things to those who were grieving. One of Jayne's aunts had had the gall to tell her at Patrick's funeral, "Maybe this was a blessing. Now, you can help your mom at the studio." Those callous words were etched in her memory.

"It's going to be quiet around here," Victoria lamented, turning to face Jayne. "I always knew when Melinda was home. Her music. Her dancing. Her talking, talking, *talking*. What I wouldn't give to hear her voice right now." Her shoulders shook. "I can't believe I'd tell her to be quiet sometimes because I couldn't think. If only I had known . . ."

David appeared, kissed his grieving wife's forehead, and tucked her against his chest. "We'll be okay."

"If there's anything I can do . . ." The tender display was achingly beautiful.

"And I'll be around." Carol Anne joined their small circle. "I'm not going anywhere."

Jayne couldn't be sure, but she thought Victoria winced.

David squeezed Carol Anne's shoulder. "Your mom will send over the troops if you stay here too long."

Carol Anne rolled her eyes. "I'm twenty-six."

"Then maybe it's time you found your own place." Carol Anne's father patted his oldest daughter's arm and laughed.

It was Carol Anne's turn to wince. "I'm . . . Oh, never mind."

Jayne tried to catch Carol Anne's eye—reassure her—but she never lifted her gaze from the floor.

A suffocating awkwardness settled around them. Poor Carol Anne had always exuded a subtle—and sometimes not-so-subtle—clumsiness surrounding her eagerness to please people. When Victoria had first started dating David, Carol Anne used to come over and try so hard to be everyone's best friend, including Jayne's.

Carol Anne's mother had allowed her to transfer from the public school to Saint Aloysius School. Back then they were both in seventh grade, and peers could smell the stench of desperation wafting off the needy kids. Jayne was in the same class as Carol Anne and was always friendly—it being Catholic school, and all—but when she had a choice, she chose not to get saddled with her. Thinking back, she was ashamed. But when you're that age, you don't want to be a loser by association.

She finally caught Carol Anne's eye and smiled. Maybe now would be the time to reach out and be a better friend. A little part of her felt like she'd be betraying Melinda, though—the younger girl had begrudgingly accepted her stepsister when she came to visit, but preferred to have David and Victoria to herself. Funny, Jayne thought. After all these years, she had never even met Carol Anne's mother.

Later. Jayne would reach out to Carol Anne later. Once everything was settled.

The familiar need to distance herself filled Jayne with self-recrimination. Yet, with a heavy heart, she let Carol Anne walk away and join some elderly relative in conversation.

Since Victoria was being so appreciative, Jayne decided to broach a delicate subject, if it could mean locating Melinda's tablet. She cleared her throat. "Victoria, I was wondering if you needed help going through Melinda's things? I know how hard it was after Patrick died." A pang of guilt sliced through her. Oh, how she hated manipulative people.

"I'm not ready to do that." Victoria pulled out a kitchen chair and sat down as if God was slowly lowering her with marionette strings. "It seems too final."

As if burying her only daughter hadn't been final enough.

Jayne sat across from her.

"I don't want anyone to go in her room. Not yet." Victoria pulled Jayne's hand toward her and hugged it to her chest. "I don't know what I'd do without you, Jayne. Melinda loved you so much. You were like a sister to her."

Jayne lifted her eyes and noticed Carol Anne watching them. Jayne gave her another sympathetic smile, knowing this had to be tearing Carol Anne up. She had lost her stepsister and she was still struggling to fit in. Jayne often resented her own meddling family, but at least they embraced her.

Even if a bit too tightly.

TWELVE

"Y ou don't have to take me home. I have a car." Kyle jangled his car keys in front of Danny's face. If he had been anyone other than the mayor's son, Danny would have slapped them out of the smug kid's hand and proceeded to wrench his arm behind his back. But Danny wasn't looking to cause a scene. So he snatched the keys out of Kyle's hand and stopped there.

Score one for the sober guy.

"Hey!" Surprise registered on Kyle's face. "Give me those!"

"Humor me," Danny bit out.

Kyle paused. "Let me run in. Say good-bye."

"Make it fast."

Danny was relieved when Kyle came right back out. He'd hate to have to drag him out of the house again, unwilling to have a scene with this punk in front of a family who had lost their daughter.

As they strode down the driveway, Danny said, "I assume you live at the mayor's residence. I'll drive your car so you don't have to go home without it. Then I'll walk back."

"Whatever." Kyle scrubbed a hand across his face, and, for the first time, a ripple of sympathy coursed through Danny. Sure, this kid exuded a cocky vibe, but he *had* lost someone he cared deeply about. That was obvious.

Danny helped Kyle into the passenger seat of the nondescript sedan. Danny would have pegged this kid as driving a yellow sports car or maybe a souped-up monster truck. Maybe this car was another one of Kyle's father's choices. The mayor wouldn't want his troublemaker son catching the eye of more people than necessary in something flashy.

Danny jogged around the other side of the vehicle and climbed in. The kid pouted as they pulled away from the curb, so Danny decided to break the silence. "How long were you and Melinda dating?"

"Since sophomore year in high school. A long time."

"That is. I'm sorry for your loss."

Kyle grunted and shifted to face the window. "She was supposed to go out with me Friday night."

Danny waited for the kid to continue, an alarm clamoring in his head. Kyle's disposition seemed off.

"Doesn't matter. I wasn't going to keep crawling back to her." He coughed. "Guess now it doesn't matter."

"I understood she had plans with her girlfriends." Danny kept his tone even, studying Kyle's reaction.

"Yeah, that's what she said." He tugged on the strap of his seat belt. "Her girlfriends."

"You can't blame yourself, you know, if that's what you're feeling."

"What, are you trying to shrink me?" Kyle muttered, still facing away from him.

"I know what it's like to lose a good friend."

Kyle snapped around, sitting up straight in the passenger seat and jabbing his finger in Danny's direction. "Oh, that's right. You're the one who got your partner killed."

Danny drew in a long breath and let it out slowly. He wasn't going to take the bait. Not with this punk. Score one for the punk, though.

Even score.

Danny decided to do a little digging since he had a captive audience. "Where was Melinda heading when she got into the accident? I heard she was supposed to meet her friends at Burgers and Buns, the other direction from the lake."

"Burgers and Buns. Pfft . . . That cheesy place?" He crossed his arms over his chest. "I have no idea why she was on Lake Road."

Danny wished he weren't driving so he could better study Kyle's body language, eye movements, and facial expressions.

"That's my house there."

Danny didn't need directions to the mayor's house, an official-looking white structure with three columns and a circular driveway. It was set farther back than its immediate neighbors.

He slowed to turn into the driveway.

"I live in back, above the garage. You can park in front of one of the bays."

"Okay." Danny did as he was told, impressed with the carriage house. They both climbed out of the car and walked around to the front of it. "Promise me you'll go inside and sleep it off."

"I'm not drunk." Kyle rolled his eyes.

"Go inside and play a video game, then."

"Whatever."

Danny pressed the keys into the young man's hand and watched him jog up the steps that hugged the side of the garage. Then Danny turned on his heel and started the mile walk back to the Greens' house. He'd grab his suit coat from the chair in the yard where he'd left it, then he'd head home. Maybe catch a few hours of sleep before his shift started.

Melinda's mom didn't want anyone to go into her daughter's bedroom, but Jayne *had* to get her hands on Melinda's tablet. She had to find out why Melinda was on Lake Road, even if no one else seemed suspicious as to why she was out there when she was supposed to meet her friends in town. In the other direction.

Jayne wandered the small ranch house, picking up plastic cups from end tables and empty corners, the ones Carol Anne had missed. The last few remaining guests didn't seem in a hurry to go home, as if saying good-bye today would be too final. Jayne understood that. She remembered with vivid clarity the stillness of her own house—a house that had usually been filled with the raucous laughter of four children, three of whom were very loud boys—after their father's funeral. It was like the spirit of her family had died. The Murphys had regained some of that joy, but had been torn apart yet again when Patrick died about a decade later.

After attending Melinda's funeral, Jayne fully understood why some people avoided funerals. They brought back too many hard memories. But sometimes you had to suck it up. It wasn't even about Melinda. It was about showing love and support for those Melinda had left behind.

So Jayne felt a little traitorous as she plotted her clandestine strategy for retrieving the tablet from Melinda's "hands-off" bedroom. *If* the tablet was in her bedroom.

She tilted her head. Through the thin sheer over the front picture window, she noticed Victoria and her husband talking to an elderly relative who had been saying her good-byes for the past ten minutes. Trinket was sniffing around a tree.

The back hallway that led to the bathroom and three bedrooms stood empty. The door to Carol Anne's bedroom—more like an extra TV room with a pullout futon for the random times she stayed over—remained closed. Carol Anne had disappeared soon after her father's gentle jab about being more independent at age twenty-six. Jayne wondered how much she made as a waitress, anyway. Could Carol Anne afford to be out on her own?

Focus.

Adrenaline zinged through her.

Setting the garbage bag down in the corner of the kitchen, she crept toward Melinda's bedroom, keeping her eye on Carol Anne's door.

The *Melinda* nameplate on her bedroom door, adorned with a kitten, made Jayne's breath hitch. It had been on the door for as long as Jayne could remember. Melinda must have been six and Jayne eleven when she first babysat. Jayne had been a very mature eleven-year-old, though.

Suddenly tears blurred the cute little tabby in the corner of the nameplate. *Focus.* Jayne racked her brain to utilize her partial police training.

Was she compromising anything by entering Melinda's room? No, how could she be? No one believed a crime had been committed.

She glanced over her shoulder. No one was in the kitchen. She ran her sweaty palms down the front of her skirt.

Now or never.

She turned the doorknob. The door opened with a pop and released familiar smells: a floral scent from Bath & Body, hairspray, and Melinda's expensive curl definer, a product Jayne had introduced her young friend to. Crazy-curly-haired girls had to stick together.

The memory made her smile.

Taking a deep breath, Jayne stepped into Melinda's bedroom and slowly closed the door behind her with a muted *snick*. A rush of competing emotions pummeled her. The posters of ballerinas and hip-hop artists swirled in her blurry vision. Jayne dragged her fingers across her wet cheek. Melinda's presence was so strong in this twelve-by-twelve space. Suddenly Jayne fully understood Victoria's need to preserve the room. To declare it off-limits. It was all that remained of her daughter.

Shut off your emotion. Focus.

"Come on, Melinda. Where did you keep your tablet?" she whispered to the empty room. She knew Melinda had one. She had seen her using it at the dance studio.

A sinking feeling settled in the pit of Jayne's stomach. She pressed her cool fingers to her forehead.

She lowered herself onto the corner of the bed and cringed when the bedsprings creaked. A headache formed behind her eyes. Hearing a rustling sound behind her, she glanced over at the window overlooking the yard. From here she could see her own house. As a teenager, she had loved being able to see her house when she was babysitting Melinda. She'd had adult responsibilities, but she'd felt protected because her parents were only a yard away. She could run to them if Melinda was choking or if a creeper got in the house.

Jayne once saw an episode of *48 Hours*, or maybe it was *Forensic Files*—a high-school student's gym teacher was stalking her and he showed up when she was babysitting. She let him in, thinking maybe she had forgotten to turn in some gym homework or something—the girl wasn't exactly high on the IQ scale. Gym homework? Anyway, she escaped her gym teacher by locking herself in the baby's room and climbing down the portable fire escape with one hand. She held the baby with the other. Turns out, the young babysitter hadn't been so dumb after all.

Melinda had been a bear to get to bed *that* night.

Sitting in Melinda's bedroom now, the harsh reality of her death took the wind out of Jayne, like a sucker punch to the gut. Covering her mouth to muffle any sound, she folded in half and had her first long cry.

A soft knock sounded on the door. Her heart leapt in her throat. Now wasn't exactly the time to have a good old-fashioned cry. How would she explain what she was doing in there?

Mind racing, Jayne sprang to her feet and flattened herself against the wall behind the door. The door handle turned and the door eased open. She sucked in a breath.

"Hello?" *Carol Anne.*

Jayne closed her eyes and imagined herself as invisible.

A soft click prompted Jayne to open her eyes. The door was closed. The room was empty. A rush of breath escaped her lungs and her resolve spurred her on.

One last look—the closet—and then she'd sneak out. Feeling like she was going to toss her cookies from the stress, she slid open the closet doors and noticed Melinda's school backpack stuffed in the corner.

Of course.

Holding her breath, she unzipped the bag. *Melinda's tablet.* Afraid to turn on the device and alert anyone to her location, she held it close to her chest and moved to the door. Voices floated in from the hallway.

A *scratch, scratch, scratch* and a whimpering sounded on the other side of the door. Trinket was back inside, which meant Melinda's parents had come back inside.

Rubbing her free hand along the fabric of her skirt, Jayne came up with plan B. Once, when she was babysitting Melinda, they got locked out of the house. She had placed a small plastic slide under the bedroom window and used it to climb in.

Going out should be easier, right?

Voices grew louder outside the door. She couldn't think straight. *Some cop I'd make.*

Without wasting any more time, she crept to the window, unlocked it. She swallowed hard. The scratching at the door intensified. The old wood, expanded in the frame, rumbled as the window slid up. Clenching her jaw, Jayne glanced over her shoulder; the door to the hallway remained closed.

Thank you, Lord.

She grasped the tabs on the screen and slid it upward. Her passage to freedom revealed, she grabbed the tablet in its lime-green cover from the floor and held it to her chest. She swung one leg over the sill, careful to gather the fabric of her skirt. She eased toward the outside, ducking her head under the open window and stretching her toe toward the ground. She wasn't exactly the athletic type, but even she knew she couldn't reach, not without letting herself drop.

Realizing her precarious predicament, she tossed the tablet out the window and it landed with a soft thud on the thick grass, just beyond the landscaped flowerbeds.

Did Melinda really find footsteps under her bedroom window?

With her hands free, Jayne wiggled her other leg through the opening, but the heel of her shoe got caught on the sill.

She broke into a flop sweat and tugged with all her might. Her shoe flung into Melinda's bedroom as gravity did the rest. Jayne landed with a thud on her side between the dying marigolds and the droopy stems of dandelions that had bloomed months ago. Dampness seeped through her skirt.

"Ugh." She pivoted in the most ungraceful of moves.

"You passed the physical-ability test in the police academy, right?"

Muttering under her breath, Jayne glanced over her shoulder and saw Danny, his suit jacket draped over his arm.

Her voice got lodged in her throat. Probably just as well, because any words she had for Danny right now wouldn't have been kind. Or ladylike.

The crooked slant of Danny's smile should have annoyed her, but instead it caught her off guard. Why had she always considered him a nuisance while growing up? If she had only looked right in front of her, she could have had a date to the prom and occupied her Friday nights with more than babysitting duty for the Greens.

That was assuming a lot. Danny Nolan would forever and always consider her Patrick's little sister.

"Need a hand?"

"Ha." She rotated her wrist, checking for pain. A clump of mud fell from her palm. What she wouldn't do to dig a hole and never show her face again.

She rubbed her hands together, then accepted his offer of help. Danny pulled Jayne to her feet, and she stopped her forward momentum with the palm of her hand flat against his crisp white dress shirt. She snatched it back and grimaced. "Sorry about that." She feverishly began to rub at the dirty handprint, only making it worse. She tuned in to the solidness of his chest.

Waves of tingling awareness made her lower her eyes. The bright green cover of Melinda's tablet glowed against the lawn. She swooped down, snatched it up, and held it to her chest. Despite her efforts, she doubted she was pulling off calm and cool.

Understandable, considering the circumstances.

In the next yard, Jayne noticed a young woman dressed all in black staring curiously at them while taking a long drag on her cigarette.

Jayne forced a smile and waved. "It's all good. Nothing to see here."

Shrugging, the girl turned her back to them and disappeared around the other side of her house. Jayne had seen the girl before. She and Melinda had christened her "Goth Girl" because of her attire. GG's family had moved in next door to the Greens about a year ago, but they weren't the neighborly type.

"Care to explain?" Danny deadpanned, forcing her to turn her attention back to him and the tablet in her hands.

Biting her bottom lip, Jayne looked back at the open window, then down at her bare foot. "I'll explain everything. But first, I need a favor."

He frowned, waiting.

"I lost my shoe." She pointed at the open window.

"You know they have a door."

Jayne would have swatted him if it wouldn't have meant another handprint.

"Just help me out. I did something I shouldn't have."

"You have to be kidding me." He leaned back and looked toward the driveway. Then stretched to look through the open window. "Here, come on."

She set the tablet down on the grass and shook out her hands as she watched Danny brace himself under the window, his dress shoes planted in the dirt. "You can't just reach in?" she asked.

"Seriously?" Danny laced his fingers. "Here. If you don't hurry up, you're going to be explaining to Melinda's mother why your shoe is in her daughter's bedroom."

"What's the plan?" Jayne glanced toward the driveway, then back at him.

Danny held up his laced fingers and gave her a pointed stare. "Aren't I being obvious enough? I'll boost you up. Lean over the edge and grab the shoe. Easy-peasy."

"Okay . . . Here I go." She planted her clean hand on Danny's shoulder and put her bare foot in his clasped hands. With little effort, he pushed her up to the window. She leaned her belly on the sill and popped her head through the opening. The door leading to the hallway was still closed.

Thank you, Lord.

Jayne stretched, the sill digging into her belly.

"Ugh," she groaned. Stretching . . . stretching . . . stretching . . . her fingers finally caught the heel of her shoe.

The door handle rattled.

"Pull me back."

Danny planted his solid hands on her waist and lifted her down. She grabbed his hand and crouched down below the window. "Come on," she whispered. She snatched up the tablet and crouch-ran around the corner of the house and stopped in the grassy alley between the two small homes.

Thankfully, Danny followed her lead without question.

"Someone came into the room." She pressed her hand against her beating chest. Trinket's high-pitched *yap-yap-yap* could be heard through the open window.

"What have you done?"

"Me? You're the one who made me go get my shoe."

"And if you hadn't?"

"I could have gone home minus one shoe." An uncontrollable giggle bubbled up. That tended to happen when she wasn't supposed to laugh.

Danny pulled her down against the faded siding of the Greens' house. They were hunkered down like two little kids playing hide-and-go-seek. "What would have happened if their little doggy brought them your shoe?" he asked in a harsh whisper. He cupped her bent knee with his hand and gave it a shake. "You're trouble. You know that?"

"That's what my brothers tell me."

THIRTEEN

Danny and Jayne emerged from the side of the Greens' house and walked briskly around the block to Jayne's. She was still coming off the adrenaline high of throwing herself out of Melinda's bedroom window, and she explained to Danny along the way why she'd gone to such measures to retrieve the tablet. Only a twinge of guilt dulled her excitement about finally—*hopefully*—finding out who'd sent Melinda that text.

When they reached her front porch, Danny turned to Jayne. "You have to be careful."

"I will."

"Promise?"

Jayne sighed. "I don't know what I would have done if you hadn't come along."

He took a step back and lifted a skeptical eyebrow. "I suppose you'd be running through the yard with one shoe."

She tapped her heels together like Dorothy making a wish. "I owe you."

Danny ducked his head and looked at her with those puppy-dog eyes. "You don't owe me anything. Just . . . just stay out of trouble.

Please. And . . ." He pointed to the tablet she'd held down by her side, hoping not to remind him that she still had it. "Return it to the Greens' house. *Please.*"

"After I read her texts. My conscience would keep me awake at night if I kept it any longer than that. Nine years of Catholic school, remember?" She laughed and rubbed her chin along the shoulder of her sweater. "Once I took a pen home from Lake Union Bank. I had to drive all the way back to return it."

Jayne found herself jabbering on, unwilling to let him leave. "I feel a little guilty that I bailed on Victoria. I wanted to finish helping her clean up."

"You've done a lot already."

"Yeah." Drawing in a deep breath, she glanced over her shoulder. "Sounds like my mom has company."

Maybe it was the television.

"Well, thanks for saving . . . my shoe." She playfully lifted her foot and swatted him on the thigh with it.

With ninja-like reflexes, he caught her ankle and a twinkle lit his eyes.

"Hey." Jayne did a little hop-step, and she clutched his solid bicep to steady herself.

"Hey, yourself," he said, his voice hoarse. He released her ankle.

Laughter floated out from inside. Jayne smiled shyly and dropped her hand to her side. "I better go check on Miss Natalie. She *does* have company." Jayne couldn't imagine who. There were no cars parked in the driveway, so she assumed it was a neighbor.

"I'll talk to you later." Danny took a few steps backward, dropping his hand.

Her lips parted, but she had no idea what to say. Needing a distraction, Jayne pointed at his stained shirt. "Please send me the dry-cleaning bill."

He shook his head, a playful glint in his eyes.

"See you later." She went inside, set Melinda's tablet down on the hall table, and walked slowly toward the back of the house. In the family room, she found her mother sitting across from Gigi Jones—Miss Gigi, her mother's former student and the current owner of the only other dance studio in town.

Jayne stopped in the middle of toeing off her shoes. "Hello, Miss Gigi." Her ingrained politeness had her biting back what she really wanted to say: *What are you doing here?*

Miss Gigi stood, her thin frame and perfect posture indicative of her years of dance.

"Hello, Jayne, how are you?" She had a stiff smile on her bright-red lips. Rumor had it that she was going through a nasty divorce and her father was tired of supporting her new business venture.

Jayne lowered herself onto the arm of her mom's chair and kissed the top of Natalie's head. "Hi, Mom." She'd be lying if she didn't admit to herself that she was relieved her mom was exactly where she had left her before she'd gone to the reception. One less thing to stress over right now.

"Hello, sweetie. Isn't it nice that . . ." The smile slipped from her mother's face and a vacant look descended into her eyes.

"Yes, it's nice to see Miss Gigi. It's been a long time. Two years?" Jayne plastered on a false smile and she really didn't care if Miss Gigi saw through it. "Two years" was a personal jab, the amount of time since Gigi had bailed on her mother.

"Well, I saw you both at the funeral this morning. And I stopped by the Greens'. Paid my respects."

"I didn't see you."

Miss Gigi flicked her wrist. "I slipped in, checked on some of the dancers, and slipped out. I know I'm not always welcome."

"No, I suppose not." Jayne stifled an irrational need to tell Gigi that she knew about her attempts at "stealing" Melinda. *What does it matter now?*

Her mother shifted forward on her seat, as if to stand. "Would you like some tea?"

The look of sympathy in Miss Gigi's eyes indicated that she understood what it was like to be the caregiver of someone who was slowly losing their faculties. Jayne didn't want her pity. Miss Natalie would have despised it.

A commercial for that night's newscast drew Jayne's attention to the TV screen. On it, a young reporter stood in front of the jagged edge of the broken guardrail where Melinda had crashed through before drowning in a watery grave. A knot twisted in her stomach. Below the reporter on the screen, a ticker rolled past: *Teens and texting. Tonight at 6*. Gritting her teeth, Jayne leaned over her mother and scooped up the remote from the side table. She pointed it at the TV, and the screen went dark.

Lines of confusion edged her mother's eyes. "Is my program over?"

Jayne tossed the remote on the table. "We'll catch up with it after Gigi leaves." She couldn't help but put emphasis on the word *leaves*.

Jayne draped her arm around the back of the chair behind her mother. "It's been a long day, Miss Gigi. Is there something I can help you with?"

Miss Gigi ran her hands down her black pants, then worked at a piece of lint Jayne couldn't see. She supposed it was her way of gathering her thoughts.

"Miss Natalie and I had a nice visit." She bowed her head. "Such a shame about Miss Melinda. She was a beautiful dancer. A wonderful teacher." She let out a breath between tight lips. "I fear these young kids today think they're invincible. One moment of distraction and then this . . ."

"What happened to Melinda?" her mother asked in a worried tone.

Jayne reached for her frail hand and gave it a squeeze. "Don't worry, Mom. We'll talk about it later."

Miss Natalie yanked her hand out of her daughter's hand. "I want to talk about it now. Don't dismiss me."

Miss Gigi glanced up, her long lashes framing wide eyes. "Oh, I didn't mean to cause more stress . . ." The woman had an annoying way of not finishing her sentences.

Jayne clamped her mouth shut, unable to say what she really wanted to in front of her mother.

"I can see I've upset you. That wasn't my intention."

"What was your intention?" The fiery liquid passion to protect her mom turned to steely resolve. "We're tired. Like I said, it's been a long day."

Miss Gigi folded her hands, then unfolded them. "I'd like to suggest a business proposition. I thought now might be a good time."

"Now's not a good time to talk business," Jayne said curtly. Her mother trembled under Jayne's touch, obviously agitated. "Mom, I'm going to see Miss Gigi out." Jayne picked up the remote on the end table. She felt Miss Gigi's confused gaze on her. Jayne turned the TV back on and found one of her mother's favorite programs, a rerun of *King of Queens*. Laugh tracks accompanied the silly antics of Kevin James.

Jayne slid her hand across her mother's shoulders. "I'll be right back."

She led the other woman out to the front porch.

"I don't appreciate your coming here and upsetting my mother."

Miss Gigi held up her hands in an apologetic manner. "That wasn't my intention. I had to see how you were all doing after Melinda's accident."

"We're fine." Her curt answer held a challenge.

Miss Gigi crossed her arms. "How did it happen?"

"The accident?" Jayne's pulse beat steady in her ears.

"Yeah . . . I mean, what are the police saying? Bad weather? Texting?"

Jayne studied Gigi intently. *Why all the questions?* "I don't really know more than what I've heard on the news." She was purposely vague. "I hate to ask questions. Upset her mom. You know how it is."

Gigi waved her hand in dismissal. "Of course." She cleared her throat. "And I really didn't mean to upset *your* mom. I know you're helping her with the studio and it's not really your thing . . ."

"Why make an offer now? You could have returned to Murphy's Dance Academy last year if you really wanted to help out." Jayne planted her hands on her hips, but even as she asked the question, she knew the answer. Miss Gigi offered now because Murphy's Dance Academy had lost its best teacher. The studio was vulnerable.

Goose bumps blanketed her flesh. *How convenient for Miss Gigi.*

"Can I ask you a question?" Miss Gigi opened her purse and pulled out a pack of cigarettes and a lighter, but when she caught Jayne's watchful eye, she stuffed them back in.

Jayne tilted her head as if to say, *Go ahead.*

"You quit dance when you were twelve."

Jayne shrugged.

"So . . . why do you want to run the studio?"

A nervousness fluttered in her stomach. "It's my mother's studio."

Miss Gigi fidgeted with the flap of her purse as if she were itching to get her hands on the cigarettes inside. She took a step closer and Jayne stepped back, her thighs bumping against the metal railing. Miss Gigi ran a hand across her smooth hair. "I had heard rumors about your mother's health, but until I had a chance to visit with her, I hadn't realized . . ."

Jayne gritted her teeth, unwilling to confirm or deny.

"You lost two of your students to my studio at the beginning of the school year."

Jayne leaned back and braced her hands against the railing. Prickles of rust bit into her palms, but she forced herself to remain impassive. "Dancers leave . . . change schools all the time."

"There are only two dance schools in Tranquility. Why don't you let me buy you out? I know that old Victorian house needs a lot of improvements." She grimaced as if she had swallowed something bitter. "*You* don't want to do this. This was your mother's dream. Not yours." Then she leaned in conspiratorially. "Your mother won't even remember."

Jayne pushed off the railing, forcing Miss Gigi to take a step back. Jayne descended the steps, needing to create distance. She turned and glared at her former friend. "I would remember."

Miss Gigi sputtered as she came down the steps and joined Jayne on the walkway. What did she have against personal space?

"I didn't mean . . . I mean . . . It's just that dance isn't your thing."

Disgust made Jayne's hands shake. Miss Gigi had studied at her mother's studio. Attended parties at their home. She had been like family.

"My mother loves dance." Without dance, she'd lose herself—but Jayne didn't admit this last part out loud. That was none of Miss Gigi's business.

"But you don't."

"Love dance?"

Miss Gigi shook her head slowly, a light glinting in her eyes.

"I love my mother."

"Of course you do." Miss Gigi shifted her stance. "Sweetie"—the endearment she used when about to correct one of her students' technique—"this town isn't big enough to support two dance studios."

Tilting her head, Jayne weighed all the ways Miss Gigi would have benefited from Melinda's death. Her mind drifted to the tablet she had placed on the hall table. The answers she was looking for were on that tablet. She just knew it.

Miss Gigi opened her purse and pulled out the cigarettes and lighter again. This time she tapped one out and lifted it to her mouth but didn't light it. "I heard your studio is closed for a week out of respect for Melinda. I wonder if Miss Quinn will be looking for more reliable employment?"

Jayne swallowed hard, refusing to take the bait.

"Give it a week. Think about my offer. I'll make sure your mother's compensated for her studio. Give her a little retirement nest egg."

"She has my father's pension."

"Are you saying she couldn't use a little extra money? She should go out on a high note instead of watching everything she's worked for her entire life swirl down the toilet."

Miss Gigi strode down the walkway, lighting her cigarette as she went. A cloud of smoke trailed behind her as she climbed into her sedan across the street.

Still fuming from Miss Gigi's absolute gall—coming to her home and offering to buy Miss Natalie out of Murphy's Dance Academy, her mother's life work—Jayne busied herself by putting on the teakettle. She tapped her fist on the counter, trying to channel her anger. She would *not* take the offer.

"Mom, I'll make you some tea. Are you hungry?"

Miss Natalie scooted forward on her large recliner.

"No, don't get up. I'll bring the tea to you. How about a few cookies?"

"Sounds nice, thank you." Miss Natalie leaned back in the chair and turned her vacant stare toward the television screen. Guilt at sitting her mom in front of the TV wove through Jayne. All the more reason to keep the studio open.

Jayne closed her eyes and said a silent prayer, feeling the pressure of everything weighing on her shoulders.

The whistle on the kettle sent out a shrill shriek, startling Jayne. Annoyed that she hadn't lifted the kettle from the burner sooner, she filled two teacups and set out a plate of cookies.

After settling her mom in with her snack, Jayne grabbed the tablet from the hall table where she had left it and joined her mom in the family room.

Holding the teacup in her hand and balancing the tablet on her lap, she held her breath, feeling like she might have the answers at her fingertips.

Jayne muttered under her breath when the tablet prompted her for a password. Biting her lower lip, she tried to figure out what Melinda might have used. Jayne worried that she probably only had ten tries before the device reverted to factory settings, and then any information that might lead to the killer would be erased forever.

Way to get dramatic. You don't know that Melinda was killed.

Jayne took a sip of her tea to quell her dry mouth, then set the teacup in its saucer on the side table. Anticipation hummed through her as she tried the most obvious numbers: the month and date of Melinda's birthday.

The screen buzzed its rejection.

The year she was born.

Buzz.

Jayne's stomach pitched.

Eight more tries. She wiped her palms on her thighs.

Four digits. Numbers that meant something to Melinda.

The Greens' house number was four digits.

Buzz.

Running her finger across her bottom lip, Jayne stared absently at the soap opera her mother had enjoyed watching for as long as Jayne could remember. How was it possible that the same actors were still on it? How was it possible they still looked the same?

"Didn't that guy go to prison for killing his brother?" Jayne asked her mother.

Miss Natalie slowly shook her head, her brow furrowing as she seemed to give it some consideration. Then her eyebrows flew up. "Oh, yes, he did, but then his brother, Marcus, came back. He wasn't really dead, so they had to release his brother."

Jayne smiled at the predictability of life on a soap opera, and she was secretly pleased her mother had recalled that information. Every victory, however small, was something to be celebrated.

She traced the outline of the tablet, wondering if her life seemed a bit soap opera–like.

Staring at the black screen with the number keypad, Jayne tried to think of a number that would have significance to Melinda. The young woman had been very excited about graduating from college next spring. Graduation date?

She put the tablet aside and went and grabbed her smartphone from her purse. She Googled the graduation date of the college Melinda attended and, after a few tries, found it: May 19.

She stared at the date for a long time.

0519

That *had* to be it.

You enter that and you've used up four tries. Six more wrong entries and you'll lose all the data. Forever. Maybe.

Squaring her shoulders, she entered the number.

0-5-1-9

A collage of apps zoomed onto the screen.

"Yes!" She gave a little fist pump, drawing her mother's attention. Jayne smiled sheepishly. "Just figured something out."

Her mother smiled.

Jayne tapped the pads of her fingers together, a block of ice settling in her gut. She felt like she was about to open a Pandora's box of secrets. Not that Melinda was a secretive person, but someone's digital footprint was very personal.

Would Melinda have resented Jayne for reading her private information?

Melinda used to grumble that Carol Anne liked to snoop.

Was this snooping?

Jayne pushed up her sleeves. No, Melinda and Jayne were kindred spirits when it came to true crime.

But this wasn't rehashing the case from some TV show. This was real life. *Melinda's* life. Anything Jayne discovered on this tablet, Melinda wouldn't be able to explain or defend.

Jayne clicked on the message app that should have captured all the texts that also came to Melinda's phone. Butterflies flitted in her stomach, and she stared for a long moment at the names and numbers filling the sidebar. Her finger hovered over the screen before she mustered the courage to click on her own name. The last string of messages popped up:

Jayne: Netflix Night? ☺

Melinda: I wish. Meeting Bailey at Burgers and Buns. Wish I could just go home and veg. ☹

Jayne: You'll have fun. <Confetti horn emoji> Drive safe.

Then a few minutes later:

Melinda: Ugh. Bailey just texted. Girls night now at Henry's Waterfront Cafe. Hate last minute changes <crazy face emoji>

Jayne: Go have fun. Be safe.

Jayne's vision blurred over her last words to her dear friend: *Be safe.*

Blinking away the tears, Jayne clicked on other messages from Melinda's friends. From Bailey. Plans to meet at the Burgers and Buns in town. So *why* had she headed out to Lake Road?

Then she clicked on Melinda's boyfriend Kyle's messages.

```
Kyle: Hey Babe, grab pizza after work?

Melinda: I told you I had plans with my
friends.

Kyle: Cancel them

Kyle: Where are you?

Melinda: No

Kyle: What took you so long to answer?

Kyle: Mel?

Kyle: Come on, baby

Kyle: <angry face emoji>

Kyle: I miss you

Kyle: Stop ignoring me

Kyle: Why ya gotta be like this?
```

And then the texts stopped. Kyle's growing frustration was evident. Melinda never got back to him. Never told him about her change in plans.

Jayne absentmindedly twirled a strand of hair around her finger while she studied the screen. There was another number there without a name attached. She clicked it and her pulse spiked:

```
716-555-2436: Hey. Change in plans! Meet
us @ Henry's Waterfront Cafe.-B
```

Then, about ten minutes later:

```
716-555-2436: Don't text & drive
```

Her breath sounded in her ears. Someone *had* changed the location. Someone claiming to be "B." *Bailey.* And what about the second text?

Jayne's finger hovered over the reply box.

She felt like she was plucking petals off a flower. *Loves me, loves me not. Should I? Should I not?*

What could it hurt?

Wait, wait, wait. She took a screen shot as proof of the message and sent it to her phone.

With fingers that felt fat and clumsy, she tapped out on Melinda's tablet:

```
Melinda: Who is this?
```

And she waited, her pulse beating wildly in her chest.

Please reply, please reply.

"I don't like when that actress wears her hair like that. It makes her look like she has a really long face. Like a horse."

"Mom!" Jayne snapped her attention away from the tablet. "That's not very nice." But she couldn't help but laugh. God had seen to it that her mother maintained her wicked sense of humor.

"Well, I'm not telling her to her face. I can only imagine she thinks the same thing when she looks in the mirror."

Jayne rolled her eyes. Dementia was slowly removing her mother's filter.

She looked down at the screen. Little bubbles appeared that indicated someone had opened the message and was active. Tingles raced across her scalp.

Come on . . . come on . . . come on . . .

716-555-2436: Who is THIS?

Excitement fluttered in Jayne's stomach. She had actually gotten a reply. Her fingers hovered over the keyboard.

Melinda: A friend of Melinda's.

To which the anonymous person replied:

716-555-2436: How did you get her phone?

Jayne ignored the question and asked again:

Melinda: Who is this?

The little bubble indicator returned. Jayne swallowed hard, waiting. Then a reply popped up:

716-555-2436: Someone who knows not 2 text & drive.

"Oh, oh, oh," Jayne muttered, getting flustered. Her blood pressure spiked with the back-and-forth. She glanced over at her mom, who was staring at the TV. How she responded was going to be crucial. She closed her eyes and prayed for guidance. Okay . . .

Melinda: Did you witness Melinda's accident?

Jayne stared at the tablet for what seemed forever until the bubble indicator disappeared and she had to conclude that the person was done texting her.

Tapping her fingers on the edge of the tablet, she feared she'd go out of her skin. Jayne scrolled up through the messages and found that the last one sent on the night of Melinda's accident was at 9:07.

Untucking her legs from under her, she dialed Danny's number. She had to know.

"Hey, how are you?" Danny answered.

"Fine." She cleared her throat. "You have access to records of when calls come in to dispatch, right?"

"Yeah." Skepticism dripped from that single word.

"Can you look up the time that Mr. King called in Melinda's accident? I need the exact time." She fidgeted with the cross pendant on her necklace.

"Why?"

"I can explain later. Do you have it?"

"Hold on."

Clicking sounded in the background. He was obviously typing something into his patrol car's laptop. "The call came in at 9:11."

"Okay, I think I have something. I mean, I do . . ." Jayne sputtered. "Melinda received a text at 9:07 from an anonymous number. Four minutes before Mr. King called in the crash."

"What did it say?"

"'Don't text and drive.'"

"'Don't text and drive'? Really?" Danny scratched his forehead in disbelief. He had pulled his patrol car into the parking lot of one of those stores where nothing cost more than a dollar. Where nothing was worth more than a dollar.

"Yes." Jayne sounded breathless. "This must mean someone was toying with her. I Googled the number that sent the text, but I couldn't get any information. It all came back as private or restricted. You have resources I don't. You can find out who has that number. What if the car Mr. King saw swerved, and, between that and the text, Melinda got distracted, overcompensated, and ended up in the lake?"

"That's putting a lot of pieces together." Danny rubbed his jaw. Jayne had a knack for forcing pieces together that didn't necessarily fit. He had been at the receiving end of that suspicion when her brother died. And it wouldn't be a great career move to get caught up in her suspicions again.

"Hold on." A long silence stretched over the line before Jayne came back on. "Kyle was texting Melinda that night." Danny figured she was reading the messages. "He wanted to do something with her. But she brushed him off because she already had plans. She ignored a long string of texts from him. Nothing out of the ordinary for a couple having a fight, I guess. I mean, do you think he's capable of hurting her?"

Resting his elbow on the door, Danny ran his hand across his forehead. "I don't know him well enough. I drove him home earlier. Seems like he's distraught over her death. Who wouldn't be?" With a subtle nod, Danny acknowledged a driver who rolled slowly past in the parking lot.

"What did his last few texts say?" he asked, curious despite trying to dissuade Jayne from jumping to conclusions.

"'I miss you. Stop ignoring me.' The instructors don't use their phones while teaching. She might not have been intentionally ignoring him. But she didn't reply when class was over, either. And then . . ." Danny envisioned Jayne leaning over the tablet at her kitchen counter, tucking a wayward strand of red hair behind her ear. "Just around nine, the text from the strange number claiming to be B—for Bailey—saying they changed the location of their get-together."

"But Bailey didn't send the text changing the location?"

"No, like I said, I talked to her at church and saw her phone myself."

Danny scrubbed a hand across his face. "Any other friends with the initial *B*?"

"No. This person wanted Melinda to think it was Bailey. I just know it." Jayne's voice grew high pitched.

"The person would have also needed to know that Melinda had plans to go out." The vents in the dash pumped heat into the cab of his patrol vehicle.

"How hard would that be? It's not like Melinda and her friends are secretive. I mean, if it was Kyle, Melinda told him as much."

The text wasn't exactly a smoking gun, though, and Kyle wasn't exactly any kid. "He's the mayor's son."

"So, what does that mean? Does he have diplomatic immunity or something?" The hard edge to her sarcastic comment suggested her frustration.

He bit back his own annoyance. "We can't harass him simply because you have a hunch."

"You don't think it's strange?"

"Have you discussed this with either of your brothers?" Danny felt a little guilty wanting to pass the buck on this one. Melinda's accident was tragic, but he was having a hard time getting behind Jayne's suspicion that someone meant her harm.

"They'll blow me off. Please. Help me do a little digging, for my peace of mind, at least."

Danny turned down the heat. "Okay," he said, resigned. "We'll talk to Kyle. If you look him in the eye, will that satisfy you that he's innocent in all this?"

"When?" The sound of hope in her voice made his stomach pitch. *Have I just thrown fuel on the fire?*

"I'll pick you up at eleven tomorrow."

"Thank you," Jayne said, her tone a mix of gratitude and relief. "One more thing."

"What's that?"

"I texted the strange number. Someone replied." Jayne read off the string of texts.

"Enough with that for now. We'll talk to Kyle tomorrow." He didn't fully trust that Jayne wouldn't find a way to get herself into trouble before then. "Don't get any ideas to go over and talk to Kyle yourself."

"I wouldn't dream of it."

She ended the call, and Danny stared at the phone with a very bad feeling in the pit of his stomach.

FOURTEEN

I'm not a fan of funerals. Or small talk. Or annoying people in general. And people can be *so* annoying. Especially at funerals.

Today, I had to deal with all of those things. Amazing I held it together. It's nearly impossible to act all sympathetic under the circumstances.

"You must do things you don't want to do to get the things you want most," the raspy guru's voice says, filling my head with much-needed wisdom while I sit on my bed with my eyes closed, trying to block out the world.

I suppose some people read the Bible for life advice; I listen to Bud Byrdie on audio. Over and over.

You must overcome your anger to focus.

Don't let other people steal your power.

Act, don't react. Go out and get what's rightfully yours.

The mantras roll through my mind, helping me cool my anger, yet also making me wonder if they could hire a voice actor to read Bud's books. His ideas are revolutionary, but his voice is grating. I image his arrogance wouldn't allow for a narrator other than himself.

Maybe I'm just in an exceptionally bad mood. I'm entitled to that. I'm entitled to more than that.

My phone vibrates on my pillow and dread scrapes up my spine. *Easy, there.* It's not even the same phone that I texted Melinda from. Frowning, I realize I shouldn't have responded to those texts earlier. I didn't *really* expect it to be Melinda, but seeing her name pop up nearly gave me a heart attack.

Back from the dead. Too much *Walking Dead*, I suppose? Need to cut back on the TV viewing and focus on my life goals.

No one ever achieved their dream by sitting in front of the boob tube. Bud certainly didn't.

Bud didn't go from a poor kid on the east side of Buffalo to a world-renowned motivational speaker by being passive. *He* went after what he wanted.

So far, that's gotten me nowhere.

Planting seeds for future harvest.

I laugh, a strident sound even in my own ears.

Yes, I'm definitely in a bad mood. If only people would stop being so . . . annoying. Get out of my way.

Somehow, someone must have found Melinda's phone. How could it possibly survive being submerged in the lake? Mine didn't work after I accidentally dropped it in the toilet. I suddenly stop mindlessly tapping my phone against my lower lip, feeling a little queasy.

Maybe someone got into her account or laptop or tablet or something.

Could they have? Why didn't I think of that?

My stomach knots. That was a stupid move. I should have ignored the text. But, no, wasn't it an amazing coincidence that I happened to look at my disposable phone tonight? A phone designated solely for sending Melinda anonymous texts.

It was meant to happen.

Act, don't react.

A new idea worms its way into my brain. Did the police retrieve all of Melinda's messages? Was it a police officer who texted me? My queasiness wells and crests, and I slowly breathe in through my nose.

Is there an ongoing criminal investigation? Things like weather, curve, unfamiliar road, and possible distracted driving have been bandied around. No investigation. Nothing criminal. Just a traffic cop measuring skid marks and closing the file. Cops aren't looking to complicate a case, especially when there's no evidence.

Relax. Relax.

There's no evidence. None of the anonymous messages can be traced to me, especially if there's no criminal investigation.

My jaw aches from grinding my teeth. I can't relax. It's not in my nature.

Stupid. Stupid. Stupid.

What was I thinking?

I wasn't. I fist my hand but resist the urge to pound my head.

That's your problem. You leap, then decide to look. My stomach pitches again and I swallow back my nausea.

Stupid, disgusting food. I should have refrained from eating anything at the reception. Melinda was so loved, so perfect, but when it came down to it, she had only been worthy of appetizers like grape jelly rolled in a piece of doughy Wonder Bread. Melinda's mom must have splurged on prepared food from a low-end catering company. Nothing like pulling out all the stops for their darling daughter.

Their perfect, darling daughter.

She wasn't so perfect.

Now, without Melinda, I can focus on me. Focus on my dreams.

My time. My time is coming.

FIFTEEN

After sitting on the couch with her legs tucked underneath her while watching a soap opera, a talk show, and now the start of the news, Jayne suddenly realized both her legs and her brain were numb. She changed the channel to a light comedy.

Jayne traced the edges of the tablet sitting on the couch cushion next to her. She had tossed it aside, but its neon-green cover glowed like a spotlight urging, "Open me, read me, check me out." *Figure out who's responding from the unlisted phone number.*

And Jayne wasn't a complete technology newbie. She could investigate without deleting data or anything. She'd successfully found the password, right? She could be sitting on a wealth of information. Critical, timely information.

What else is on Melinda's tablet?

Balancing the device on her lap, she clicked through a few other social-media apps, seeing that some of the more popular ones were busts with their generation, and another one was password protected. People their age only had Facebook accounts so that their parents and grandparents could tag them in photos or random stuff they found while reading other people's Facebook threads.

"Sorry, Melinda, for spying," Jayne whispered under her breath.

"What's that?" The one time her mother actually heard her when she kept her voice low.

"Are you hungry for dinner?" Jayne changed the subject.

"No, I don't think so." Uncertainty edged her voice; dementia had also affected Miss Natalie's eating habits. She'd once asked, "How do you know you're hungry?" So it was Jayne's job to make sure her mom ate at regular intervals.

"I'll warm up soup for us soon, okay?"

"Sounds nice," her mom said, not seeming to really care one way or another.

Jayne opened the photo app on Melinda's tablet and swiped through the pictures. Nothing out of the ordinary, if she counted a ton of sticking-out-your-tongue selfies ordinary. Which she supposed they were. She imagined these photos had also been uploaded on social-media sites where Melinda measured her popularity by the number of likes or hearts or whatever. Jayne had found herself posting on social media, seeking the approval of others, too, until Patrick's death. Then the cruel comments of random strangers were like a knife to the heart; they couldn't be softened by the far more common expressions of sympathy. For some reason, *Die pig die* stuck in her memory far more than a string of emoji hearts encircling the world.

It was then that Jayne had sworn off social media.

Tracing the outline of Melinda's beautiful face in one of her selfies, Jayne tried to block out that very dark time in her life.

Scanning the apps, she stopped on the one for e-mail. She figured all she'd find were sale ads and other spammy things. Fortunately, the e-mail password had been saved and Jayne got right in. She scrolled through the messages. The only e-mails Melinda had viewed pertained to her college classes. The rest remained unopened.

Young adults rarely used e-mail unless they had to, like for college applications, college classes, and then, four years later, job applications.

Jayne kept scrolling. A subject line caught her eye: *Open Me.* Apparently, Melinda hadn't felt compelled. The sender's e-mail— mrrhee@yahoo.com—didn't spark recognition in Jayne. Nor could she recall a friend of Melinda's by that name. It was probably some guy across the globe looking to scam Melinda, like the ones Jayne sometimes received:

> Dear Beautiful One: I come to you with news of inheritance. But first, you must send to me to prove your sincerity, 1000$. I look forward to conducting best business with you. I wait. Sincerely, Scammy Sam.

Yet a force unseen had Jayne clicking on the e-mail. A link was attached with a small thumbnail of a photo. She tapped on it and sucked in a gasp.

With trembling hands, she lifted the tablet close to her face, studying the details of the strange photo. It had been taken from outside of Melinda's bedroom window, through the screen. A chill coursed down Jayne's spine and she suddenly didn't feel like soup—or anything, for that matter—for dinner. From where the person was standing, he would have left footprints right where Melinda claimed she had seen them.

Melinda *had* seen footprints outside her bedroom window.

Jayne pushed off the couch, tablet in hand. "I'm going to step outside. Get some fresh air." She went to the front porch and looked up her neighbor's phone number on her smartphone.

Knees weak, she slowly sat down on the top step and listened to the phone ring as she stared at the house across the street.

"Come on, Ricky," she muttered. "Come on." She secretly hoped his wife Peggy wouldn't answer. Jayne generally didn't mind a little chatty, but Peggy was a lot chatty.

"—Lo." Jayne caught the last part of a greeting at the same time as her heart plummeted. *Peggy.* Apparently she'd started saying hello before she put the phone to her mouth.

"Hi, Peggy, this is Jayne Murphy."

"Why, hello, Jayne." Then her cheery voice immediately went down three octaves. "I'm *so* sorry about Melinda Green. What a tragedy."

"Yes, it is." Jayne got right to it. "I was wondering if Ricky could help me with a computer issue."

"Of course. Hold on." Peggy screamed to her husband, then she came back on the line. "Oh, I see you're sitting on the porch. I'll send him right out."

"Thank you."

"And sweetie, I have you all in my prayers. I know how close you two were."

"Thank you." Jayne ended the call and fingered her silver cross necklace, sliding it back and forth across the chain while she waited.

A few minutes later, Ricky strolled across the street in a T-shirt with a stain on the shoulder. His hair had a pronounced cowlick near the crown of his head, as if he had been sleeping on it.

"Hey, Jayne." Tucking his hands under his armpits, Ricky rolled up on the toes of his untied Converses. He jerked his chin toward the tablet in her hand. "Peggy said you needed help with something. Did you find Melinda's tablet?"

"Yeah." She swallowed hard. "Don't tell anyone, though. I plan to put it back before anyone misses it."

Ricky stuck out his bottom lip and nodded his approval, apparently deciding Jayne was more rebel than he'd given her credit for. She wished she could get in the head of a guy like Ricky. He was smart on all things technology—smarter than anyone she knew. But he seemed socially out of the loop. Maybe *he* was more rebel than Jayne gave *him* credit for.

"I found this photo."

Ricky held out his hand, and she reluctantly passed the tablet to him. Her invasion of Melinda's privacy had gone up a notch. But this was important. If someone had been creeping on Melinda, who's to say he hadn't lured her to a different location, then run her off the road? Or lured her to a different location with plans to attack her, and the accident was just an unintended consequence of being out on Lake Road on a stormy night? Jayne's nerves were frazzled, and she could barely contain herself.

Ricky twisted his face in concentration. "We don't have to check the photo's metadata to find out where it was taken, because that's obvious. I take it you recognize this room?" He had an even way of talking that would make a lesser person feel dumb.

"Yeah, I do. Can you track the e-mail?" Jayne slid in next to him and clicked through to the e-mail app. She pointed to the message with the creepy photo attached from mrrhee@yahoo.com.

"Anyone can go on Yahoo or Gmail or something and create a random, anonymous e-mail address." Ricky clicked on the link. "Did you try to reply?"

Jayne shook her head. "No, but I did respond to a text from an unfamiliar number that was sent to Melinda the night she died."

"Really?" Ricky did a double take. "Who was it?"

"They didn't say. Can you do a reverse lookup or something on the phone number?"

Ricky scrubbed a hand across his jaw. "If you want to leave the tablet with me, I can poke around. IP addresses can be tracked, stuff like that. I bet the phone number is restricted. They do sell disposable phones that are hard to track. But I can do some digging when I have time."

"Can you?" Hope calmed some of the churning in her stomach. If Ricky could track the information, she wouldn't have to bother Danny.

"Yeah, I'm kinda buried with work. But I can look into it." Ricky roughly scratched his head, leaving more tufts of hair jutting out at awkward angles.

"There you are!"

Feeling like she had been caught kissing her best friend's boyfriend, Jayne spun around to find Carol Anne walking around the side of Jayne's house with a glass dish. Jayne tried to ignore the tablet in Ricky's hand. Maybe Carol Anne wouldn't recognize her stepsister's device.

"Hello." Carol Anne held out the dish. "I wanted to return this."

Jayne shuffled her feet and made a big show of checking out the dish. "Oh, that's not mine. I'm sorry to say I didn't bake anything. I brought over some prepackaged cookies from the grocery store." She laughed nervously.

"Oh." Turning the empty dish over in her hands, Carol Anne stuck out her lower lip. "I don't know why I thought this was yours." She shrugged, then smiled at Ricky. "Hello."

"Hi." He cleared his throat, obviously out of his comfort zone. "I'm sorry about your sister."

Carol Anne closed her eyes and nodded slowly, as if emotion had suddenly stolen her words. Jayne understood that. She couldn't wait to get away from all the well-wishers after her brother had died.

"Is that my sister's tablet?" Carol Anne asked on reopening her eyes. "Where did you find it?"

"Um . . ." Ricky stammered, and Jayne's mind swirled.

Sweat slicking her palms, Jayne plastered on a fake smile as a fully formed lie popped into her head. She wasn't a liar, but this was a matter of self-preservation.

"Melinda left it at the studio. I didn't realize it was hers until I started going through it."

"You went through her tablet?" Jayne sensed Carol Anne was trying to hide her disdain for what Jayne had done, but the hard set of her jaw gave her away. She had a right to be angry.

Maybe Carol Anne also had a need for answers. *She* had lost her stepsister.

Yet, suddenly, Jayne was afraid to let the tablet out of her sight. She took the device from Ricky's hands and said, "I'm all set. Thanks for your help."

"Don't you still need my help?" Ricky asked.

"Maybe later." Jayne patted his arm. "I appreciate you coming over. Maybe we can talk again in a few days."

"Okay." He rubbed his head, and his hair was just as mussed as ever. He flicked his hand. "'Bye."

Jayne watched her neighbor cross the street, then she turned to Carol Anne, wrapping her fingers tightly around the edges of the tablet. She needed to put off Carol Anne without offending her. But mostly, she needed to keep this tablet. For now.

Jayne plastered on a friendly smile. "I need your input on something. Do you think you could help me?"

"What is it?" Carol Anne asked with the curiosity of someone eager to be in on the gossip. With the fervor of someone who usually wasn't.

Almost immediately, Jayne questioned her sanity for bringing Carol Anne into this. But did she have a choice? Carol Anne would have expected to take her sister's tablet home and Jayne wasn't ready to hand it over.

Maybe Carol Anne sensed her indecision, because she touched Jayne's arm. "Why did you take the tablet to him? Why didn't you give it to Victoria?"

Jayne cleared her throat. "I will return it, but I was looking at the tablet and found something. Ricky's really good at technology, and I wanted to make sure I didn't do anything to lose the data." She tapped her thumb on the cover. "I know how much seeing her photos would mean to Victoria. And you."

"Oh . . ." Carol Anne pointed to the tablet with her free hand. "What did you find? It has to do with Kyle, right?"

"Her boyfriend?" Jayne's mouth went dry. She turned to track a minivan driving down the street. A mother. A father. Two kids in the backseat. Maybe headed out for ice cream after dinner.

Another day in an ordinary life.

Oh, what Jayne wouldn't do to only be worried about sprinkles or no sprinkles on her ice-cream cone.

Carol Anne slowly shook her head. "Her ex-boyfriend. They had broken up. Melinda said he was hassling her."

Jayne buried her surprise underneath an invitation to come in for coffee.

Carol Anne smiled. "Sounds nice. Just for a bit. Victoria's not doing well. I don't want to leave her alone for long. She needs me." Jayne had a sense that Carol Anne liked to be needed.

A realization whispered across Jayne's brain: *don't we all.*

Jayne climbed the porch steps and held the door open for Carol Anne. As her guest slipped past, Jayne touched the back of her hand. "It'll take some time for Victoria to heal. Give it time. I'm sure it brings her comfort that you're here."

"Pfft . . ." Carol Anne made a face. "You and I both know Victoria never liked me."

"I'm sure she likes you. Maybe she doesn't know how to show it." The white lie tasted foul. Apparently Carol Anne sensed what Jayne already knew. Melinda's mother had never liked her husband's daughter, and she had told Jayne as much. As a teenager, it had struck Jayne as odd that an adult would openly talk negatively about another teen—her parents certainly never did. Her mother never even swore in front of her children. *Ever.* So Jayne had been secretly thrilled to be included in such tawdry gossip. To be included in a conversation that seemed so . . . adult.

Other than her dislike for her stepdaughter, Victoria, by all accounts, was a good person and a doting mother. No one was perfect.

"Let me check on my mom," Jayne said, "then we'll chat."

Miss Natalie was dozing in the family room, and Jayne realized with a start that she hadn't prepared the soup she had promised.

Gesturing to a kitchen chair across from hers, Jayne sat down, too tired to make Carol Anne the coffee she had promised. "What do you know about Melinda and Kyle's relationship?"

"Well . . ." Carol Anne clasped her hands and rested them in her lap, as if she were pleased to be the center of attention. "She wanted to cool things down, and he kept coming around. He couldn't take no for an answer."

"Did he ever hurt her?"

Carol Anne's eyes flared wide. "Not that I ever saw. It was more subtle."

Jayne tilted her head, waiting for Carol Anne to continue.

"He didn't want to lose her."

Jayne tapped on the tablet, and the image of Melinda's bedroom taken from outside her window opened on the screen. She spun the tablet around on the table to face Carol Anne.

Carol Anne leaned close to study the photo. "*He* took this."

"The message was unread. It was sent from an e-mail address I don't recognize—mrrhee@yahoo.com. Does that sound familiar?"

"No, not at all." Covering her mouth with one hand, Carol Anne tapped on the photo with the other. "She told me she saw footsteps in the dirt outside her window, but when we looked, I didn't see anything."

"She told me, too. I figured it was the landscapers." Jayne scratched her forehead. "Did Melinda ever tell her mom?"

"I think she wanted to, but was afraid Victoria and my dad wouldn't let her go to New York City if she was too scared to live here in Tranquility."

"Was Melinda planning a trip to New York City?"

"You didn't know? Melinda planned to move there after she graduated from college."

"*Move* there? I had no idea." Surprise and disappointment edged her tone.

I wonder why Melinda hadn't shared that with me?

Jayne tried to hide the hurt.

Carol Anne shrugged as if she, too, had no idea why Melinda had kept that information a secret. What other secrets had Melinda kept from Jayne? But wasn't a young woman allowed to keep some things private? Jayne kept her share of secrets.

Crossing her arms tightly across her chest, Jayne wondered if she should have left well enough alone.

She blinked rapidly, trying to keep her disappointment in check.

"Did you try to contact the person who sent the e-mail?"

The weight of Carol Anne's steady gaze unnerved her.

"I don't know if I should."

"You could send it from Melinda's e-mail." Carol Anne laughed. "Might freak them out."

"I'm sure it would." She wondered about the person at the other end of that private phone number. "This may be a police matter. Maybe Melinda had a stalker. Maybe he ran her off the road . . ." As soon as the words came out of her mouth, Jayne reached across and grabbed Carol Anne's wrist. "Don't repeat that to Victoria. I don't want to cause her any more worry in case I'm way off base. It's just that Melinda got a text from a strange number the night of her accident. And because of that text, she ended up on Lake Road and not at the restaurant where her friends were."

"You think someone forced my sister off the road?" Carol Anne's voice grew loud, panicked. Jayne glanced over her shoulder, relieved Miss Natalie was still sleeping, her head slanted at an awkward angle.

"I'm probably being paranoid." Her nervous laugh didn't sound reassuring. "Who do you think got Melinda hooked on all those crime shows?" She clutched Carol Anne's hands on the table and leaned close.

"Please forget I said anything. I'd hate to cause your mom—I mean Victoria—any more pain. And I didn't mean to worry you."

What was I thinking?

"Who do you think sent the photo?" Carol Anne's voice had a strange quality to it, a mix between fear and curiosity.

"Maybe it was a joke. People take photos of everything nowadays, don't they?"

"Hmm . . ." Melinda's stepsister seemed to be considering. "I wouldn't put it past Kyle for a joke . . . or otherwise. He wasn't too thrilled with her moving to New York City, and I once heard him tell her she'd never cut it there. At first I thought he meant as a dancer, but now I wonder if he meant because she was such a chicken, afraid of everything."

"Kyle knew about her plans to move, too?"

Carol Anne drew in a long breath and nodded.

A ticking started in Jayne's head. Did everyone besides her know about Melinda's planned move to New York City? She slumped in her chair. None of that mattered anymore. She stared at the photo until it went blurry. "I'll ask Officer Danny Nolan"—she was careful to make it sound all official—"to look into this. I'm out of my league. If it's nothing, he'll know." She didn't want to tell Carol Anne that they already had plans to talk to Kyle.

Carol Anne placed her hand over the tablet and met Jayne's eyes. "Sometimes an accident is just an accident. No other explanation." She tilted her head, studying her. "Victoria's fragile. If you ask these kinds of questions and you're wrong, she'll be hurt even more. Like you said, she needs time to heal."

"I'm well aware of that." Jayne ran her palm back and forth along the edge of the table. "That's why it'd be best if you didn't share this conversation with her. I'm probably chasing ghosts."

Carol Anne frowned, as if considering. "Do you plan on hanging on to her tablet?"

"For now. If it's okay with you," Jayne quickly added. "I'll return it when I'm done."

"Okay." Carol Anne looked like she wanted to add something else, but didn't. She pushed away from the table and the loud screech made Miss Natalie open her eyes, but she didn't say anything. Carol Anne grabbed the dish that she had brought with her. "I guess I better find who belongs to this."

Jayne stood and followed her to the door. "I'd appreciate it if you kept this conversation between the two of us."

"Of course." Carol Anne gave Jayne an awkward side hug. "Night," she whispered into Jayne's hair. Then she pushed open the door and jogged down the steps.

Jayne stared out the front door long after Carol Anne had disappeared around the side of the house. Maybe she should have kept her mouth shut. But Carol Anne had given Jayne two new pieces of information: Melinda had broken up with Kyle, and she had planned to move to New York City.

Had Kyle subscribed to the if-I-can't-have-her-no-one-can school of thought? Or had Jayne watched one too many if-I-can't-have-you-no-one-can crime dramas?

There was only one way to find out.

SIXTEEN

I need to confront Kyle. See what he knows." Jayne fidgeted in the passenger seat of Danny's truck. They had dropped her mother off at her friend Barbara's house down the street for a visit. Jayne seemed encouraged that her mother wouldn't be spending the morning in front of the TV.

"It's not too late. We can call this off. I'll talk to him on my own. Leave you out of it." Danny braked a few blocks away from the mayor's home.

"I need to look him in the eye." She fumbled with the tablet in her lap.

"And you really need to return that."

"Who's going to miss it?" Her tone cut through him, and she turned her back to him. "Melinda's dead. And I want to find out what happened. Her parents probably don't even know she had this."

Danny pulled over and unclicked his seat belt, hoping to draw her attention. "Are you going to ignore me?"

Her shoulders rose and fell on a heavy sigh. After a long moment, she shifted in her seat to face him. A hesitant look flashed in her eyes. "Do you think I'm crazy?"

"I think you're looking for answers where there might not be any. Sometimes bad things happen. Period."

Jayne patted his chest. "I feel it in my gut. Something else was going on here. Melinda broke up with Kyle and had plans to move to New York City." The sting of that secret was evident in her tone. "That's enough to make a clingy boyfriend snap."

Danny covered her hand with his, and she lifted her bright-blue eyes to meet his eyes. A shy smile tilted the corners of her lips.

Good grief, this is Patrick's little sister.

He patted her hand, then removed it from his chest. "You want to find answers."

"Exactly!" Some of the light dimmed out of her eyes. "But you don't think there are answers. You think I'm crazy."

His fingers traced her hairline and tucked a strand behind her ear. "No, not at all. What I do think is that Melinda had a few secrets. I think Kyle is probably a jerk. Do I think he had a hand in her accident?" Danny twisted his lips. "I can't see it. He's needy. Not malicious."

"I have a bad feeling . . ."

Danny took her hand and traced an arc with his thumb. "I also know you're a good friend. Let's go see what Kyle has to say. Put your mind at ease."

He palmed the gearshift and pulled it back to drive. Jayne covered his hand. "Wait."

He jammed it back into park before they'd moved away from the curb.

"Maybe I should go alone. Keep you out of this."

"Why would I want that?" He played coy. The chief was going to kill him for continuing to mix it up with the mayor's son, especially when the mayor was down nine points in the polls.

"Kyle is the mayor's son. Your dad's boss."

"I said I'd take you and I'm not going back on my word." Helping Jayne see this through to the end was what he needed to do, even if the only thing he'd ultimately give her was peace of mind.

Jayne unbuckled her seat belt and leaned over, cupping his face with her soft hand. She left a gentle kiss on his cheek. Then she slumped back in her seat and smiled. "Thank you."

Danny stared at her a minute, the warmth of her kiss coursing through him. *What have I gotten myself into?*

"The only way I'd ever run for a political office is so that I could live in a place like this," Jayne said, admiring the fancy chandelier visible through the glass transom above the double doors of the mayor's home.

"Still not worth it," Danny muttered.

"Probably right." Jayne laughed, despite the nerves jangling in her stomach.

Danny pointed to the white structure behind the main house, an apartment above a three-car garage. "Kyle lives in the carriage house in back."

"Impressive." Jayne leaned toward the windshield when she noticed one of the garage doors opening.

Kyle appeared, ducking under the door, his hands stuffed in his jacket pockets. Based on the man's expression, he hadn't seen them pulling up the driveway. Danny put the gear in park and climbed out. Jayne joined him around the front of the truck, the edge of Melinda's tablet cutting into her palm.

"You again? What's going on?" Kyle asked, seeming a little fidgety despite his cocky tone.

"We're trying to put a few pieces together from the night of Melinda's accident." Danny's well-practiced, firm tone would have elicited an honest response from Jayne. No messing with him. Kyle, however, seemed unfazed, except for his fingers tapping something out on his thigh.

"Wasn't she meeting friends out? All I know is that she blew me off."

"Her friends were at Burgers and Buns. Other side of town," Danny said, not taking his eyes off Kyle. "But last-minute, someone changed the location to a place out by the lake. Was that you?"

Kyle drew his shoulders up and smirked. "Why would I do that?"

With the tablet in hand, Jayne clicked through a few screens and found one of the last text messages Melinda had received that night. She set the tablet on the hood of the truck, grabbed her cell phone from her purse, and dialed the number. She could hear the phone ringing on her end.

"Do you have your cell phone on you?" Jayne approached Kyle, her cell on speakerphone.

Brrringgg . . . Brrringgg . . .

"No." The single word was uttered as a challenge.

Jayne pointed toward the stairs leading to his apartment. "Any chance your phone is ringing right now?"

"What are you talking about?" Disgust dripped from his voice. "What is she, your junior detective?"

Danny pinned Kyle with a pointed stare.

"Do you have one of those burner phones?" Jayne asked, resting her elbow on her hip and holding up her ringing cell phone.

Kyle smirked. "What? Are you binge watching *Sons of Anarchy* or something?"

For some inexplicable reason, Jayne's cheeks grew hot. She was not going to allow this guy to talk down to her.

Footsteps sounded from inside the garage. Jayne lowered the phone to her side when she saw Quinn emerge from the shadowed garage bay.

"Um, hi." Quinn rocked back on her sneakers. "What's going on?"

"Nothing." Kyle spoke first. "For some reason this crazy lady wants my cell phone. Thinks I sent Melinda anonymous texts."

"Jayne's my boss." Quinn kicked his shoe softly in a subtle warning. "Sorry, he's a little rough around the edges."

"I didn't realize you were . . . friends with Kyle."

Blotches of pink blossomed on Quinn's face. "Yeah, we've known each other for a while." For a graceful dancer, she flung her arm awkwardly toward the bikes parked in the garage. "We were going to go for a bike ride. It's such a nice day. We wanted to get out. Try not to think about Melinda and all." The quiver in her voice suggested she wasn't so sure anymore. "Is something wrong?"

"We're trying to figure out what happened the night Melinda died," Danny said.

Something unreadable flashed in Quinn's eyes. "What do you mean? Wasn't it an accident?" She brushed the back of her hand across Kyle's arm. "What are they talking about?"

"I don't know." If Kyle had been a cartoon character, smoke would have been billowing up from his nose and ears. "*She* thinks she's going to find the answers on my phone."

Jayne's lips parted slightly as she struggled with the idea that Quinn was hanging out with Kyle less than a week after his girlfriend died.

Ex-girlfriend.

"Is she?" Accusation flashed in Quinn's leery gaze.

"Of course not." Contempt pinched his mouth. He was either highly offended or a good actor.

Quinn pressed a hand to her forehead and looked a little queasy. "I'll be right back."

When she was out of earshot, Jayne asked, "Are you and Quinn dating?"

"We're hanging out. That's all." Kyle glanced toward the steps inside the garage leading up to his apartment. A second set of steps hugged the outside wall. "Listen, I loved Melinda, but I have to move on."

"Glad to know you're so choked up about it," Danny said, his tone even.

Jayne drew in a deep breath. "Carol Anne told me you and Melinda had broken up."

Kyle groaned. "No. We just hit a rough patch. We were going to work things out."

"Were you?" The sun beat down on Jayne's neck. She'd pay for that later with a strip of sunburn. "You were planning on having a long-distance relationship?"

Kyle sucked in his lips. "What are you talking about?"

"You know, when she moved to New York after graduation."

Kyle bowed his head and rubbed his neck.

"Are you telling me you didn't know she had plans to move?"

Kyle snapped his head up and ran a hand across his mouth. "She'd never go through with it."

"Wishful thinking on your part?" Jayne couldn't help the jab.

"I know she wouldn't have." Kyle crossed his arms, jamming his fists in his armpits.

"Because you made sure she didn't," Jayne spit out.

Danny held up his hand and gently touched Jayne's arm. She shot a sideways glance over at him to get a read on the situation, but something caught his attention in the open garage.

Quinn strode out with a cell phone in hand. "Here, look. I have Kyle's cell phone. You can check for yourself."

Jayne expected Kyle to protest, but he only stood there with a stoic expression on his face.

Jayne put her phone on top of the tablet on the hood of the car, then took Kyle's phone. "You seem pretty confident."

Quinn lowered her eyes and mumbled, "Kyle's a nice guy, despite the stuff Melinda said. There's always two sides of a story when a couple breaks up."

"We hadn't broken up. Not really." Kyle scratched his head.

A tingling started in Jayne's fingers and moved up her arms. She handed the cell phone to Danny. "Hold this." She grabbed her phone and dialed the restricted number again, but Kyle's phone didn't ring.

She twisted her mouth, thinking. "I wanted to see if he had downloaded one of those burner apps on his phone."

"See, I told you," Kyle said. "I didn't text Melinda to meet me out at that restaurant on Lake Road."

"It doesn't mean you don't have another phone." Jayne ran a hand over her hair, warm from the sun. "One of those cheap ones you can buy at a drugstore."

Kyle held up his palms. "I don't."

"Wait." Jayne tucked her phone into her back pocket and took Kyle's phone from Danny. She touched the screen without looking at Kyle. "What's your passcode?"

"Wait, what are you doing?" He took a step toward her.

Jayne lifted her eyebrow. "If you have nothing to hide . . ."

"I don't." Kyle sounded like a petulant child. "Here." He took his phone, entered his PIN, then handed it back to Jayne as if to say, *See for yourself.*

Jayne flipped through the first few screens. There were too many apps to tell if he had one that let a caller disguise their phone number, but she could check something else quickly.

Jayne clicked on the photo app and scrolled through his photos. Surprisingly, Kyle didn't have a gazillion selfies on his phone. However, Jayne wasn't much older and she also wasn't a fan of the vanity trend.

When she landed on the photo she was looking for, her pulse slowed to molasses in her veins. She clicked on it, and the shocking reality—that Kyle had stood outside Melinda's bedroom window and taken a photo like a stalker—chilled her to the core.

She held the phone out to him, screen forward. "Can you explain this?"

"Hey, you didn't say you were going to check my photos. You said texts. Just texts."

"I asked if I could look at your phone and you gave me permission." Jayne didn't take her eyes off Kyle. His nostrils flared.

"Let me see that." Danny took the phone and glanced down at the photo, then up at Kyle. "Why did you take this?"

Kyle's shoulders sagged. "Oh, man, it was a *joke*. Did Melinda say something to you about it?" He shook his head in disbelief. "I didn't even know if she got it. She never said anything."

"How would she have known you sent it? Would she have recognized the e-mail address you sent it from?"

"No," Kyle admitted. "I used a junk e-mail address I use for all kinds of spammy stuff."

"Why didn't you just text her from one of your fake phone numbers?"

Kyle paced in front of Danny's truck, the gravel crunching under his choppy steps. He stopped abruptly and pointed at Jayne. "I don't *have* a fake phone number. Like I said, the photo was a joke. You know how worked up she got about all those crime shows."

"Kyle," Quinn said, "why would you want to scare Melinda?"

"It was a joke." He snatched his phone from Danny's hand. "Why did you have to stir up trouble? It's nothing."

Quinn shook her head in disgust. "I'm going home." She slowed and smiled at Jayne. "See you at the studio."

Jayne nodded. Quinn put on her bike helmet and then pushed her bike out of the garage. Kyle turned to Jayne once the clicking sound from Quinn's bike reached the end of the driveway.

"I'll be straight with you. I was mad at Melinda. She was talking about spending more time apart, but that's not what she really wanted. I was stupid to take that photo. I wanted to freak her out. She was wrapped up in all those stupid crime shows. And dance. If she was scared enough, she'd run back to me. Give up the crazy idea of New York. It was dumb, I know that now. But I had nothing to do with her accident. Nothing." Water formed in the corners of his red eyes, but he never actually cried.

"I saw the texts you sent her. You seemed pretty upset. Angry, even."

"See?" Kyle jabbed his finger in the direction of the tablet. "If you saw my texts, you know I used this phone. *My* phone number."

"Doesn't mean you don't have a second phone." Jayne gritted her teeth. "If you had anything to do with Melinda being on Lake Road, even as a joke, I'm going to let everyone know what a jerk you are. And if you . . ." A throbbing pulsed behind her eyes.

"Jayne?" Danny tried to break through her red-hot anger, but she wasn't ready to back down. Not yet.

"I had nothing to do with those texts," Kyle spat out. "I only sent the photo as a joke. That's all. Did you see the e-mail address? Mr. Rhee at yahoo dot com?" He said it more slowly. "Mr. Rhee. *Mystery.*" He smirked at his cleverness. "She was into all that crime and mystery stuff because of you. Anyway . . . I figured she'd eventually get the joke, even if it did make her second-guess her decision to move to the big city with all the crime."

"What a nice guy." Jayne felt a shortness of breath at the depth of his betrayal. *What kind of guy does that sort of thing?*

Kyle dragged his hand through his hair. "Oh, what did it matter, anyway? I had pretty much come to the conclusion that your stupid dance studio—*dance*—was her life. I could never compete."

Jayne moved closer to Kyle, secretly pleased that she was a few inches taller than he was. "Dance had nothing to do with it. You would have lost Melinda anyway because you're mean and petty." She glowered at him. "And small."

A muscle worked in Kyle's jaw and his cheeks puffed in frustration.

"Let's go," Danny said, gently taking Jayne's arm.

Danny opened the truck door for Jayne, and she climbed in and buckled her seat belt with jerky movements, missing the latch a few times before it clicked. The exchange had made her lightheaded. When Danny climbed in behind the wheel, she said, "I never liked him."

"I could hardly tell."

SEVENTEEN

The dance studio looked like someone had swallowed a box of pink tissues and thrown up a gazillion flowers. The transformation of Studio A was an homage to Melinda, who as a little girl loved to fold tissues into the shape of flowers and then pin them in the center with a bobby pin. Every dancer and her mom always had a million bobby pins around, except when they really needed one.

Tonight would mark a full week since Melinda had been killed, and tomorrow morning they would host a final farewell to Murphy's Dance Academy's favorite teacher.

The local florist had also dropped off four bouquets of flowers, one for each corner of the studio. A nearby bakery donated cookies shaped like ballerinas. The residents of a small town pulled together in times of tragedy. This was generally a good thing, except when you wanted to run to the grocery store and grab a gallon of milk without someone expressing their shock and dismay at your brother's brutal murder.

Not a fun conversation to have back in dairy by the Danimals Smoothies.

Jayne pinned the last tissue flower and stood back. The studio had been closed for instruction since Melinda's accident, and Monday they'd reopen for business.

Jayne had tentatively hired two former students who were enrolled at the nearby university to fill in for some of Miss Melinda's classes. Quinn had offered to cover more of the classes, but Jayne felt as if she had as many as she could handle. Neither of the temporary instructors seemed interested in long-term positions. Nor was Jayne sure they'd be the best fit to maintain Murphy's Dance Academy's status as a top-notch studio.

Miss Natalie and the parents demanded the best.

Jayne was looking forward to getting back to normal. *If* that were possible. Until she had her answers, she'd always wonder about Melinda's death, and part of her feared she'd never get answers. Taking a creepy photo from outside your girlfriend's bedroom window made you creepy, not necessarily a murderer.

It did make sense, in a warped kind of way, that Kyle would use Melinda's obsession with true crime to try to scare her from moving to New York City. Still, there was the unanswered question of who'd sent the anonymous texts.

Jayne stretched her arms out to her sides to ease the kinks from her back. She had been hunched over the table for hours, folding tissue flowers with her mother.

Miss Natalie hummed quietly to herself as she tore the plastic off a pack of silver napkins. The only time she came to life and seemed happy was when she was at the studio. Jayne couldn't sell the studio to Miss Gigi, no matter how many times the idea had crept into her mind since Miss Gigi'd had the nerve to bring it up.

On one hand, selling the studio would provide much-needed funds for her mom's long-term care, if and when it became necessary. However, if her mom didn't have the studio, Jayne imagined she'd decline faster than she already had. The physician had said it was key to keep her mom active. Busy. Both mentally and physically.

A person had a lot of time to think about things while folding tissue flowers.

"It looks pretty." Miss Natalie fanned the last package of napkins out on the table. Her smile began to falter. "Are we hosting a baby shower?" Uncertainty trembled in her voice. She was in her midsixties but could easily pass for a decade younger. Her physical fitness and beauty were a contradiction to her weakening mind.

Jayne slipped her arm around her mother's shoulders. A lump of emotion trapped the words she needed to say. *Do I need to say them? Could she lie to her mom?* It would be an innocent lie that God would certainly forgive. Protect her from the knowledge—yet again—that one of "her girls" had died.

Jayne sniffed and Miss Natalie looked up at her, concern alighting in her eyes. "What's wrong?"

"We're having a little party to celebrate Miss Melinda's life."

"Oh?"

Jayne squeezed her mother's shoulders. "Yes, Mom. I'm sorry. Miss Melinda was in a car accident."

Her mother shook her head in a mix of dismay and disbelief. "You did a nice job. Everything looks so pretty."

"The dancers are coming in the morning. It will be a fitting memorial to Miss Melinda."

Her mother squared her shoulders. "Yes, yes, it will."

"There's one more thing we have to do." Jayne grabbed a large manila envelope from the end of the table. "We can tape these to the mirror." She turned over the envelope, and photos of a life cut too short spilled out onto the table. "I pulled some of these from social media. Victoria provided the rest."

Her mother picked up a photo of a young Melinda on her backyard swing, her feet pointed toward the sky, a huge smile on her face. Long, dark pigtails flying out behind her. Pure joy on the child's face. Miss Natalie traced the outline of the photo. "Too much sadness lately."

"I know." The back of her throat ached. "Yes, too much sadness."

Her mother lifted her eyes to meet her daughter's. "You've experienced far too much sadness. Dad. Patrick. And now Melinda." She waved the photo in her hand.

Jayne sucked in a breath. Her mother's lucidity was fragile and fleeting, and Jayne wanted to hold it close and carefully, like a bird in the palm of her hand—she didn't want it to fly away, but she knew if she held it too tight, she'd destroy the bird. End the moment.

Her mother yawned and set the photo down as if it were a priceless crystal.

"Sean's going to pick you up, Mom. I'll finish up."

"Oh, don't bother him. He's so busy with work and his new house." Her brother had purchased a small fixer-upper. He was spending every spare minute working on it.

Jayne smiled to herself. Her mother never wanted to bother her sons, but she didn't think much about the fact that her daughter had deferred her dreams of becoming a police officer to help both around the house and at the dance studio. It was a fact that made her neither angry nor resentful. It just was.

Just like Patrick hadn't been able to choose his fate, Jayne wasn't able to choose hers. Between the two siblings, she had the better deal. As the familiar dark emotions crowded in on her, Jayne turned her mind to her long-held beliefs. One day, she'd be reunited with all her family in heaven. The thought immediately brought her peace.

If only she could hold on to it.

A quiet knock sounded on the front door.

"Hold on, Mom. I think that's Sean."

"Oh, is he going to help us?"

Jayne patted her shoulder, knowing it wasn't important to correct her. "I'll be right back." Through the top half of the door, she saw Sean holding her niece Ava's hand, and her heart burst with love. Patrick's precious three-year-old daughter.

Jayne pushed on the door and struggled to release the deadbolt. She sighed heavily when she finally opened the door.

"Is something wrong?" her brother said, smiling down at his niece, probably realizing little kids had big ears, which sometimes led to lots of questions followed by bad dreams.

"No, everything's fine," she said in a baby voice as she crouched down to Ava's level. "How are you, sweetheart?" Ava dove into Jayne's arms, and they both squeezed each other tight. The smell of baby shampoo filled her nose. "Guess who's here. Grammy!"

Ava's eyes brightened. "Gammy." The little quirk of her lips always reminded Jayne of her brother. A smile sent from heaven.

"Yes, she's right back here." Holding the sweet child's hand, she led her into Studio A.

"Flowers!" Ava pointed at the pink tissue flowers. Melinda's favorite color.

"Yes, aren't they pretty? Would you like one?" Jayne handed her a soft flower by its bobby-pin stem, and her little niece pressed her button nose into its fake petals.

Miss Natalie reached for her granddaughter, who ran over to her and gave her a giant squeeze. God certainly knew what He was doing when He gave them Ava. Jayne just wished He hadn't had to take Patrick. Flattening her hand against her chest, she reminded herself not to question the why of things when it came to her faith. She struggled with enough whys of the earthly variety.

"Mom," Sean said, "want to help me babysit Ava?"

"Of course." She smooshed a kiss on the toddler's chubby cheek. "We should probably get her home and into PJs." Outside of dance, her mother's bliss was her granddaughter. Jayne's heart warmed as she watched Ava take her Grammy's hand and glance up at her with such pure adoration.

"We'll have to get her into dance lessons soon, right, Mom?" Jayne asked.

"Oh, yes." Miss Natalie swung her granddaughter's arm. "Would you like that?"

"Can I wear a princess dress?"

"Of course." Jayne smiled at her niece. "We should ask your mommy first," she added, not wanting to jeopardize the relationship with their sister-in-law. Patrick's widow. The Murphys had a decent relationship with Cara now, but Jayne often wondered if that would change over the years, especially if Cara remarried. Jayne tried not to dwell on that possibility.

"You good here?" Sean asked his little sister as he walked toward the door.

"Yes, I'll finish up and then swing by your place to get Mom. How long do you have Ava?"

"For a few hours. Cara wanted to run errands." He patted his niece's head. "I think she's"—he lowered his voice to barely a whisper—"dating someone."

Jayne's eyes flared wide. Exactly what she feared. Not that Cara didn't have a right to; Jayne just wanted to keep Ava close. She ran a hand over her niece's soft hair and went for the magnanimous response: "She deserves happiness." That's what people said when young widows found new love, right?

Something crossed Sean's eyes that Jayne couldn't quite read. "Does that bother you?"

"Well, she's still here. Our brother's not."

"Yeah," Sean said, seeming noncommittal.

Jayne opened the door on the large Victorian home. "I'll help you buckle Ava in."

He gave her a mock offended stare. "I'm more than capable. I run police checks on car seats."

"An aunt can't buckle her niece in?"

She followed them outside, settled Ava, and gave Miss Natalie a kiss on her soft cheek. Then she stepped back and waved as they drove away. Imagine that, her tough brother with a car seat in the back of his car.

That should be Patrick with his daughter.

Jayne drew in a deep breath. It seemed her entire life of late involved one sad thought folding into another.

Dear Lord, please give me comfort and peace. Let me cherish each moment and not dwell upon the bad.

Her nose tingled. Her loved ones were in heaven, but knowing they weren't here on earth hurt. A lot. She'd have to dig deep. Find the strength to get through tomorrow's memorial.

A gust of wind whipped up, and dried leaves scraped across the sidewalk as a sudden chill slithered up her spine. The huge house surrounded by a parking lot and acres of land left her isolated. Alone. She spun around and hurried up the steps and into the studio, locking the door behind her.

The lights on inside Murphy's Dance Academy called to Danny like a beacon as he patrolled that part of town. Jayne's car was parked in the lot. He didn't think they were reopening the studio until Monday. Maybe she had preparations to make.

Danny hesitated a moment before turning into the lot. It couldn't hurt to check in on her. If Jayne's hunch was right and Kyle had something to do with Melinda's accident, who's to say he wouldn't turn his animosity on Jayne? Danny had seen firsthand the hatred in Kyle's eyes when they'd confronted him yesterday.

A weasel like Kyle wouldn't act on his aggression, would he? Danny's gut told him Kyle was more the sneaky type, rather than the in-your-face-I'm-going-to-hurt-you type. He was the type that would take a photo of his ex-girlfriend's bedroom without her knowledge.

Or maybe Danny was simply looking for an excuse to see Jayne.

He jogged up the steps and rapped lightly on the door, smiling when he saw Jayne through one of the glass inserts, peeking around the corner from her office with worry in her eyes. Her tight expression relaxed when she recognized him. Holding up her finger in a hold-on-a-minute gesture, she disappeared into the office, then came back and unlocked the door.

"What are you doing here?" Jayne gave his uniform and then his patrol car a once-over. Concern lingered in the depths of her eyes. "Is it one of my brothers?"

Danny waved his hands apologetically. "No, no, I didn't mean to alarm you."

Her shoulders sagged.

"I wanted to"—he stopped himself from admitting he wanted to see her—"make sure everything was okay here."

"Well, I'm here and I'm fine."

"Are you almost done? I can walk you out."

"Let me put a few things away. We have Melinda's memorial service in the morning." Returning to her desk, she pushed the chair out of the way and made a few piles on her desk. She patted one. "All this can wait. Not as exciting as police work, but stuff that needs to be done."

"It's been a long week."

Jayne sighed. "It has. Hard to believe it's only been a week." She picked up an envelope, then slowly sat. The corners of her mouth tugged down as she stared at the name on the envelope. "Melinda's paycheck. The system automatically printed it."

"I'm sorry."

"Nothing you can do." Resigned, she tossed the envelope aside.

"Ready for tomorrow?" Danny shifted his stance, feeling a little uncomfortable.

"We're as ready as we'll ever be. Melinda's not going to be easy to replace." She planted her elbows on the desk and supported her chin in the palm of her hand.

Danny wanted to touch her exposed neck. Instead he backed up, his heels hitting the doorframe. "You'll move past this."

"Do you ever move past losing someone?" She bowed her head and rubbed her forehead.

"I suppose not."

Jayne stood. "Let's go talk in the lounge in back. I want you to understand I'm not a loose cannon. Just because . . ." She slipped past him in the doorway and gestured to the back room with her open palm.

"Sounds serious," Danny joked.

"I need to officially clear the air."

Sensing where this conversation was headed, he waved his hands in front of him. "I'm fine with leaving everything in the past."

"Please." Her pretty blue eyes implored him. "This will always be lingering between us unless we discuss it. It's like the elephant in the room."

"This *does* sound serious. And big," he joked again.

"Come on." Jayne grabbed Danny's hand and led him to a cluster of couches set up at the side of the house in what must have been an add-on, a sunroom of sorts.

"Wow, this is nice. Can I sign up for dance classes?"

"Ha." Jayne let go of his hand and held hers out, indicating he should take a seat.

"Why do I feel like I should be standing for this?"

"Don't make this awkward. I can't say what I have to say with you glowering down at me." Jayne sat and tucked a leg under her, facing the empty half of the couch.

He sank into the oversized cushions. "For the record, I don't glower."

She grabbed her shin and pulled her leg closer. "You've been known to glower." A trace of a smile touched her eyes before she grew serious, leaving him to question his decision to stop by the studio.

"Thank you for not dismissing my concerns about Melinda's accident." She ran her hands along her thighs. "I know there's not much to go on, but I had to go down the path, otherwise I'd never be able to sleep at night."

"No problem," Danny said, casually crossing his ankle over his leg. "Part of my job."

"Not really. The chief is ready to write Melinda's crash off as an unfortunate accident. All indications show that it was, but you've been . . ." She pulled her foot closer to her and shifted toward him. "You didn't shut me down, and you had every right to after how I treated you when my brother died."

Out the windows, the blackness of night heaved and grew closer. Shifting forward on the cushion, Danny fought the overwhelming sense of dread making him want to flee. "We don't need to talk about this."

"When my brother was killed in the line of duty . . ." Her voice trembled and her cheeks grew pink. She swallowed hard before continuing, "I wanted to blame someone." She shrugged, but it wasn't a casual gesture. "And you were the easiest person to blame."

Danny nodded, his words getting lodged in the ache at the back of his throat.

"I wasn't fair. I lashed out, and once all the details came out revealing what really happened, I wasn't strong enough to apologize. An apology would mean I was accepting Patrick's death. And I wasn't ready."

The memory of Jayne cornering him at Patrick's wake hollowed out his gut. She'd demanded answers. She'd wanted to know where Danny was when that first 911 call went out. Why the gunman had targeted Patrick. Admitting he'd been sitting in his patrol car waiting for his sub seemed so pathetic that he chose to say nothing. And admitting that the situation escalated when he did arrive on scene, resulting in the death of his partner and a young man, felt too much like failure to discuss it.

"You were in pain," Danny finally said.

She scooted toward him and pulled his hands into hers. "We were all in pain. But it was wrong of me. After I went on the news accusing you of not getting to my brother in time, why didn't you defend yourself? Explain what really happened?"

Danny shrugged. "It wouldn't change the outcome." He cleared his throat. "And I felt like if I defended myself publicly, it would look like I was making excuses. I tried to keep my head down and do my job. I let the department's official statement stand."

And since Danny's father was the chief of police, the official statement appeared to be all about the police protecting their own.

"I didn't help you with that." She bit her lip. "In typical Jayne fashion, I jumped to my own theories. Finn finally got through to me about what really happened, but by then my pride and my spirit had been broken." She lowered her voice. "Can you forgive me?"

He searched her face. "Of course I forgive you." He just hadn't forgiven himself.

The intensity of the moment unnerved him. Pushing against the arm of the couch, he stood. "It's all cool."

"No, it's not."

Danny'd recognize his father's voice anywhere. The chief stood in the arched doorway to the dancers' lounge.

"Chief Nolan." Jayne struggled to pull her leg out from under her and stand. She tugged on the hem of her shirt, pulling it down over her jeans.

The chief tipped his chin toward Danny. "Your patrol car's out front. Trouble here?"

"Not at all."

"Aren't you supposed to be on patrol?"

Danny ground his teeth at his father's scolding. The dance studio was within his patrol area. If dispatch had a call, he'd respond in a timely manner. But he didn't need to explain that to his father. The chief knew that. He was here for another reason.

The chief shifted his stance to face him. "I got a phone call from the mayor."

And there it was.

"How's the mayor doing? I heard he's behind in the polls." Danny didn't care that he sounded like a petulant child.

Anger flashed in his father's eyes. "You realize if Mayor Duggan's not reelected, I'm out of a job."

"This is about politics." Anger simmered below the surface.

"It's about my job," the chief said. "Why did you and Jayne talk to Kyle yesterday?"

Danny wondered why it had taken his father a full day to confront him.

"I had a valid reason." Danny exhaled slowly through gritted teeth. "Kyle was in a relationship with Melinda Green. He had e-mailed her harassing photos prior to her accident."

"Why didn't Melinda report the incident before her death?" The chief pushed his hat back and stared at his son expectantly.

"She may not have opened the e-mail."

The chief crossed his beefy arms over his broad chest. "You were off duty when you went to speak to him and you brought a civilian."

Jayne stepped forward. Danny wanted to warn her off, but decided that probably wouldn't go over well. With either Jayne or his dad.

"Sir, I uncovered a few things on Melinda's tablet. I fear she may have been lured out onto Lake Road."

Danny watched his father's inscrutable expression.

"There's no indication anyone else was involved in her accident," the chief said.

"A witness saw another car down the road, but the driver didn't stop. No indication the car was involved or even saw the accident. The driver may have been slowing down due to the inclement weather conditions. But it was worth checking out," Danny said.

The chief sniffed. "Unless we have something concrete, you can't harass people."

"Kyle admitted to sending a photo that could be construed as stalking, or, at the very least, he's a Peeping Tom," Jayne said.

A muscle ticked in the chief's jaw. He quickly checked himself, smoothing out the lines of surprise around his eyes.

"Listen"—he dropped his arms to his side and softened his posture—"I'll admit. The mayor's son is a wild card. He's not the brightest bulb, but those are separate issues. And unfortunately, Melinda's not around to report the incident."

Danny discreetly brushed his hand across Jayne's lower back, and he sensed her tense.

"You both remember the relentless news coverage after Patrick's death." The chief didn't wait for a reply. Their small-town paper had raised a lot of questions. Words like *nepotism, incompetence, culpability* were thrown around.

Danny had grown numb to the accusations. No one could be harder on him over his best friend and partner's death than he had been. Still was.

"Well, the same reporter who got a lot of mileage from Patrick's death was at the mayor's home for something else yesterday. She recognized you talking to the mayor's son. She called my office asking questions. If this blows up, a lot's at stake."

"The mayor's race," Jayne muttered.

"Yes, the mayor's race. And my job." The chief tapped his fist on the doorframe. "Stop whatever it is you're doing. Now. There's no evidence that Melinda's accident was anything but that."

Jayne's heart beat wildly in her chest. "There's no evidence because we haven't uncovered it yet. We can't ignore the accident just because we're in an election year."

Danny's gaze burned hot on her cheeks.

"Okay, Chief." Danny capitulated to his father's request.

She reeled around on him. "Are you serious? Someone made a point of sending Melinda anonymous texts to get her on Lake Road. Kyle sent her a creepy photo from a random e-mail address so Melinda wouldn't know it came from him. I don't know how or if they're related, but something was going on prior to her death."

The chief rested his elbow on the top row of cubbies that the dancers used to store their backpacks, coats, and boots. "Your dad and I went through the academy together. I've looked out for all the Murphys. Your brothers are fine young men. Fine officers. Tore me up when Patrick . . ." The chief dragged his big, beefy hand across his mouth in an uncharacteristic show of emotion. "Your dad wouldn't want you going around playing cop. Let the police do their work."

"What are you going to do about this?" The throbbing behind her eyes grew so strong she thought her head would explode.

"You've been through a lot. I understand Melinda Green was an employee here, a neighbor of yours."

"She was more than that!" Jayne hated that her voice had grown high pitched, but she couldn't help herself. "She was like a little sister to me."

"You've suffered tremendous loss. One after the other." The chief nodded and put on an expression that Jayne interpreted as *I'm about to give my I-know-this-is-hard-but-this-is-how-it's-gonna-play speech.* "It was a tragic accident. One split second of distraction and a beautiful young life taken. I'm sorry." He didn't sound sorry. "We don't have a bad guy to arrest. The sooner you accept that, the sooner you'll begin to heal." The chief pushed off the cubbies to stand straight again. He patted the doorframe with his open palm and looked at Danny. "I expect you back on patrol."

Out of the corner of her eye, Jayne saw Danny give his father a curt nod. Jayne stood silent—fuming—until she heard the front door click. "I should have locked the door."

"He would have knocked. That conversation was inevitable."

Jayne fisted her hands. "Why didn't you support me on this?"

"I gave him the facts. The chief won't be swayed by opinion. Not yours. Not mine."

She stared at him, dumbfounded, unsure of what to say. "You believe it was an accident."

"The truth?"

Jayne gave him a pointed glare. "The truth."

"I'm leaning toward accident. But I'm not leaving you alone on this."

Jayne's shoulders sagged. She wasn't in the mood to keep going round and round about it.

Danny brushed past her. "You almost ready to go?"

"Yeah."

"Listen, I can help you look into this in an unofficial capacity. Okay? I can't have you investigating it on your own."

"Thank you. I appreciate it." She glanced over at the couch where they had been talking only moments ago. "About our conversation about Patrick."

Danny waved his hand. "I need to get back on the road. Let's get moving."

Jayne stared at him for a minute, then hustled to the office to gather her things.

"Jayne . . ." Danny lingered in the doorway. "Be careful what hornet's nest you poke. This is a small town, and if you decide to become a cop, you might find you've been stung."

"What about you? You afraid of jeopardizing your career?"

Half his mouth pulled into a grin. "My official job is to protect the fine residents of Tranquility, New York. Last I checked, you were one of their fine residents."

"Fine, huh?" Amusement bubbled up inside her.

"Don't overanalyze the situation."

Their gazes lingered, then Jayne rolled her eyes.

"Thanks for the escort home."

"Any time."

EIGHTEEN

Between worrying about the memorial service that morning and the chief's voice on repeat in her head, Jayne hadn't slept much last night and found herself transferring desserts from a cart to a table in Studio A in a bit of a dream state. The chief wanted her to stop investigating Melinda's accident, but more specifically to stop bothering Kyle.

Normally, Jayne would have been all over following the rules, but this time, it didn't feel right.

Or was she just looking for someone to blame like she had when Patrick died?

"Hi, Miss Jayne." A few dancers strolled in, appearing markedly different with their long hair flowing down over their shoulders versus their usual tight buns.

"Hi, girls. How nice of you to come." Jayne studied their faces. "Everyone okay?"

"Yeah . . . ," a few of them muttered. For many of the young students, this was their first experience with death. Jayne wouldn't wish this on anyone, but maybe for once, some of them would be thinking of someone other than themselves.

"There are some beautiful photos of Melinda taped to the mirror, going back to when she first started at the studio when she was three years old." Vision blurring, Jayne quickly looked away. Melinda had had the world at her feet and now . . .

"Oh, wow! Look!" Cindy said. "Miss Melinda had braces. And look at those eyebrows."

Jayne laughed through a strangled sob. Leave it to a teenager to critique a dead person's photo taken in middle school. The ordinariness of the comment reassured her that all these girls would be okay. They were resilient. And apparently judgmental.

Who wasn't?

More voices carried into the studio from the front door. Jayne tugged on the hem of her shirt, smoothing it over her long skirt.

"Jayne." Carol Anne rushed into the studio. "You did a beautiful job. I would have helped you. All you needed to do was ask."

"Miss Natalie and I had it under control."

Carol Anne leaned in conspiratorially. "It'll be good to have this last memorial service for Melinda and then move on. Victoria needs time to heal without all this . . ." She waved her hand around to the tissue flowers, bouquets, ballerina cookies, and dancers.

"You need time, too." Jayne struggled to muster as much sympathy as she should after that dismissal of her efforts.

Carol Anne's mouth twitched. She and Melinda had had a strained relationship—not unusual for sisters, especially stepsisters. That had to add an extra burden of guilt. Perhaps since the realization of a "someday reconciliation" was no longer possible.

"I know you guys had your ups and downs . . ." Jayne tilted her head. "But Melinda loved you and she knew you loved her." Jayne didn't actually know that for sure, but she felt it was the right thing to say.

"If you say so." Carol Anne shrugged. "Hey"—she pointed toward the door with her thumb—"Kyle's outside in his car." She lowered her voice. "I think he's been drinking. He's with your other dance teacher. Quinn, I think?"

Jayne frowned. She didn't want any confrontations today. Just then, Danny strolled in from the back, where he had gone to get more chairs. "Hold on a second, Carol Anne." Jayne informed Danny, who promised to handle Kyle. With more than a sense of apprehension, she watched as he disappeared out the front door.

"I'm sorry you have to deal with that," Carol Anne said. "I never understood what Melinda saw in him."

"Thanks for letting me know."

Carol Anne nodded with an air of wisdom. "Remember when my dad first married Victoria?" she reminisced. "He told me there was a little girl my age living in the house behind his new house with his new family."

Jayne smiled at the long-ago memory. Carol Anne and Jayne, both twelve at the time, had initially hit it off, each excited to have a new friend who shared the backyard. How cool was that?

"I miss those days." There was a faraway quality to Carol Anne's voice. "We had so much fun on that swing set."

Over Carol Anne's shoulder, Jayne noticed Paige walk in and scan the room before rushing over to give Jayne a hug. "The room looks so pretty," she said. "Melinda would love it."

Hugging Paige tightly, Jayne asked, "Are you okay?"

Paige shrugged, as if she couldn't talk.

"If you need anything, you know where to find me, okay? It's hard to lose someone you care about."

Paige pulled away and bowed her head, a long curtain of hair falling over her face. "I feel bad—she was out that night because of my lesson."

"Honey . . ." Jayne paused and waited until Paige met her eye. "You can't blame yourself. The circumstances of her accident had nothing to do with you."

The despair on Paige's face broke Jayne's heart.

"You brought Melinda joy. She *loved* working with you."

"I didn't give her my all that last night."

Jayne pulled the young dancer into another embrace. "Stop beating yourself up over every little thing. Melinda wouldn't want that." Long-forgotten words washed over Jayne, but she let them slip away. It was so much easier to provide comfort than to accept it.

"Okay," Paige breathed into Jayne's hair.

Jayne gave her one last squeeze, then let her go. "Your friends are waiting for you."

Paige stood there awkwardly for a second. "Thanks, Miss Jayne. You're the best."

Jayne pulled her sleeves over her hands as she watched Paige rush to her friends, who embraced her in a group hug.

"You're good with the girls. No wonder Melinda liked you so much." Carol Anne watched the group of girls with a hint of envy in her eyes.

I am good with the girls. She had resented giving up her original plans in order to help her mom at the dance studio, but in the end, she was still making a difference in other people's lives, just in a different way.

"Melinda loved you, too." Jayne reached out and touched Carol Anne's hand briefly.

"If one more person tells me I was lucky to have her while I did, I'm going to scream." Carol Anne's porcelain skin grew blotchy.

"Or how about God only gives us what we can handle?" An awkward laugh whispered past Jayne's lips. "He must think I can handle an awful lot."

"You're one of the most capable people I know," Carol Anne said. "I try to comfort my stepmom, but I'm not sure she appreciates it. It's like she wants me to leave."

"Don't take it personally. Everyone grieves in their own way."

"I know." Carol Anne sounded resigned. She plucked one of the photos of Melinda from the mirror, the tape dangling from the top. In the photo, Melinda was about seven, holding both Jayne's and Carol Anne's hands. She was smiling up at Jayne. "We both lost someone we love."

"We did. I don't know how my mom's studio is going to manage without her."

"Beautiful job here." Jayne turned to see Victoria approaching them with her arms outstretched. She drew Jayne into a big hug and whispered in her hair, "Thank you. It means a lot. The dance studio meant everything to Melinda. *Every* . . . thing." Her voice broke on the last syllable.

Tears Jayne had been holding back all morning spilled over. "*She* meant everything to us."

When Victoria pulled out of her embrace, she smiled sadly at Carol Anne. Then David surprised Jayne by giving her a big hug. "This studio gave Melinda purpose." Uncertainty flashed in his eyes. He reached into the breast pocket of his sport coat and handed her an envelope.

"What is it?"

"Open it." David wrapped his arm around his wife's shoulders and beamed at Jayne.

Jayne peeked into the envelope and gasped when she saw a check of a sizable sum.

"What's this for?"

"Melinda loved this place. It was her second home. Use it for renovations. Whatever makes sense."

Jayne shoved the envelope toward him. "Oh, I can't . . ."

"Oh, but you must," Victoria said. "It would mean a lot. We were saving to help Melinda get her start in New York City." Her chin trembled. "It would mean so much to David and me to donate this money to the studio. Help future dancers pursue their dreams. Something Melinda will never get to do."

Holding the envelope to her chest in disbelief, Jayne's face grew warm. "Are you sure?"

Victoria's smile didn't reach the sadness in her eyes. "I've never been more sure of anything. You're like a daughter to us, Jayne. Please, take this money."

"Thank you. I can't thank you enough." She made eye contact with Victoria, David, then Carol Anne. "Thank you," she repeated.

"That was a nice party," Miss Natalie said.

"Yes, it was nice." Most everyone had left. The girls had kindly put their garbage in the cans, but a few miscellaneous paper cups and plates littered the studio.

"I'll take the bags of garbage out back," Danny said, gently brushing his fingers across Jayne's arm, leaving tingles of awareness in their wake.

"Thanks." She smiled. "And thanks for handling Kyle." Jayne would have hated to see the memorial service ruined by a drunken ex-boyfriend. Danny had quietly driven him home, then returned midway through the service. "Do you know what happened to Quinn?"

"She walked away when I put Kyle in my car. I figured she came into the studio."

"No." A weight settled in her chest. Why wouldn't Quinn come to Melinda's memorial? Sure, they'd had their differences and were competitive during the high-school years, but to blow off this final tribute? Jayne ran her hands up and down her arms, trying to shake this chill. "Thanks for all your help."

"Anything for you." He winked, then wrapped up the garbage and headed out back.

Out of the corner of her eye, Jayne saw Paige lingering in the doorway. She crossed the room to the girl. "Are you feeling any better?"

Paige bowed her head and dragged her toe along the edge where the hardwood studio floor met the slate of the entryway. "I won't be at the studio on Monday."

"Oh . . ." Jayne jerked her head back. Paige never missed dance class. Jayne touched the girl's arm. "What is it?"

"I'm going to change studios."

Jayne's arms dropped to her sides. "Miss Gigi's?" Of course, Miss Gigi's. It was the only other studio in Tranquility.

Paige nodded.

"Why?" Heat flooded Jayne's face. Across the room, Miss Natalie picked up garbage along the windowsill. Jayne was glad she couldn't hear this. "Aren't you happy here?" The desperation in her tone fueled her anger. "Did Miss Gigi approach you?"

Paige's lips trembled and she shook her head. An emptiness expanded inside Jayne's belly. These decisions often were out of the girls' hands. The parents—no, the mothers—drove the decisions based on what they considered best for their daughters.

Is this for the best?

Jayne's mother had built Murphy's Dance Academy into an award-winning school over four decades, but now holding on to it was tenuous at best. Maybe canceling classes for the week had been a mistake. Maybe Jayne should have found a way to cover them. Instead, she'd gotten distracted with investigating Melinda's accident, and now one of her best students was leaving.

Jayne blinked slowly and drew in a steady breath through her nose. It wasn't Paige's fault. "It's okay." She looked beyond the young woman toward the doors. "Is your mom in the car?"

"Yeah, she'd planned to send you an e-mail Monday morning. I begged her to let me say good-bye." Paige dipped her head.

"If you don't want to go . . ."

"I have to. My mom said that if I don't keep progressing, I'll never be able to pursue dance professionally."

"We've hired two new dance teachers. They're great. I promise."

Don't make promises you can't keep. Melinda was gone. Her mother was slipping away before her eyes.

"Miss Gigi has a proven track record." Paige's voice shook. Jayne suspected she was repeating her mother's arguments.

The heavy sense of loss pressed down on Jayne's lungs. Tiny stars danced in her eyes. She couldn't fight this battle right now. She opened her arms and embraced Paige. The dancer returned the hug, fiercely. "You'll do great wherever you go. Come visit, okay? Let us know how you're doing."

Paige nodded, fighting mightily to keep it together. "My mom's probably wondering what's taking me so long."

"You better get going, then." Jayne forced a smile even as she felt the earth shifting at her feet.

She expected Paige to turn and stroll out the door; instead she sashayed gracefully across the room—in the way only a dancer could—and said good-bye to Miss Natalie with a long hug. Now it was Jayne's turn to fight to keep it together.

Little by little, piece by piece, Jayne was losing everything important to her.

NINETEEN

Does counting sheep actually help a person fall asleep? I roll over and punch my pillow, convinced that guilt—no, maybe rage—doesn't allow a person to sleep.

But I need sleep. I'm so tired.

Everything's messed up. Melinda's gone, but it doesn't change anything. Nothing at all. My life is out of control. I twist my sheets, wishing I could wring a few necks.

But I don't do sloppy seconds.

It's all Melinda's fault. Everyone is so focused on her death, they're forgetting about those of us who are alive.

It's time to move on.

But things are happening so fast, and not how I planned.

No one seems to want to let Melinda rest in peace.

Hot anger burns my gut. I can't stop thinking of her. The rage. I thought if she was hurt and couldn't dance, my life would change. Then when she had the misfortune to die, it was meant to be. Wipe her out of our lives. Permanently.

Still my rage grows.

Everyone keeps talking about her more and more.

I need to move on.

Shut up. Shut up. Shut up.

The voices just won't shut up.

And Jayne won't stop questioning Melinda's accident. Now the police are involved. Of course the police are involved. Jayne has cop brothers. Cop friends. She's asking far too many questions. Why can't she accept that Melinda's death was an accident?

I scratch the top of my head, frustration coursing through me.

If I want to get away with this, I'll have to make sure Jayne lets it go. Give her something else to worry about.

Distract her.

Then an idea hits me. Why didn't I think of it sooner? Stretching across, I grab my phone from the bedside table. I click on an audio app and a wise voice fills my ears.

Bud Byrdie.

"Go after what you want. The world is yours for the taking. Don't let those who have their feet mired in molasses stop your forward momentum." His words float on a drawl that is uncharacteristic of his roots. My annoyance grows.

Don't we all try to hide who we really are?

"Be who you were born to be."

TWENTY

A new week.

Jayne prayed it would be far less eventful than the last one. She slammed the trunk and jogged up the steps of the old Victorian house with plastic bags of supplies—toilet paper, soap, tissues. Stuff they'd need for their first full week back at dance. She reached out to unlock the front door, but it swung open.

Her knees grew wobbly and a hot flush of unease washed over her. Her mind raced, trying to remember if someone was supposed to be at the studio. Dread knotted her stomach. *No one should be here. Not this early.*

"Hello." Her limbs grew weak as she called the names of her cleaning staff, but they came in on Sunday. And they had absolutely come in yesterday, because Jayne needed to make sure they cleaned the dance floors after Saturday's memorial service.

Keeping her feet firmly planted on the porch, she leaned inside the doorway and listened. Silence, save for her obnoxious mouth breathing.

Snapping her mouth closed, she took a step backward. The floor-boards on the porch creaked. She knew enough not to explore the building herself, for fear she'd get brained before she was able to check each of the studios.

The news headlines would proclaim, *Local Woman, 26, Murdered in Family's Dance Studio.*

Or *Sister of Slain Tranquility PD Officer, Patrick Murphy, Dies.* Her name would probably be excluded from the headline. Dead office managers weren't big news. Maybe third page, below the fold.

Letting the bags dangle and untwist from her grip, she dropped them on the porch. She retreated to her car and scavenged through her tote bag for her phone. Holding it in her hand, she stared at the old Victorian in need of a new roof, paint, and windows.

And, apparently, a new lock.

Her stomach knotted.

She glanced down at the phone and had a battle with herself. Call 911? Or call Danny directly? Danny wasn't on duty. But if she dialed 911, she might incur the wrath of Chief Nolan, who already believed she was too flaky for the police force. She couldn't have him thinking that if she ever hoped to become a police officer.

But someone broke in, right? This was a very real crime and not one caused by her paranoia.

Who'd been the last to leave the building on Saturday? She had, right? Her mother hadn't gone back in and left the door ajar. No, not possible. She pressed her fingers to her temple and sighed heavily.

Then that familiar guilt sloshed in her gut. She couldn't help but feel like she'd been waiting for something to change so she could get on with her life. But that wasn't fair. Not fair at all. Her mother had been all about her family—still was—and had given up her dream of becoming a professional dancer in New York City to instead marry Jayne's dad, who'd had dreams of being a cop.

Now it was her turn to be there for her mother.

Staring through the windshield at the front door, Jayne half expected someone to explode out the door onto the porch. She didn't own a gun. Nothing. Hands trembling, she swirled her finger absent-mindedly over the smooth glass of her smartphone.

The studio seemed deserted.

That's because it is, doofus.

Why was she just sitting there? She dialed Danny's number, then sat and watched her mother's dance studio. By the time Danny pulled up in his truck and rolled down his window, Jayne was going out of her mind.

"What's going on?"

"I stopped by with supplies." She pointed to the bags on the porch as if she needed them for evidence. "The front door was open."

A sense of urgency creased the corners of his eyes. "Stay here, I'll check it out."

Despite being dressed in plain clothes, Danny pulled a gun from a shoulder harness. Envy whispered through her. *She* was supposed to be a police officer with a gun, not the damsel in distress.

Jayne scrambled out of her car and hung back while Danny climbed the steps, pushed the door all the way open, and entered the studio.

She paced in front of the car. An eternity stretched before her until he stepped back out onto the porch. All his senses were on high alert. Something was wrong.

Very wrong.

"What is it?" She rushed to the bottom of the steps.

"Whoever was here is gone, but . . ." He searched her face.

Anxiety welled up inside her. She had to see for herself.

Pushing past him, she charged up the front steps. The door bounced off the wall, reverberating in her ears. She froze in the entry-way. Someone had smashed the full-wall mirrors in Studio A. Shiny shards littered the floor. All the beautiful photos of Melinda were torn among the glass.

Knees feeling weak, Jayne lowered herself onto the bench in the foyer. The same bench where little girls slipped on their ballet shoes or tied their tap shoes.

The place where dreams began. She bowed her head and buried her face in her hands.

Danny sat and pulled her into an embrace. "I'm sorry."

Jayne nodded as the words lodged in her throat. After taking a moment to compose herself, she looked up into his kind eyes. "Maybe I'm kidding myself. Maybe this is a sign. Maybe it's time I gave up the dance studio."

"You can't give up."

"Sure I can. Remember how I gave up the police academy?"

Danny took her hand and threaded her fingers in his. A shock of warmth and awareness and confusion snaked up her arm.

"You didn't quit because you were no good. Or because you were lazy. You quit because your family needed you. You're doing a good thing here."

Staring at their joined hands, she whispered past the ache in her throat. "It doesn't feel like a good thing. Everything is falling apart around me." She held out her other hand. "Who would do this? Do you think Kyle could be lashing out at me? He did leave here pretty drunk Saturday, right?"

"It's tough to say. I did have to drive him home."

"Do we . . ." She hesitated. "Do we call the police?"

"I am the police."

Jayne rested her head on his shoulder and sighed.

Danny rubbed her arm in a comforting gesture. "Come on, I'll take you home, and then I'm going to track down that punk."

If Jayne hadn't had to get home to check on her mother, she would have insisted on going with Danny to chat with Kyle Duggan. Based on the anger rolling off her, that probably wouldn't be a good idea. Sure, the kid didn't comprehend the word *no* and had a huge chip on his shoulder, but Danny wanted to chat with him with a cool head. And unofficially. He wasn't rolling up on Kyle as Officer Nolan; no, he was showing up as Jayne's overprotective friend.

Scare the kid into compliance.

With no witnesses.

Uniform or no uniform, Danny feared this chat was going to come back and bite him in the backside. Part of Kyle's MO was reframing the story and using it to his benefit with his father.

Being Daddy's Boy was part of the problem. What did they call it? *Affluenza?*

After Danny dropped Jayne off, he checked Kyle's apartment, with no luck. Then he drove through the center of town, guessing where he might find him. A lot of kids hung out on Main Street. He'd try down there. He cruised down one side and then the other. How many times had he and Patrick hung out on Main Street without a care in the world, other than how they were going to get a few bucks to buy a burger or take some cute girl to the movies?

Life had gotten far more complicated since then.

That's when Danny spotted Kyle. He parked his truck illegally and hopped out. He crossed to where Kyle sat at a picnic table, holding court with a few friends, more like-minded individuals on the fast track to nowhere. Young adults with the time to hang out in the middle of the day. Danny imagined not many of them had the connections Kyle had.

"Need to talk to you," Danny said abruptly.

Kyle grimaced and scoffed. "Yeah, whatever." He shifted so his back was to Danny.

"Now," Danny persisted.

Something in his tone must have given Kyle pause. He stood and swaggered toward Danny, working to maintain his cool in front of his friends. Danny would give him that, but not for long.

Kyle squared his shoulders. "What do you want?"

"When I dropped you home Saturday, you were pretty ticked off."

"You banned me from going to my own girlfriend's memorial service." Kyle stuffed his hands in his jeans pockets and hunched up his shoulders. "You've been harassing me ever since my girlfriend died in a car accident." Danny noticed an imperceptible change in his tone. A softening. Did that indicate Kyle was truly grieving for his former girlfriend, or was his tone more out of remorse for a role he might have played?

Apparently Jayne is getting to me.

As a police officer, Danny had honed his garbage meter. It horrified him that so many people lied without compunction. Yet Kyle was a tough nut to crack.

Danny decided to go for the direct approach. "Do you know anything about a break-in and vandalism at Murphy's Dance Academy? Perhaps a little retribution for Saturday?"

"No way. I wouldn't do that. Sure, I was mad about Saturday, but not that mad." Kyle tilted his chin in defiance and crossed his arms over his chest. "Cut a guy a break. Melinda's accident was like a punch to the gut. I had asked her to do something with me that night, but she insisted on going out with her friends." He pressed his fist to his chest. "If she hadn't blown me off, this never would have happened." He twisted his mouth, which could be read one of two ways: grief or *too bad for her*. Danny's ill feelings toward Kyle made him lean toward the latter.

"Did you make her see the error of her ways?"

"What are you talking about? You think I ran her off the road? Is that why you and Jayne have been all over me, thinking I changed the location of her girls' night? Why would I do that?"

"Because you were mad she turned you down that night."

Huffing, Kyle fisted his hands.

"You were mad that she had broken up with you. That she was moving to New York City."

"We would have gotten back together." Kyle took a step backward and let his arms drop to his sides. "You're crazy."

"Listen, whatever issues you have with Jayne, you better knock it off."

"I have no issue with Jayne. I barely even know the woman."

Danny pointed his finger toward Kyle's chest. "I'm going to be watching you. I'm going to put the word out that you need to be watched. The second you do something wrong, I'm going to see that you pay. Even a smart man like the mayor knows he can't keep looking the other way when his kid's breaking the law. It's not good politics."

Kyle's nose flared. "My dad could fire your dad in a minute."

Driving his fist into Kyle's smug face would achieve nothing but a momentary sense of satisfaction. He took a step back. "None of that is going to help you, because I'll still be watching you whether I'm in uniform or not. You want to know what it's like to be stalked?" Served him right for taking secret photos from outside Melinda's bedroom.

"That photo was a joke!" Kyle sputtered.

Danny stared Kyle down like the creep he was. "I don't like you. Guys like you think they can do anything they want and never have to pay the consequences. You think you can hide behind your daddy."

Kyle made a face. "What, are you going to shoot me?"

The explosive noise of a gun firing sounded in Danny's ears. He gritted his teeth, shoving the memory away.

"I'm not the only one who hides behind my *daddy*," Kyle continued. "Heard you were slow on your feet. You totally botched the situation. Killed a scared kid and got your partner killed."

"That scared kid had a violent rap sheet."

"So your daddy said."

Kyle was trying to bait him. Danny swallowed back his anger. "You worry about yourself."

Kyle smirked as if to say, *Whatever*. He turned to walk away and muttered, "You can't watch me all the time."

Jaw tensing, Danny decided to walk away himself. Be the bigger man. The kid had gotten his message. He'd let him save face.

For now.

But Kyle's words got to him. Would Danny ever move past Patrick's death? Even though he had been cleared, the public outcry had been loud. And vicious.

But no voice of recrimination had been louder than his own.

TWENTY-ONE

"Where are you going?" Miss Natalie asked Jayne for the tenth, maybe eleventh—maybe twenty-seventh—time. But who was counting?

Lord, I love my mom. Please give me patience.

Jayne held the door open for her mother, and the older woman stepped out onto the driveway.

After a full week of work—and paying the cleaning crew extra to clean up the glass—Jayne was flat out of patience come Friday night. The glass company was coming out to the studio sometime next week to replace the mirrors. Thankfully, the dancers this week took everything in stride and managed to dance without looking at themselves.

"The Greens invited us for dinner." Jayne held a salad in a plastic container as they cut across the backyard. "It'll be nice to get out. Relax a bit."

Miss Natalie's face brightened. "Oh, the Green girl is such a beautiful dancer. She has wonderful things in her future." Then she pinched her mouth, as if something didn't seem right. "Is she going to New York? Someone said she's going to New York. I dreamed of going to

New York." They reached their neighbors' driveway, and Jayne fought the urge to take her mother home. Maybe this wasn't such a good idea.

"Did Melinda leave already?" Miss Natalie persisted and her voice hitched. "Did something happen?" She lifted a shaky hand to her mouth. "I'm so worried about her." Her eyes darted around the yard. "Maybe we should go home."

This was going to be a long dinner. "Mom . . ." Jayne rested the salad container on her hip and wrapped her arm around her mother's thin shoulders, mustering up every ounce of compassion. "Maybe we should talk about something other than dance tonight. Mix it up a little bit."

"Okay," Miss Natalie said agreeably. "We can talk about something other than work." She said it as if it had all been settled.

"You good?"

"Wonderful." Miss Natalie gave her daughter an uncertain smile.

Jayne lifted her hand to knock and Carol Anne appeared before her fist met the metal frame.

"Heard your voices." She pushed open the screen door and propped it open with her hip. "Come on in." She reached for the salad. "You shouldn't have." Then a bright smile crossed her face. "But we're glad you did," Carol Anne said before calling, "Miss Natalie and Jayne are here."

The house smelled of sauce and garlic. Victoria stood at the stove stirring the sauce. She set the spoon aside and rushed over to greet Miss Natalie and Jayne with warm hugs. Victoria seemed thinner, frail, a shadow of herself.

"Carol Anne, take the salad and put it on the table." Annoyance edged Victoria's tone, indicative of all the stress she was under. She lifted her apron over her head and hung it on a hook near the door. "Come on, Miss Natalie, I'll get us a drink."

Jayne was about to protest—her mother wasn't supposed to drink alcohol—but decided one drink wouldn't hurt. Or so she hoped. Her mother used to enjoy a glass of red wine after dinner on Friday nights when she had her book club over. The knot in Jayne's shoulders eased a bit. Simpler times.

Victoria guided her mother to the couch and they sat.

David went to the liquor cabinet. Jayne sidled up to him. "Do you have tonic? Perhaps my mother shouldn't have a drink after all."

He nodded in understanding.

"How are you?" Jayne asked him.

He poured himself a Scotch and tipped it back. Then frowned. "It's tough."

Jayne didn't want to pretend that losing a father and brother was the same as losing a daughter, but she understood loss.

The silence stretched between them for a moment as David swirled the crystal glass on the bar. "Carol Anne seems to be a help. She and her stepmom never got along." He frowned. "Maybe now . . ."

Jayne made a few listening noises, not sure what an appropriate response would be. It was unlikely Victoria would embrace Carol Anne as if she might somehow be a consolation prize for her only daughter.

"Carol Anne always resented the fact that I left her mom when she was a little girl and married Victoria. It's cliché, isn't it?"

Her cheeks grew warm at David's revelation. As much time as she had spent at the Greens' house babysitting Melinda, most of her interactions had been with Victoria. The mister always breezed in and went straight to the liquor cabinet or his office, or to retire for the night.

Jayne accepted her mother's drink. "What do I know? I'm twenty-six. I don't even have a boyfriend."

"Ah, to be twenty-six again." David sighed heavily and glanced up, a tired, glazed look in his eyes. "The different choices I would have made."

Jayne picked up the glass he had poured for her, feeling a bit uneasy about the personal nature of their conversation. "I'm so sorry about Melinda."

David lifted his glass. "Me, too." He took a long sip of his drink, then gave her a pointed stare. "I heard you did some digging into her accident."

"Um . . . I . . ." He'd asked her himself to look into it, but she hadn't wanted to share any developments until she had some proof. She didn't want to cause him any more unnecessary pain. "The police still say it was an accident. It was raining. She missed a curve." Jayne kept her voice low so as not to be overheard by Victoria, who chatted with Miss Natalie on the couch, fairly out of earshot. "It's just that I don't understand why Melinda ended up on Lake Road."

"Carol Anne started to tell Victoria you have Melinda's tablet." David took another sip, then seemed to wince, as if he had tasted something sour. "I told Carol Anne it was no big deal. That you'd bring it over at some point."

Jayne wasn't sure how to feel about that indiscretion. Betrayed, she supposed. She glanced at Carol Anne, who stood at the sink in the kitchen, rinsing a few dishes. "I'll make sure I return it."

He held up his hand. "I'm not worried about the tablet. Just be careful what you tell Victoria." He took another long drink. "It would destroy her if she found out Melinda was texting while driving. She warned her. Constantly." Pain radiated from his eyes.

"I understand."

He nodded slowly, as if he wasn't sure if he could believe her.

Changing the subject, she said, "The money you gave the studio came in handy to replace some mirrors that were recently damaged. Thank you."

"I heard about that." He shook his head. "Crazy world."

"Well, without your generous donation, we may not have been able to replace them as quickly."

"Happy to hear it." He tapped the side of his fist on the bar. "How's your mom?"

"Getting a little forgetful." Jayne wondered how much longer she could keep using that same old tired phrase.

"My dad had Alzheimer's. I know what it's like. I did a lot of research on facilities. Long-term care."

"She's fine at home."

David nodded, as if to say, *For now*. He ran a hand over his face, the exhaustion visible in the dark circles under his eyes. "My dad ended up getting cancer. That killed him before he got to the wandering phase."

"I'm sorry."

David studied her for a moment with an expression she couldn't read. "Best thing that could have happened to him. Alzheimer's is a bear. Cancer took him quick."

Sweat beaded up under her arms—flop sweat, she jokingly called it, but tonight she didn't feel much in a joking mood. She rarely heard someone talk so glumly and flat-out honestly about the ravages of dementia. Even though she knew or suspected the hardships to come, people often gave her false reassurances and accolades.

"You're doing such a good thing."

"What a wonderful daughter."

"Your mother's blessed to have you."

Perhaps it took a drunk, grieving father to lay it out like it really was. To paint her a realistic, dark portrait.

"Dinner's almost ready," Carol Anne called cheerily from the kitchen.

Suddenly, Jayne wasn't very hungry anymore.

Jayne, Natalie, Victoria, David, and Carol Anne made small talk while eating dinner, trying to avoid any topics that might send one of them spiraling into the depths of despair.

There were a lot of topics to avoid.

Miss Natalie pushed her noodles around on her plate and answered any questions that were thrown her way with one- or two-syllable answers. Jayne wondered if her mother had eaten anything at all. Perhaps she was no longer able to handle the stimulation of a dinner party.

Jayne was relieved as they wound things up, and she eagerly helped Carol Anne clear away the dishes. Victoria set out tea and coffee and a plate of cookies, no doubt purchased at the bakery of the local grocery store. Jayne helped her mother dunk the tea bag in the hot water, then pull it out and set the wet bag on her saucer. Her mother finally seemed at ease enjoying her tea and cookies.

Even though she knew she'd pay for it with a night of staring at the stick-on stars on her bedroom ceiling, Jayne filled her own mug with coffee. Those chocolate-chip cookies demanded to be washed down with coffee.

"Oh . . ." Carol Anne lifted her hand to cover her mouth, half stuffed with dessert. "Did Jayne mention she found Melinda's tablet at the studio?"

Nearly choking on her coffee, Jayne figured she had one thing to be grateful for: her cardigan masked round two of uncomfortable flop sweat. *Thanks a lot, Carol Anne.*

"I'm sure she'll return it soon enough," David said.

Jayne swallowed hard. "Of course. I've been meaning to bring it over." She smiled tightly, wondering if Carol Anne could feel the heat of her what-in-the-world-are-you-doing dagger eyes beaming her way. "I didn't want to bother you."

"That's okay," Victoria said, taking a polite sip of her tea.

"You should have brought it with you tonight," Carol Anne said helpfully. *Not.*

"Maybe we should let Jayne keep it for a little bit." David set his glass down noisily on the table, his drink sloshing over the edges. "I don't know if I'm ready to see what Melinda was doing online. I'd feel like I was spying. Seeing a part of her I wasn't meant to see." The alcohol slurred his words.

"Dad, anything on there was stuff she posted to social-media sites. Not exactly private," Carol Anne said, seeming oblivious to her father's pain.

Ignoring his daughter, David turned to Jayne. "Will you hold on to it for a while?" He reached over and covered Victoria's hand—she had gone silent during all this. "Hold on to it until we're ready to go through her things."

"I will." Jayne clutched her hands in her lap, feeling like she was going out of her skin in this small space. "Let me know and I'll return it. Whenever you're ready." She cut a sideways glance to Carol Anne, who was chomping away on a chocolate-chip cookie.

TWENTY-TWO

J ayne was always amazed at how the Monday of one week rolled into the Monday of the next. Routine was good for her mother, but the boredom was beginning to settle in. She had left her mom at home tonight since they only had a couple of classes and her mother seemed content in front of her nightly lineup of sitcoms.

Despite her initial suspicions that Melinda's death wasn't an accident, neither Jayne nor Danny had been able to dig up any additional information. She had tried to catch Ricky again to look into the restricted phone number, but she didn't want to make a pest of herself after Peggy had said he'd been working long hours.

So basically, dead ends all around.

The initial shock and anger and wanting to blame someone had begun to numb and morph into bad-things-happen-to-good-people-and-then-you-die acceptance.

But not completely. Not yet.

Sitting behind the computer in her small office at the dance studio, Jayne took matters into her own hands and researched a few PI blogs, which led to websites that tracked phone numbers.

Tapping the edge of the credit card against her lips, she tried to decide if it was safe to enter her financial information. Two young dancers giggled as they pushed through the oversized door and into the foyer. They carried their dance bags to the back room and stuffed them into cubbies.

One of the dance moms knocked on Jayne's door and explained why her tuition payment was late. Another mom popped her head in "for just a quick sec," questioning why her daughter had been moved from the first line to the third. After she left, Jayne closed the door and hoped for quiet.

Leaning back, she closed her eyes against a subtle pounding in her head. *How has Mom done this for her lifetime?*

Her mother had been following her passion. That was the big difference.

Jayne's dreams for her future never included responding to a parent e-mail complaining that their little dancer got the red costume when she would have rather had the pink one. Just the idea of crafting a polite response that didn't include the words, "Really?!? Are you kidding me?!!! (#FirstWorldProblems)" taxed her underutilized brain.

A quiet rap sounded on the door. Jayne resisted the urge to groan. She looked up and saw Paige standing there. She pushed back from her chair and gestured for her to come in. "Hello." Jayne gave her a once-over, surprised to see their former student. "How are you?"

Paige smiled shyly and held up a set of car keys. "I got my driver's license. I wanted to stop by and tell my friends in person."

"Miss Quinn's in the middle of class"—she stood to guide the girl by the small of her back—"but let's go tell them. This is big news."

Jayne and Paige walked over to the studio and lingered outside the door. Miss Quinn turned off a catchy little tune, the type of song that was perfect for seven-year-olds who loved to tap. Undoubtedly, the song would worm its way into her brain until she found herself humming it when she was alone in the car on the way home.

"Hello," Quinn said. "Look, girls. We have visitors."

Paige held up her hand. "Oh, I shouldn't have interrupted. I was just excited because I got my driver's license."

Quinn smiled brightly. "Freedom!" She lifted her hands and spread her fingers for emphasis. *Jazz hands!*

"I'm sure the girls would love to show you their dance before they go home for the night." Quinn planted her fists on her hips, showing a strong command of the classroom. Maybe Jayne had underestimated her abilities.

The dancers gave a collective sigh.

Tap-tap-tap-shuffle-shuffle-tap-tap-tap.

A cute little girl with dark-blonde hair rolled her eyes and gave off some attitude that could rival someone twice her age. "Miss Melinda didn't keep making us run through the number."

A little girl standing behind her, oblivious to anything—including any possible tap combination they had learned—had a will of her own. *Tap—shuffle-tap—tap-tap-tap.*

Jayne was impressed with how calm Miss Quinn remained—and how quickly she regained control of the classroom, despite the attitude the tired young dancers were throwing off. None of the instructors could risk blowing a gasket in front of all the little Emmas, Sophias, Bellas, and Madisons. If one of these little special flowers cried from hurt feelings, they'd run home to their moms, who would call the studio and complain. Or even worse, they'd pull their little Emma out of Murphy's Dance Academy and sign her up across town with Miss Gigi.

Quinn turned on the music, and the girls ran through the number for Paige and her. Jayne couldn't help but smile as the young girls fell into dance mode: smiles, lots of energy, and most were on the right count.

When the music sounded out its final beats and the girls gathered in the center of the dance floor in the final formation, Jayne and Paige gave them an enthusiastic round of applause.

"Okay, girls. Have a good night. Don't forget to practice." Quinn stood with her hands on her hips.

All the little dancers rushed to the door in a cacophony of *tap-tap-tap-tap*. The class was over and the parking lot would be filled with SUVs and minivans and moms eager to get on with their next errand. Or home to wine and Netflix.

"Practice, practice, practice." Quinn forced a cheery tone over the chatter and clatter. "See you next week."

Most of the girls had already run out of the studio and were stuffing their feet into expensive faux-fur-lined boots even though there was no snow on the ground.

A few of the older dancers strolled in and shared in Paige's excitement over her license. Quinn finally clapped her hands to get their attention. "Okay, ladies, time to stretch."

"Congratulations, Paige." Quinn smiled. "Nice to see you."

"You, too." There was a wistful quality to Paige's voice.

Jayne took a step toward the office. "Do you have time to visit for a bit? I'd love to hear how things are going at Miss Gigi's."

They walked back to the small office and sat down. Paige ran her hands down the arms of the chair. "It's fine, but I miss my friends."

Jayne frowned. "You're welcome here any time you'd like."

Paige glanced over her shoulder as if she didn't know what to say to that. She turned back around and tilted her head to look at the computer screen. "What are you doing?"

"Ah, my pet project, I suppose. I'm trying to track down the owner of a phone number."

Paige stood, planted her palms on the desk, and squinted at the screen to get a better look. "Why?"

Jayne hesitated a moment, uncertain if she should share the information with one of Melinda's former students. Then she remembered Paige had been one of the last people to see her alive. She clasped her hands and placed them on the desk. "Did Melinda tell you she had plans to meet her friend Bailey at Henry's?"

Paige slowly shook her head. "No, we didn't talk about anything other than dance." She cocked her head. "Are you investigating Melinda's accident?"

"Something about that night doesn't add up."

"Like what?" Paige crossed her arms and lowered herself onto the edge of the chair.

Jayne waved her hand in dismissal. She probably shouldn't have said anything.

"You wanted to be a police officer before this," Paige said, straightening. "Are you sorry you have to run this dance studio?"

"Sometimes life takes unexpected detours." Jayne looked into Paige's eyes, seizing the unique opportunity this job did offer her to influence young women.

"Like moving to Miss Gigi's studio." Paige laughed.

"Yes, definitely a detour."

"Hey!" Paige's eyes lit up. "You could be a private investigator or something. Do it right here. You could still run the studio and do all sorts of spy work. I bet you're good at investigating things."

"Why would you say that?"

"Your background. You studied criminal justice in college and then you went through the police academy." She pointed to the open laptop on the desk. "And look at you, still trying to figure out what happened to Melinda."

Jayne dragged her hand through her hair. "Something to think about."

"Well, unless you were going to close this place up."

Paige's comment startled Jayne. "No, of course not." She clicked a few Xs and closed down the tabs on her computer screen. "How did Melinda seem the night she was working with you? The night of her crash?"

Paige twirled a strand of hair around her finger. "She seemed fine. Like normal."

But it wasn't normal. Jayne slid her credit card back in her wallet and glanced at the clock on the computer screen. The sound of girls chatting grew closer.

"Well, I better go. I don't want my mom to worry." Paige jumped up from her chair and leaned across the desk to give Jayne a quick, spontaneous hug. "I've missed you."

Jayne gave her a little squeeze back. "Missed you, too." She pulled back and pointed at the young woman. "Drive safely."

Paige jangled her keys. "I will." She skipped out of the office, and Jayne's attention was drawn to the door where two other dancers walked out, their heads tipped in conversation. They moved out of the way, and Sean stepped through the door. His stern expression sent Jayne's blood running cold.

Instinctively, she flashed back to when her eldest brother, Finn, had come to the house to tell her that Patrick had been involved in a shooting.

Involved.

Such an innocent word for *shot and bled out before help could arrive.*

The quiet, contained trembling of her mother was imprinted on her brain.

Jayne rose on shaky legs. "What's wrong?"

"Where's Mom?"

"At home. She doesn't have any classes today. She was watching TV. She looked tired." Her vision tunneled and a tingling raced across her scalp. "Did you stop by the house? She's watching TV, right?"

Of course she wasn't, that's why her brother was standing over her glowering at her.

"No, she's not. Cara stopped by for a visit with Ava and found the side door unlocked and the TV blaring. She called me right away. I was on patrol a block away from here, so I drove over." Accusation laced his tone. Sean unhooked his cell phone from his duty belt and made a call. Heat infused Jayne's cheeks as she listened to his end of the conversation. "Put out a Silver Alert for my mom, Natalie Murphy, five foot one." He turned to Jayne. "What was Mom wearing?"

Jayne pressed her fingers to her temple. "Um . . ." The buzzing in her head grew louder. *Louder.* Making her dizzy. "She was wearing a long purple skirt with her black leotard. Her hair was in a bun." She nodded, certainty strengthening her spine.

Sean relayed the information and ended by saying he'd text a photo of his mom over shortly so it could be sent out to all the patrols. Thankfully, most of the officers already knew what Natalie looked like.

"Come on." Sean strode toward the door. "Let's go."

Jayne glanced around the office with the paperwork for next month's dance convention scattered across her desk. But her loyalty— her responsibility to her mom—was not in question. "Hold on." She jogged to the main studio where Miss Quinn was working with the next class.

The older dancers were on the floor with their noses pressed to their extended legs, stretching. She waved Quinn over. "I'll be back to lock up before classes end."

"Oh, okay," Quinn said. "Everything all right?" Her eyes drifted to Sean in his police uniform.

"It's my mom."

Quinn went pale. "Go, go, I have everything here. I'll wait till you get back. I won't leave the studio unattended. Go make sure Miss Natalie's okay."

When Sean and Jayne got back to the house, Jayne raced through all the rooms, sending up a silent prayer that her mother was somewhere in here—safe, of course—and just hadn't heard Cara's calls.

When they met back in the kitchen, Jayne asked, "Where's Cara?"

"She didn't want to leave, but she had to take Ava to an evening doctor's appointment that had taken months to get. I told her to go." Sean shook his head, his disappointment obviously targeted toward Jayne. "You shouldn't have left Mom alone."

Jayne opened her mouth to answer, when Sean cut her off. "Where's a good photo of Mom?" Following behind him as he stomped into the family room to scan the framed photos on the wall, Jayne wondered if anyone had ever made her feel as incompetent as her big brother was doing right now. The photos of the Murphy kids and the one grandchild stared back at them with big grins and bright eyes, oblivious to the stern expression of Officer Sean Murphy. Not a one of Miss Natalie.

An idea hit Jayne. She rushed into the dining room and found the photo of her mom and Patrick at his wedding. "Here," she said, rushing back into the family room.

Sean opened the camera app on his phone and zoomed in on his mother's smiling face.

Glancing around as if her mom might suddenly appear in their long-overdue-for-a-remodel family room, she muttered, "She couldn't have gone far." Still, an empty feeling of hopelessness pulsed through her veins. "Maybe she went for a walk," Jayne offered, her voice lacking conviction.

"Why did you leave her alone? It's your job to take care of her."

Jayne drew in a deep breath. *My job?!* But it wasn't in her nature to lash out at her brothers. "Mom was tired. She's never wandered away from the house before. I was only going to be gone for two hours max." Then hot anger edged out her fear. "I'm doing my best around here. I'm running the studio and taking care of Mom. Who do you think you are to tell me what I should or shouldn't be doing?"

"Who am I?" He paused long enough to make her feel like a criminal he was about to book. "The son who has to put the alert out for his missing mom. That's who."

The outrage rushed out of her on a breath. "I'm going to look for Mom. She has to be close."

"I'll patrol the area. Other patrols will also be looking."

They both left the house and Jayne stopped in her tracks. "What if she does come back while we're gone?" She scratched her head. "I'll run over to the Greens'. Carol Anne's car is in the driveway. Maybe she can sit here until I get back." But as soon as the words came out of her mouth, she had an uneasy feeling. Did she really want Carol Anne in her house alone? Where had Jayne left the tablet? She was being ridiculous. It didn't matter how Jayne felt. She had to do whatever it took to find her mother.

Sean nodded his agreement. "Keep your cell phone on." He jogged toward his patrol vehicle, then yelled over his shoulder, "Call me the minute you find her."

TWENTY-THREE

Worry ate away at Jayne while a headache formed behind her eyes. *Where is Carol Anne? Her car is in the driveway.* Just Jayne's luck, they were probably out to dinner and wouldn't be back for a while. She paced the black pavement at the top of the Greens' driveway while keeping an eye on the back of her own home, hoping, praying her mother would suddenly appear, strolling up the driveway, all apologetic that she had caused all this worry.

"Oh, Mom, where did you go?" Jayne whispered, her anxiety growing with her mom's absence. "Where did you go?" The headlights of a patrol car cruised the street as dusk closed in. She held her breath, thinking maybe an officer would stop, get out, and open the back door. But nope, it continued past. Jayne was grateful her family's connection to the Tranquility Police Department meant additional patrols searching for her mom.

As Jayne turned to walk back home, the smell of cigarette smoke reached her nose. She followed the scent toward the front of the house and found Goth Girl sitting on her dark porch next door; the only thing that gave her away was the orange glow of her cigarette.

"Hi. My name's Jayne. I live on the street behind you." Though the young woman's family had moved in a year ago, Jayne hadn't met them. The only sign of life in the house was this girl, whom Melinda and Jayne had christened "Goth Girl." She lurked in the shadows, always looking unapproachable, but more than likely she was just trying to hide her smoking habit from her parents.

"Yeah," Goth Girl said in such a noncommittal way Jayne wasn't sure whether the girl recognized her or not.

"Anyway, have you seen an older woman who looks lost?" Jayne crossed the grass to where Goth Girl sat.

A cloud of smoke released on a long puff of air. "Nope." Flattening her hand on the pavement, she pushed to her feet. "Is something wrong? I mean, is your mom . . ." She seemed to search for the right word. "Is your mom likely to get lost?"

Jayne was taken aback at how respectful the young woman was. She had assumed Goth Girl would be aloof and indifferent.

"My mom wandered off. She has—" Jayne hated to use the word *Alzheimer's*, so she didn't. "She's forgetful sometimes. Did you happen to see her? She probably had her hair up in a bun. A long purple skirt. She looks a lot younger than sixty-five." Jayne rambled on. "I didn't get your name."

"Hi, I'm Goth Girl."

Jayne forced herself to hold her ground even though she wanted to reel back and hide the shame burning her face. "I . . . um . . ."

Goth Girl threw her head back and laughed, a genuine laugh. Jayne wasn't sure how to read it. "Houses are close together. I've heard you and your friend talk." She took another drag on her cigarette, eying her neighbor.

"I'm sorry. That was rude of us. We should have never said that."

The young woman waved her hand up and down, indicating her long black trench coat, black hair, and heavy black eyeliner. "No offense taken. That's the look I'm going for," she said, talking around the cigarette pinched between her lips.

"Still." Jayne ran a hand over her mouth, unable to shake the feeling that this young girl had overheard two adults and not at their finest. Fingering her cross necklace, she turned and squinted down the street. No sign of anyone, not even anyone out walking their dog. And it was getting darker.

What was she doing standing here when her mother was missing?

"I'm sorry. I heard about the accident," the young woman said. "Melinda seemed pretty cool." She smirked. "She had me pegged."

"Hmm . . . Thank you."

Melinda's neighbor came off as warm and friendly, a contradiction to her wardrobe.

"I'm sorry about the Goth Girl comment."

The young girl held up her hands. "I guess I came by it honestly, right? I decided when I moved from Buffalo to the burbs, I'd try out a new me."

"What was the old you?"

"Invisible."

Jayne smiled, not sure if she should feel sorry for the young girl or inspired by her go-for-it attitude.

"Okay, Goth Girl," she teased, sensing her new neighbor had a sense of humor. "What's your name?"

"Hannah."

"That's a pretty name."

"Pfft. Until your so-called friends start calling you Hannah Banana when your misguided mother dresses you in a yellow sweater the first day of second grade. Kids have long memories. Good thing Dad got a new job in Tranquility. Most people would hate moving during high school, but for me it was a chance to reinvent myself."

"Why do I think you can handle yourself?" Jayne scanned the sidewalk, searching for her mom.

Hannah shrugged, then her eyes brightened. "Want me to help you look?"

"Would you do me a huge favor?"

"What's that?"

"Sit in my house, so there's someone there if—*when* my mom returns. I'll give you my cell-phone number."

Hannah slid her hands into her deep trench-coat pockets. A person could carry a purse's worth of items in there. "Won't it be odd that a stranger is sitting in her house?" Her sudden hesitance reminded Jayne of someone used to being set up to be the butt of a practical joke.

Jayne hadn't been popular in high school, but she also hadn't been unpopular. She was smart and independent and had never gotten caught up in the drama. And if someone even tried to harass her, they knew she had three older brothers.

Being a kid with a target on her back mustn't be a fun way to go through school. Dressing Goth to avoid invisibility seemed like trading one problem for another.

"I'll pay you," Jayne offered when Hannah stubbed out her cigarette with her black boot. She bent over and tossed it in the bushes.

Time was slipping away. Jayne rubbed her hands up and down her bare arms. Her mother probably wasn't dressed appropriately. The night would only grow cooler.

"You don't have to pay me. I'd do anything to get away from *her* for a little bit." Jayne assumed "her" meant Hannah's mother, but she didn't have time to ask.

"Let's go, then." Jayne hustled back across the backyard with Hannah in tow, hearing the *swoosh-swoosh-swoosh* of her trench coat flapping around her black leggings.

Jayne yanked open the door and called out to her mom, hoping, praying she had returned.

"Mom and I are in here," came her brother's reply.

"Oh, thank God." Jayne instinctively reached back and touched Hannah's wrist. "She's home."

"Since you're all set." Hannah shuffled backward, her black ankle boots squeaking on the linoleum.

"Come in. Say hello. You can meet my mom."

Hannah waved her off. "I'm not into the whole family-reunion scene." She pushed open the screen door. "Glad your mom made it home safely."

"Thank you." Jayne met the young girl's dark-rimmed eyes. "It was nice to meet you, Hannah."

"Bye," she muttered as she slipped out the door, revealing a bit of the shy girl she had once been. Still was . . .

Jayne stared after the unusual girl for a moment before spinning around and jogging through the kitchen and into the family room. She banged her foot on the doorframe, but she ignored the pain as a rush of relief—unlike any she'd ever known—coursed through her. She knelt down in front of her mom, who raised her eyebrows at her only daughter. Jayne gathered her mother's cool hands in hers. "Are you okay, Mom?"

Miss Natalie gave her a watery smile. "What's all the fuss?" Still clutching her daughter's hands, she leaned back in her recliner. "Are you going to call your brothers every time I go out for a walk?" She pursed her lips and shook her head. It was a defensive tactic.

"Mom," Sean said, "Cara happened to stop by and you weren't home. *I* called the patrols."

Miss Natalie kept shaking her head. "I'm your mother. Don't treat me like I'm helpless. I sometimes forget things, but I'd never lose my way home."

Jayne stood and was about to sit down in another chair when she noticed Carol Anne sitting in a kitchen chair nearby.

Annoyed that Sean seemed to be pinning this all on her, Jayne exhaled sharply and turned to Carol Anne. "Did you find her?"

Carol Anne slid to the edge of her seat. "She was walking down the street. I knew that—" For some strange reason, she looked to Sean for approval. "I wanted to make sure Miss Natalie wasn't lost."

"I wasn't lost," her mother bit out. She straightened her back and looked every bit the well-poised dancer that she had been all her life. Jayne had once heard a health-care professional refer to Alzheimer's as the long good-bye. The words had clung to Jayne like an ill-fitting wool sweater on a cold winter day. Too useful to discard it and too itchy to forget she had it on.

Jayne squeezed her mother's hands. "It's okay, Mom. Are you cold? Would you like some tea?"

Miss Natalie blinked slowly. "Sounds nice."

"Your TV program is on." Jayne turned on the TV, then turned to Carol Anne. "Thank you so much. We were worried."

"You didn't need to worry," Miss Natalie muttered.

Carol Anne stood and moved closer to sit on the couch in the family room. "No problem. Miss Natalie is like family."

Something in her tone made Jayne bristle. Miss Natalie was Jayne's mom, not Carol Anne's. She wasn't sure why it bothered her so much, but she let the comment go without a sarcastic reply.

Sean followed his little sister into the kitchen. Jayne said, "See, she's fine."

"But what about next time?"

Jayne unthreaded the dishtowel from the handle of the stove. "She's fine."

"Ignoring the situation won't solve it."

Jayne's ears grew hot. She didn't resent giving up her career for her mom. (*Her* mom!) But what she did resent was how her brothers tried to micromanage her decision without making any sacrifices of their own.

They kept living their lives while judging hers.

"How's Cara?" Time to turn the conversation around. If her tone came off as sarcastic this time, she meant it. Jayne was grumpy. Everything from her mother's unauthorized walk to her brother's condemnation.

"What do you mean by that?" Sean crossed his solid arms, but then, just as quickly as his anger seemed to get the best of him, he relaxed them. "Did you ever think that Cara needs help now that Patrick's gone?"

She turned her back to her brother and flipped on the faucet. She put her fingers under the flow until it ran warm. With jerky movements, she filled the sink with suds and tossed her mother's unbreakable dishes, which had been around since dirt, into the sink.

Jayne slammed the handle down, cutting off the flow of water. She spun around and leaned her backside against the edge of the sink. It was her turn to cross her arms. "What am I going to do about Mom?" She asked the question that hung heavy in the air.

"Don't leave her alone."

"I'm doing all I can."

"Why didn't she go with you to the dance studio?"

"I already told you. She was tired. She's never wandered before. Besides, I had some paperwork to do. It's easier to focus when she's not asking me a million questions." All the words coming out of her mouth felt like excuses. Fear and anger warred for prominence. "I'm doing everything I can."

Jayne wanted to scream, "Why does it all fall on me?" But she stuffed it all down, not wanting her mother or Carol Anne to overhear. She glanced around her brother, and the way Carol Anne had her head tilted, Jayne suspected she had heard every word.

She rubbed the back of her neck. "I'll figure something out."

"I can keep Miss Natalie company."

Jayne angled her head to see Carol Anne standing nearby with a cheery smile on her face. *Of course she was listening.*

"I've been spending more time at my dad's house anyway. I'm right there. Close by." She gestured with her hand toward the house behind them.

Sean sought affirmation from his sister.

Something about Carol Anne's offer annoyed Jayne. Was it because Jayne realized she could no longer do this without support? Her brothers would probably argue that they did help, but it came at their convenience. Or was it because Melinda had once called her sister a snoop, so Jayne didn't like the idea of Carol Anne in her house, looking through her things? Searching for her stepsister's tablet.

"Don't you have a job already?" Jayne tossed out the most obvious question, hoping to deflect answering the real one. Last Jayne knew, Carol Anne was a server at a local Greek restaurant.

"I have flexible hours at the restaurant. I've cut back of late."

"We'll have to talk about it as a family." Jayne slowly strolled toward the young woman who had tried so eagerly to be Jayne's BFF when they were little girls. But if Miss Natalie had taught Jayne anything, it was to be gracious. "That was a nice offer." She ran her hand over her hair. "I have to figure this out."

Carol Anne reached out and touched Jayne's arm. "You're not alone."

"I suppose I'm not." Jayne glanced at the clock and had an oh-no moment. She scrambled through her purse for the studio keys. "Sean, can you do me a favor? Run back to the studio and lock up. Quinn will be waiting."

Sean held out his hand. "Of course." Palming the keys, he strode toward the door. "Keep an eye on Mom."

Jayne bit back her frustration. *All's well that ends well, right?*
For now.

TWENTY-FOUR

I t was quarter after eleven in the evening before Danny clocked out from the second shift and found himself driving down Treehaven Road toward the Murphys' house. His childhood home away from home. A light burned in the kitchen. Undoubtedly Jayne was still trying to unwind after her mother had gone missing.

Eager to check up on her—eager to *see* her—Danny parked his truck in the driveway and knocked quietly on the front door, only loud enough for someone who was still awake to hear him.

The wind rustled the leaves in the trees overhead, and somewhere in the distance a dog barked. Danny was about to call it a night when Jayne appeared in the doorway. Her hair was disheveled and her skin was scrubbed free of makeup. Under the lonely bulb in the front hall, she looked much younger than her twenty-six years.

"Hey," she said, her voice gruff, probably from not having talked to anyone in a while. She dragged her hand through her hair and angled her head, a question in her eyes.

"Wanted to see how you were. I heard the Silver Alert go out for your mom. She okay? I would have been here sooner if she was still missing."

Jayne leaned a hip on the doorframe and propped the screen door open a fraction with her foot. "She's fine." But her tone suggested that neither she nor her mother was fine.

"How are *you*?"

Jayne blinked a few times, slowly. "Do you feel like coming in?" Then she quickly waved her hand, as if embarrassed by the question. "I wasn't thinking. It's late. You were just being nice by stopping by. You must be tired after your shift."

Danny grabbed the door before it closed. "Of course I'm being nice. But if it's not too late for you, I wouldn't mind coming in. It takes me a while to unwind after work."

A half smile curved her mouth. The porch light danced in her eyes. "I'll make coffee."

They settled on the couch in front of a late-night comedian, with their untouched coffee sitting on the coffee table. *How convenient.* Jayne aimed the remote at the TV, adjusting the volume down. The images on the screen flickered in the heavily shadowed room, the only other light coming from over the kitchen sink.

"You seem pretty drained," Danny said, tilting his head to look in her eyes, but she insisted on staring at the silent TV screen.

After a long moment, she said, "I've been distracted by Melinda's accident when I should have been focused on my mom and the dance studio." She pressed her fingers to her temples. "Tonight, I thought I'd do more research about the private number that sent Melinda the text. I was going to be tied up on the Internet and I didn't want my mom bothering me. So I left her home." Leaning back on the couch and staring at the popcorn ceiling, she groaned. "I should have never left her home. If something had happened to her . . ."

"It's not your fault." Danny reached out and sandwiched her hand between his. He was a little surprised she didn't pull it away.

"*Everyone* knows that you don't leave someone with dementia alone." They both stared down at their clasped hands. She held out her free one toward the TV. "I've seen those Silver Alerts and wondered how it could happen. But now I understand."

"You're not being fair." He glanced toward the TV. Some popular actress he wouldn't have been able to name even if someone offered him a hundred bucks was laughing and chatting with the host about her upcoming movie. "Did your mom ever wander away before today?"

"No." Her angry tone suggested she wasn't going to let herself off for a second.

"Most of the Silver Alert calls I've experienced are for first-time occurrences. Mom, Dad, Grandpa never wandered before. It's an eye-opening moment. It's the moment the family realizes a loved one can't be left alone anymore." He ran his thumb across the soft skin on the back of her hand. "Even if it wasn't the first time"—he paused, searching for the right words—"people understand that caring for someone with dementia is tough." He squeezed her hand. "You're doing a great job. And your mom's fine."

"Thank God," she breathed. Tucking a strand of hair behind her ear, she arched her eyebrows. "I guess I've had my eye-opening moment." Tears glistened in her eyes in the dim lighting.

Danny nudged her shoulder and she offered him a sad smile. "Deep in your heart, you had to know this moment was coming."

"Change is hard." She twisted her mouth. "Miss Natalie still does well when she's at the studio. I don't want to be responsible for taking that away from her. Not yet."

"Why does this all fall on your shoulders? What about Sean and Finn?"

A strangled laugh escaped her lips. "This kind of thing always falls on a daughter."

"When do you get to do what you want to do?"

Jayne froze and locked eyes with him. "Sometimes life doesn't work out the way you planned." She bit her bottom lip. "One of the teen dancers said the craziest thing today at the studio. She saw me doing research on the Internet and she suggested I should be a private investigator. I mean, I have to be at the studio to manage the office. I have my days free . . ." Her words flowed with excitement. "I could take jobs when I had time . . ."

"You've been thinking about this."

"It's not crazy, is it?"

"No . . ." He dragged out the single word.

"Gee, thanks for the vote of confidence."

"It's not that. I want you to be safe." Danny slipped his arm behind Jayne on the couch.

"I have two big brothers who have made it their mission in life to keep me safe. I don't need you hovering, too."

She lifted her face, inches from his. She smelled like clean cucumbers. How easy it would be to lean forward, just a fraction, and kiss her soft pink lips. Fighting the temptation, he closed his eyes, feeling Patrick's presence in the childhood family room where they used to play video games and watch action movies. "I don't mean to hover." He squeezed her shoulder with the hand draped around her back.

Jayne rested her head on his shoulder and whispered, "I'm sorry. I didn't mean to snap at you." She twirled a strand of red hair around her finger. "I'm trying to find my place in all this. No matter what, my mom comes first."

Danny kissed the top of her head. "You're a good daughter."

"I try." Defeat crept into her tone.

He played with the locks of her soft hair that pooled around her shoulder. "Don't let tonight get you down."

"I'll try," she muttered, snuggling into him.

So not a good idea, man.

But he couldn't tear himself away. He trailed his fingers down her arm in a comforting gesture, until they both grew quiet. Until his eyelids grew heavy.

He wasn't sure how long they had stayed that way, but when he opened his eyes, a different program was on TV. He didn't recognize the unfortunate comedian who had been relegated to the late-late-late-night TV that only college students and insomniacs tuned into. He sat there for a moment, enjoying the warm feel of Jayne pressed up against him. But as one commercial for an injury attorney rolled into the next, Danny slid his arm out from behind Jayne and whispered her name.

She sat up, wide eyed and blinking. She shifted out of his embrace and finger-combed her hair in a frantic motion. Squinting at the cable box under the TV, she shook her head as if dispelling the sleep.

"We must have been tired." She laughed, wiping the corner of her mouth. "Hope I didn't drool on you." A light danced in her eyes as she patted his chest. "Nope, it's all good."

Danny wrapped his fingers around her hand, still resting on his chest. "I better go."

She stilled and their eyes locked. Blinking rapidly, she pulled her hand out from under his and stood and broke the spell.

"I'll walk you out." She escorted him to the door and stepped outside on the porch. "The PI idea was crazy," she said, as if the notion wouldn't leave her. "Forget I said anything." She must have been worried he'd repeat the conversation to one of her brothers.

Danny took a step closer to her, and she looked up at him with clear blue eyes. He slipped his hand across her soft cheek and leaned forward, secretly pleased when her breath hitched. He planted a chaste kiss on her forehead, lingering a moment before stepping back.

Under the porch light, Jayne's cheeks grew pink.

He ran his finger gently across her jawline. "It's very late. You've had a long day. Wait to make big decisions in the light of day."

Pressing her lips together, she nodded.

"Night, Baby Jayne."

She smiled. "Patrick used to call me that."

"I know. He told me you loved that old Bette Davis movie, *What Ever Happened to Baby Jane?*"

"Why would he tell you that?"

"You have a lot of time to talk when you're partners on the force." It seemed as good an answer as any. He didn't want to admit that he had asked Patrick a lot of questions about his sister, mostly questions Patrick diverted by saying, "Never mind. She's my sister."

Staring off in the distance, Jayne said, "I probably saw that movie for the first time when I was about seven. I was captivated by everything about it. Black-and-white film. The acting. The pure evil." She ran her tongue along her bottom lip, and he wanted nothing more than to press his mouth against hers.

"Never mind. She's my sister." Would he ever be able to get Patrick's voice out of his head?

"It was my first taste of the dark side of human nature," Jayne continued. "From then on, I became obsessed with thrillers and everything true crime." She touched Danny's forearm and smiled at a distant memory. "Did he also tell you he had nightmares for a week after watching that movie?"

Her hand slid down his forearm to his fingers. Danny squeezed her hand, not wanting this evening to end. "I think you're mistaken. He said *you* slept on *his* bedroom floor for two weeks."

"So not true." Jayne bowed her head, then lifted her eyes to meet his. "I miss him."

Danny pulled her into an embrace and held her. "Me, too."

The scent of Danny's aloe aftershave lingered in her nose as she climbed into bed and pulled the covers to her chin. She ran the palm of her hand over her pillow, remembering the solid feel of his chest under her cheek . . . his warm breath on her neck.

A tingle raced up her spine.

She was in serious trouble. This was Danny Nolan. Her childhood archenemy. She laughed at the notion, flipped her pillow over, and plumped it up. Tonight had been a one-off. He'd been comforting her after her stressful evening. Danny would never look at her as anything but Patrick's little sister.

Jayne stared up at the glow-in-the-dark stickers on her ceiling. Well, technically Finn's ceiling. She'd claimed the largest bedroom in the house when he went away to college. Back then, she had always been able to drift off to sleep while staring at the gazillion stars until they blurred and grew black. It calmed her.

When Jayne was a kid, her older brother would allow her to sit on one of his beanbag chairs after dark and together, they'd pick out the star formations. Even then, she knew he was pulling her leg, but she didn't care that the stickers didn't form any real constellations. She loved spending time with her brothers.

Punching her pillow to get more comfortable, Jayne tried to relax. But it was hard to after all the night's events, not least of which was her mom's disappearance. What if Carol Anne hadn't happened to see her mom walking down the street?

Shut your brain off. Sink into the comfortable mattress. Relax your feet, your shins, your thighs . . .

Relax. Relax. Relax.

Unbidden, her father's smiling face floated to mind, and a single tear tracked down her cheek. She swiped it away as if she were at risk of being found out in the darkness of her big brother's bedroom. She understood the silliness of it, but she had to be strong. Even now. Even as she lay here all alone.

She wished her dad was still here, because he'd know what to do. He had always served as a kind and firm parent. The patriarch of the Murphy family. He'd know what was best for his beloved bride . . .

His sons.

His only daughter.

His granddaughter.

I miss you, Dad.

Eventually, Jayne's eyelids grew heavy as all her worries swirled into the water around her, lulling her into a fitful sleep on her tiny raft bobbing in a wild sea.

She wasn't sure how long she had been sleeping when she startled awake.

Silence.

Maybe she'd been dreaming.

Mentally, Jayne retraced all the steps she had completed to assure her mother's safety that night before she'd gone to bed. Jayne had kissed her mother good night and tucked her in. That went a long way to relaxing her mom. Most importantly, Jayne had set the house alarm, something she hadn't always done. But she would now. The bell would chime whenever someone opened a door.

Now she prayed she'd hear the chime in her sleep if her mother got restless.

Is that what she had just heard? Had the door chimed? Had her mother left the house?

Exhaustion scratching the insides of her eyelids, Jayne threw back the covers and raced to her mother's bedroom. Holding her breath, she turned the door handle silently. A slice of light from the hallway lit on her mother's thin frame under her bedspread. Relieved, Jayne pulled the door closed with a click.

She crept back to her bedroom next door and left her door open. Better to hear if her mom needed her. The red digital numbers on her bedside clock read *2:34*.

Morning would come quickly.

Relax . . . Melt into the mattress.

Once again, Jayne's mind grew light and her eyelids grew heavy. Satisfied her mother was safely inside the house, she allowed herself to finally fall asleep.

A long tunnel smells of algae, wet feet, and cold. If cold had a smell.

Even in her sleep, Jayne knew she was dreaming—and yet she had no recourse to stop the path of the dream. It was like watching a rerun even though she hated that particular episode.

The dark shadows in the tunnel close in around her, reminiscent of an old episode of Crime Solvers *where a woman killed her best friend while jogging and dragged her body to a damp tunnel, with the* drip-drip-drip *echoing in the confined space. The police searched for a skinny white man with a goatee for six months until they realized the pretty, fit blonde had killed her best friend in a calculated move to put a surefire end to her husband's affair.*

You shouldn't watch so many crime shows, *she finds herself thinking. The thoughts of her waking self seeping into her sleeping brain and giving her the same kind of admonishment.*

Dismissing her reservations, she moves forward through the long tunnel. The sound of a steady drip-drip-drip *has her hoping the water gathering in the tunnel is from a fresh source.*

The ripe smell says otherwise.

Bile rises in her throat.

Don't think about it.

She walks slowly forward, the sound of her heels reverberating through the hollow tunnel. Strange, she rarely wears heels. A young woman never gets away when being chased in heels. A person solving crime in heels forgot to read the rule book, because rule number one clearly reads, "No heels." Or . . . it should read "No heels."

Her palms grow clammy as she reaches the edge of the tunnel. She has to hold up her hand to block the sun from blinding her. From her vantage point at the mouth of the tunnel, Jayne sees the shadow of a rowboat, a man and his pole backlit by the setting sun.

She recognizes her daddy's blue rowboat, the Miss Natalie. *She cups her hands around her mouth and hollers to him. He looks up and his face comes into full view, a phenomenon known to her only in dreams.*

He smiles his big grin. The one she imagined was reserved only for her. His baby girl.

Her dad lifts his hand to wave, when he suddenly clutches his chest, gives her a look of betrayal, and tips out of the boat and submerges under the water in an understated splash.

Her heart plunges, much like her father's body, to the bottom of the lake.

Her body's flight response kicks into gear. She tries to run but the earth swallows her shoes, her legs, up to her thighs, encasing them in cold, wet mud.

Darkness, like a thick fog, creeps across the landscape and swallows her whole, leaving her wide eyed, yet blind.

Panic slicks her skin in cold fear.

"Daddy! Daddy! Don't leave me."

Her muffled calls woke her out of a restless sleep. Jayne tossed back the covers and swung her legs over the edge. She bent at the middle and sobbed. "I'm sorry, Daddy. I'm sorry. I won't let you down again. I'll make sure Mom is safe."

TWENTY-FIVE

The scent of pine overwhelms my hiding place and reminds me of Christmases past when I still had hope for my future. When I thought life would turn out better than it did.

Don't let your past define you. Each day is a blank page. A promise.

A promise not kept. My anger grows, blinding me with white-hot fury. I wrap my fingers around the pine needles and squeeze, ripping the bundle from the tree.

Why does everything always turn up sickeningly sweet for Jayne? Her mother goes missing and then returns, and her knight in shining armor shows up for some cuddle time on the couch.

It's infuriating.

I fist my hands. The sap from the tree makes my palm tacky. I struggle to stay warm as the night grows colder.

I wait.

Jayne's friend finally leaves.

I wait. Longer.

The house goes dark. I approach the back window, the one I unlocked earlier when everyone was distracted looking for Miss Natalie. When the house was left unattended.

How can smart people be so stupid?

Yes, the inclination to leave the house open for her mother's return was strong, but still . . .

The mud under the family-room window sucks the soles of my shoes. I reach for the latch and something makes me pause. I noticed an alarm pad near the door earlier. Is the window wired to the alarm system? Or just the doors?

Stupid. Stupid. Stupid.

Why didn't I think of that before?

Luck was with me the first time I entered the house through the unlocked sliders. I can't push it again. I'm not a lucky person.

I step backward, annoyed that I'll have to scrub the mud from the grooves in my shoes. Worry whispers across my goose-pimpled skin. Will someone notice the footprints under the window?

Gritting my teeth, I realize time is running out.

I glance up at the house. At Jayne's bedroom window.

Life always seems to turn up all sunshine and rainbows for Jayne after every storm.

But no longer.

Time is running out.

I turn and slink into the darkness, more determined than ever.

An apocalyptic storm is gathering.

TWENTY-SIX

The next night, Jayne sat on the edge of her mom's bed and smiled as her mother pulled the quilt up to her chin. "This is cozy," her mother said, a soft smile on her lips. A lot of Alzheimer's patients got agitated at sundown and Miss Natalie was no exception. However, once she was tucked into bed, she seemed to relax and the edge—the unwanted gift of Alzheimer's—smoothed over. Jayne considered herself blessed that her mother naturally gravitated toward her bedroom shortly after they arrived home from dance.

Her mother liked routine.

Jayne ran her finger along the edge of a thin booklet of the Gospel of Mark sitting on her mother's nightstand. A pen marked her mother's spot. Her mother enjoyed the Bible study at the church, primarily for the small talk with her fellow parishioners and neighbors. Guilt, yet again, gnawed at Jayne's gut. She hadn't taken her mom to the Bible study in a few weeks. When her mother mentioned it, Jayne had dismissed it. Melinda's death had distracted her.

Jayne picked up the booklet. "Would you like to go to the Bible study tomorrow?"

"I haven't read . . ." With a shaky hand Miss Natalie took the booklet, removed the pen, and squinted at the page. She closed the cover and ran her fingers over the image of the stained-glass window. Sadly, Jayne's mother didn't read much anymore.

"We can review the passages in the morning before you go."

"It would be nice to see friends." Her mother handed the booklet to Jayne, who returned it to its spot.

"I'm tired." Miss Natalie scooted down farther under her sheets, and Jayne's mind flashed back to the months after her father died. Just fifteen, Jayne had all but given up trying to sleep in her own room, where the nightmares slid out from under her bed and wrapped their tentacles around her and smothered her, making it difficult to breathe.

The true-crime books that covered Jayne's bedside table had been scary. And the endless crime shows she watched made her leery of her fellow man. But the dark shadows that haunted her nightmares after her father's untimely death were unrelenting. A triple deadbolt on the front door couldn't keep them at bay.

The sadness of her father's sudden death had eventually given way to some measure of acceptance, and she and her mother would crawl into bed early and watch *Law & Order* or *CSI: Some City or Another*. This was before video streaming, and they were at the mercy of the major networks because her parents didn't believe in paying for something you could get for free.

"Do you remember, after Dad died, how we'd snuggle in your bed and watch TV?"

Miss Natalie smiled. "It was nice."

Jayne leaned over and kissed her forehead. The familiar smells of Dove soap and Prell shampoo would forever make her think of her mother. "Thank you for being such a great mom."

Miss Natalie pulled her hand out from under the bedding and squeezed her daughter's hand. A heaviness weighed on Jayne's chest.

Her mother had no idea how much Jayne needed her. Needed this. "What's wrong, sweetie?"

"I always felt guilty about Dad's death."

Her mother patted her hand. "Why, dear? It was his time. God called him home."

Jayne drew in a deep breath. "He asked me to go fishing that day. Like we always did. But I didn't go with him because I wanted to hang out with my friends. If I had been with him, I could have helped him." She didn't find it necessary to delve into the harsh reality that her dad had fallen out of the boat during his heart attack and drowned.

Her mother rubbed her thumb across the back of Jayne's hand. "You can't blame yourself. Your dad knew he had to change his diet. Needed to exercise. But he didn't. And he refused to eat dinner if I didn't make him meat and potatoes."

Jayne swallowed around a knot of emotion.

Before now, she had never been able to open up to her mom about this one thing. She had been silent in her regret.

"Your father's in heaven and someday we'll meet again. He'll probably greet us at the pearly gates with a bowl of ice cream."

Jayne laughed. "He did like his ice cream."

"Always vanilla."

Jayne shook her head, then gave her mother another kiss. "Night, Mom." She turned the switch of the lamp next to her bed.

She had almost reached the door when her mother whispered, "It wasn't that long ago that I tucked you in."

Jayne returned to her mother's side and lay on top of the covers, fully dressed. It was heartbreaking to miss someone who was right in front of you. But tonight, Jayne had been blessed with a gift of clarity. Of forgiveness.

She reached out and held her mother's hand as they both drifted off to sleep.

❖

Jayne startled awake and blinked rapidly. She ran a hand across her eyes and had to take a minute to remember where she was.

On top of the quilt.

In her mother's bedroom.

Fully dressed.

The red numbers on her mother's digital alarm clock came into focus.

8:45.

At night? She rubbed her eyes, her brain fuzzy. She glanced toward her mother's drawn blinds. No light leaked in around the edges. She smiled at the ridiculousness of falling asleep before it was even nine o'clock at night.

Immediately, the rush of emotion from the past few weeks rolled over her. The comfort her mother had provided after Jayne unburdened herself was nudged out by her worries for caring for her mom and the studio, and by the unanswered questions surrounding Melinda's death.

Jayne would never be able to go back to sleep tonight.

Holding her breath, not wanting to wake up her mom, she rolled out of bed, careful not to go tumbling to the floor in the darkness. Then she crept out of the room and downstairs. She turned a light on in the family room and then in the kitchen. As she filled a glass of water at the kitchen sink, she noticed a light on at the Greens' house.

Melinda had been exceptionally close to her mother. Victoria knew Melinda had plans to move to New York City, while Jayne had been kept in the dark. Maybe Melinda's mother knew more about the troubles she'd been having with Kyle, too.

Jayne stuffed her feet into her sneakers, smooshing their backs down, and slipped out the back door, but not before setting the home alarm. An alert would be sent to her cell phone if any of the doors was opened.

She'd only be a house away.

One house away.

Crossing her arms against the evening chill, she jogged across the yard. Her decision to stop and see Victoria was fortified when she noticed her through the kitchen window getting something out of the fridge. Jayne often wondered if more people would draw their blinds—or buy blinds—if they knew they were like marine life swimming around a lit-up tank, especially for people like Jayne who loved to study people. The photo that Kyle had taken outside of Melinda's bedroom window sprang to mind.

Nothing creepy about that . . .

Averting her gaze, feeling like a voyeur, Jayne crossed the driveway. Somewhere close by, someone smoked a cigarette. Probably Hannah. Jayne thought about visiting with her, but she needed to talk to Victoria before it got too late. She knocked lightly on the side door. She hadn't noticed David's car, which probably meant he was traveling.

Good. Easier to talk with Melinda's mom. She'd definitely be more reserved if her husband was around. Melinda's dad thought the sun rose and set on his adopted daughter. Jayne didn't want to be the reason some of the shine dulled. Nor did she want David to stop her from talking to Victoria. He was overly protective.

Justifiably protective.

The sheer blind on the top half of the door pulled away at the edges. Jayne made eye contact with Victoria through the thin fabric and waved a hand, suddenly wondering what she was doing there.

Who shows up unannounced after dark?

Apparently Jayne.

Victoria pulled open the door, holding Trinket under one arm. "Hello, Jayne. Is something wrong?" The pain of losing her daughter was still evident in the dark circles under her eyes and her papery-white complexion.

"No, no, nothing's wrong." Jayne grabbed the handle of the screen door. "Do you have time to talk?"

An uneasy smile fluttered at the corners of Victoria's mouth. "I just poured myself some wine. I'd love the company. It seems lately I have nothing but time. The days drag. And with David traveling again . . ." She waved her hand as if she had said too much. She scratched the dog's head, then set her on the floor in the kitchen. Trinket curled up under the table, apparently content to cuddle by their feet. "Come on in," she called over her shoulder. And once again, Jayne was flooded with a million memories of all the time she had spent over here babysitting Melinda.

"Have a seat."

Jayne pulled out a chair and plopped down. She tried to ignore the *M* that had been engraved into the table when Melinda had forgotten to put a magazine under her paper as she determinedly practiced writing her name in cursive. She had gotten the first letter down before Jayne freaked and told her to stop. Seven-year-old Melinda had broken down in tears, not used to getting scolded. It took Jayne an hour to convince her young charge that she wasn't in trouble.

Jayne traced the letter with her finger.

Victoria tilted her head to study the marking on the table. "I forgot that was there." She set a second wine glass on the table and sat down.

"She was a determined little girl."

Victoria traced the rim of her glass, around and around. "Remember the time she was convinced the substitute teacher in sixth grade had been featured on *America's Most Wanted*? Poor guy."

"Sorry about that."

"Never apologize for being part of our family. Melinda *loved* the time she spent with you." Victoria lifted the glass to her lips, then set it back down. "What's on your mind, sweetie?"

Jayne threaded the stem of the wine glass with her fingers and jostled it back and forth, composing her thoughts. It wasn't fair for someone to go sobbing about their loss to someone who had suffered an even greater one.

She stilled her hand. "How were Kyle and Melinda doing before her accident? I heard they had broken up, but was there any animosity?"

Victoria lifted one shoulder, the noncommittal shrug of someone who knew more than she was willing to say.

Jayne swirled her wine glass, studying the burgundy liquid before taking a long drink. "How did Kyle feel about Melinda moving to New York?" The now-familiar sting that Melinda hadn't confided in her rose up and tasted like bile.

Something flickered in the depths of Victoria's eyes. Then she blinked and it was gone. "Melinda had broken up with Kyle. It wasn't his concern."

"How did you feel about her move?"

"Melinda knew we'd support her—I mean, we didn't pay all this money over the years for dance lessons to have her *not* follow her dreams. Our only condition was that she finish college. Come May, she would have finished." Victoria topped off her glass with more wine. "I didn't like the idea of her moving away, but that's what she worked for, right? A chance to pursue her dreams in New York City. *New York City.*" She repeated the name and opened her eyes wide as if emphasizing every great thing that city promised for someone as gifted as Melinda Green.

An emptiness expanded in Jayne's heart. She straightened in her seat and set her palms flat on the table on either side of the glass.

Victoria covered Jayne's hand with hers. "Don't feel bad," she said, as if reading her mind. "Melinda loved you so much that she was afraid of hurting you by leaving. You had already suffered so much loss. Melinda also had a lot on her mind as she finished up college and made her plans to move. She loved you," she repeated.

An ache in the back of Jayne's throat made it difficult to speak. She took a big gulp of wine, nearly polishing off the glass. Victoria refilled it before she could protest.

"Melinda wasn't the kind to be pinned down, was she?"

"No, she wasn't."

Jayne stared off into the middle distance, trying to put all the pieces together. Melinda's plans to move may have set off someone who was controlling and manipulative.

"Kyle never hurt Melinda, did he?"

Victoria cut her gaze to Jayne, some of the intended sharpness dulled by the wine. "Is there a reason you're asking?" Her thin, penciled-in brows drew together. "Did Kyle do something?" This time her question ended in a high-pitched squeak.

Jayne glanced away and ran her hand down her long braid. She should have thought this through. The last thing she wanted to do was cause Victoria more pain.

Even worse, she risked hurting Victoria by searching for something that wasn't there. Inwardly she rolled her eyes, mocking herself. She was acting like a detective when she clearly wasn't one.

Paige's encouragement to pursue a career as a private investigator floated to mind . . .

"I think Melinda was smart to cool things off with Kyle. He's immature. But I . . ." She searched for the right word to avoid setting off alarm bells. "I just never liked him. That's all." She decided to leave it at that.

Victoria lifted her shoulders as if she had thought of something important, then let them drop with a long sigh. "I guess her relationship with Kyle doesn't matter anymore."

Jayne and Victoria sipped their wine in companionable silence. A warm, fuzzy feeling coated all the hard edges Jayne had been trying to push out of her mind. *I'll sleep well tonight.* Drawing in a deep breath in a bit of a dreamy haze, Jayne stood and Victoria followed suit. The older woman pulled her into a fierce embrace.

Jayne pulled away. "You know where to find me if you need me."

"Of course."

A cell phone rang on the counter. "Hold on." Victoria's mood seemed to deflate when she glanced at the screen. "Hi, Carol Anne."

She ran her finger along the edge of the counter as she listened. "Oh, that's not necessary. I'm fine. Really." She twisted her mouth and then took another sip of wine. "No, really . . . Actually, Jayne stopped over. I'm not alone." She turned her back to Jayne and took a deep breath. "Yes, thanks for calling. 'Bye now."

Victoria paused a few moments before turning around. "That girl means well, but she gets on my every last nerve." Her hand flew to her mouth. "Oh, I'm horrible. I should have never said that. She does mean well," she repeated. "But right now her neediness drains me."

As much as Jayne agreed, she didn't want to say so out loud. She knew better than to badmouth someone's family.

Victoria settled back in her chair and yawned. "Oh, I'm sorry," she said around another yawn. "This wine is putting me to sleep. Can we chat more tomorrow?"

"Of course." Jayne moved to the door. "Make sure you lock up."

Sadness lingered in Victoria's eyes. "Kyle may not have been Melinda's soul mate, but he wasn't bad." She tilted her head and really studied Jayne. "We live in a safe town. You can't always live fearing the unknown. That was part of the reason I was so proud of Melinda. She was getting over her fears. I told her she'd have to do as much if she planned to move to New York City." She blinked her heavy eyelids slowly. "Of course, there's something to be said for common sense, but you can't look for a boogeyman around every corner."

"I suppose you're right. Night." Jayne turned the lock. She pulled the door closed and double-checked that it was secure before she started across the driveway to her home.

"Hey."

Jayne's hand flung up reflexively as she spun around. The Greens' neighbor stood on the edge of the lawn. "Oh, Hannah," she breathed out. "You scared me."

The teenager laughed. "Sorry. I swore you saw me when you were walking out the door."

"You're dressed in black. At night."

"Good point." Her leather coat crinkled as she crossed her arms in front of her. "I wanted to let you know that there was a car sitting in front of the Greens' house for a long time. Kinda freaked me out."

"What do you mean?"

Hannah glanced toward the street, as if needing to convince herself the threat was gone. "I could only see the shadow of a person inside. They pulled up. Sat in the car. Never got out. I got a bad feeling about it. I went back inside. They drove off a few minutes ago."

Jayne touched Hannah's arm. "What kind of car?"

Hannah shrugged. "You're asking me? I don't know. It just seemed strange."

"It was probably nothing. Someone pulled over to make a phone call or something."

"That's odd since we live on a dead-end street."

"Call me if you ever see that car again, okay?" Jayne walked her to her front door. "Go inside. Lock the door."

Hannah's eyes flared wide. "I'm sure it wasn't anything."

"No. Probably not. But better safe than sorry."

TWENTY-SEVEN

A strange sense of nostalgia crept over Danny when he pulled up the driveway of his childhood home.

Just part of the reason he rarely went home. If he could call it that.

The house was neat and well maintained, but it lacked something. When he was a little kid, his mother changed the wreath on the front door with every season. Like now, she would have hung a pumpkin wreath. Maybe with a friendly ghost. His older brother, Francis, used to complain that ghosts were meant to be scary, not friendly. But their mother insisted on creating a warm and inviting home.

And then one day she just left.

Up until then, Danny had been like every other kid.

Mom. Check.

Dad. Check.

Big brother. Check.

But soon after his brother's First Communion and a week before kindergarten graduation, his mother had left him. Well, not him. His family. But when you're six and your mom walks out the door . . . it feels personal.

His mother had hung a tulip wreath on the door a few weeks before she left. It hung there until Christmas, after which he found it on top of the garbage cans, as if his dad had thrown away the last reminder of his mom.

All these years later this shouldn't be so hard.

Danny pulled on the door release, and the autumn breeze cooled his skin. It was far past time that he confronted his father. *The chief.* Stop second-guessing his abilities as a cop and be willing to pursue investigations even if his dad told him otherwise.

Sure, there was the chain-of-command thing, but Danny couldn't keep sidestepping issues for fear of his father's disapproval. For fear of screwing up on the job. He was human. Humans made mistakes. But he couldn't keep living in fear. Danny had to come into his own as a police officer. He couldn't let Patrick's death define him.

He was a good police officer. He was.

Swallowing hard, Danny walked up the path and lifted his fist to knock, then remembered the chief's admonition to come in even though Danny didn't live there anymore.

The familiar smell of coffee and stale cigarette smoke greeted him in the entryway. So much for his father's claims that he'd quit. The relentless happy chat of some annoying news reporters floated in from the TV room. He found the chief reclined on his rocker with a coffee balanced on his belly.

When the chief saw him, he set aside his coffee and reached down and pulled the lever of the recliner, tucking in the footrest with a thud. "Hey, to what do I owe the pleasure?" His father rose to his feet and clapped his son on the back. He gave his uniform a once-over and concern etched his features. "You're on duty. Is something wrong?"

Danny held his hat in his hand. "Nothing urgent. Just wanted to follow up on some questions about the accident on Lake Road."

The chief ran his hand over his forehead, then sat down on the edge of the recliner. It dipped forward under his weight. "You can't give it a rest?" He held out his open palm, indicating Danny should sit. So he did.

Danny set his hat on the arm of the couch. "A text came in luring Melinda out to Lake Road."

"Who did the text come from?"

"An unfamiliar number."

The corners of the chief's mouth tugged down and his nose flared. It was his tell. He didn't take much stock in what Danny told him.

"What did the text say?"

Danny pulled out his cell phone and looked at his notes. "'Hey. Change in plans. Meet us at Henry's Waterfront Cafe.'" He looked up, studying his father's blank expression. "It was signed by 'B.' Melinda was led to believe the message was from her friend Bailey. But Bailey never sent it."

"Who do you think sent the text?" His tone was flat, indicating neither surprise nor frustration.

"Kyle Duggan."

"Why Kyle?" The chief steepled his fingers and rested his elbows on his knees. A master interrogator, the chief was leading him down a path, and Danny had no choice but to follow it if he hoped to move forward on this investigation.

"We found a photo taken outside Melinda's bedroom. Sent from a fake e-mail address. Kyle confessed to sending it. He and Melinda were dating, and I think he wanted to scare her. He didn't want her to move to New York City."

The chief's blank stare made Danny remember his teen years under the roof of a father-slash-law-enforcement-official. Sometimes his father forgot where one role ended and the other began. A kid would crack under his steely gaze.

"You're thinking this was a domestic situation. Perhaps her boyfriend ran her off the road?"

Danny turned the questioning around on his father. "You've known the Duggan family for years. How would you describe Kyle? The type of kid to lose it if his girlfriend left him?"

The chief sat back in the recliner and palmed the arms of the chair. "I'm going to be straight with you, Danny. Kyle Duggan is a royal pain in his father's backside. But you can't choose your family, right?"

The chief's words cut through Danny even though he suspected they'd been thrown out casually, not maliciously.

"I personally did some digging on Kyle regarding that night."

"You were investigating Kyle?" Disbelief laced Danny's tone. "Why didn't you tell me?"

The chief ran his palms up and down the arms of his well-worn recliner, as if debating how much to share. "I did a little digging at the request of the mayor. He wanted to make sure the kid didn't have anything to do with his girlfriend's death. Kyle had been picked up for minor stuff in the past. Always got off. Perks of being the mayor's son. This time, the mayor was proactive and wanted to see what kind of fire he might have to put out if his son came up looking guilty. Trust me on this, Kyle was *not* involved in any way with Melinda's accident. I promise you."

"Why are you so convinced?"

"He has an alibi."

Danny held out his hand as if to say, *Care to share?*

"I'll tell you, but I promised her I'd keep it quiet. She's afraid of the blowback. To her personal life. To her job."

Realization washed over Danny. "Kyle was with Quinn Taylor that night."

"Yeah, that's right. How'd you know?"

"She worked with Melinda. They were both dance instructors at Murphy's Dance Academy."

"Quinn was worried that Jayne wouldn't look kindly on her dating Kyle behind Melinda's back. Something about Melinda being Jayne's favorite and how she couldn't afford to lose her job." The chief made a face as if the girl-drama was beyond his pay grade. He sighed heavily. "Since Quinn wasn't doing anything illegal, I let it go. I got what I needed: an alibi for Kyle." The chief tapped out a cigarette, pinched it between his fingers, and stood. The recliner rocked behind him. "The mayor's kid doesn't seem to have much drive, but for some reason the ladies like him."

"Why didn't you tell me?" Danny stood and crossed his arms.

"I didn't want to get you involved. Stories about politicians' kids tend to grow legs. And since the news has finally died down regarding . . ."

Patrick's death.

"Am I going to have to avoid high-profile cases forever?"

His father stared at him squarely. "No, not at all. But memories are long. If you went after the mayor's son publicly and he was found innocent, people would question your policing skills."

"Like they questioned me after Patrick's death?" Danny rubbed his eyebrow.

"Yes." A muscle ticked in his father's jaw.

"It was a good shot." It was the first time Danny had said that out loud. For the past year, he had relied on his fellow officers to prop him up, tell him he had handled the crisis well. The only way events could have turned out better was if Danny had saved his best friend.

However, the media couldn't let it go. They questioned why the chief's son had been let off the hook so easily. Witnesses said the kid was shot first. The kid was retreating. Had dropped the gun. Was only sixteen.

The only fact was the kid's age. The rest were all stories created by individuals sympathetic to him. But the fact that a police officer had been killed in the line of duty by this kid had probably quieted the call for a public lynching of the chief's son.

An investigation was done. The true circumstances surrounding Patrick's death and the death of the kid were overshadowed by the dramatic media coverage. And that was why his father didn't want him to get caught up in an investigation of the son of the mayor weeks before the election. As they said in political circles, "The optics wouldn't be good."

"If you had found evidence that Kyle was involved, how would you have handled it?"

"It would have been handled." His father clapped his hand on Danny's shoulder. "We've discussed this before. Running someone off the road in the hopes that they'd drown is a pretty inefficient way to kill someone. It's a stretch."

"What if his intention wasn't to kill her, but to harass her?"

Tension hung heavy in the air. "I only have your best interests at heart. Get out from under this one. Convince Jayne that Melinda Green died in a horrible car accident. Kyle wasn't involved."

"What about the text from the unfamiliar number?" Danny picked up his hat from the couch and tugged it down on his head.

"Wrong number? A joke? Nothing in it suggests it was criminal."

Something about that text still bothered Danny, but did it warrant a police investigation? His father was right.

"Did you hear about the break-in at the dance studio? Seems odd so soon after one of their teachers died." Danny crossed his arms.

His father scrubbed a hand across his face. "Kids, I imagine." He dropped his hand and locked eyes with his son. "Any security cameras out there?"

"No." Danny gritted his teeth.

"There was a break-in at the hardware store a few nights ago, too." He held up his hand. "People see an empty business, it's a prime target. Don't jump to conclusions."

"No, I won't jump to conclusions, but I can investigate even if it gets some politicians riled up."

The chief harrumphed and crossed his arms tightly. Danny tipped his hat in silent acknowledgment, then turned and left before the chief had a chance to give him the dress-down that was building behind the bulging vein in his forehead.

TWENTY-EIGHT

One of the challenges of managing a dance studio was that Jayne had to work irregular hours, because dancers between the ages of five and eighteen tended to have a thing called school during the day. As a result, Jayne had to work evenings and weekends and run errands with the likes of retired folks, stay-at-home moms, and the unemployed.

And, of course, those who worked in nontraditional jobs, like her.

It gave Jayne the flexibility to run errands with her mom, though, who was more lucid during daylight hours. Today was the Bible study at church. She planned to drop her mom off, because Miss Natalie relied on Jayne too much when she was around. Once, Jayne had watched from a distance and noticed her mother blossom with her church friends without her daughter as a crutch.

In the passenger seat of Jayne's car, her mother fidgeted with the booklet of Gospel readings. Jayne reached across and covered her mom's hand.

"Barbara will be there today. She always brings the best baked goods."

"Oh, should I have baked something? Oh, maybe—"

"No, it wasn't your turn, Mom. Don't worry about it."

"I hate to show up empty-handed." Miss Natalie tugged on her seat belt. "Maybe we can swing into the bakery and pick something up."

Jayne squeezed her mom's hand before letting go to turn on the directional. "They'll be happy to see you."

"Oh, I don't know."

When they pulled into the church lot, mostly empty except for the cars of the teachers at the adjoining elementary school, Jayne noticed her mother's friend, Barbara, standing in the doorway of the community center. She pushed through the glass doors and waved enthusiastically at Jayne's car.

Jayne rolled down the passenger window. "Hi, Barbara."

Barbara smiled. She was at least ten years older than Miss Natalie. She kept her beautiful silver hair fashionably cut and wore stylish clothes. A pang of envy zipped through Jayne.

Will my mom even be here in ten years?

"Hi, ladies." Barbara pulled on the door handle, but it was locked. Jayne flicked the locks and Barbara tried again. "I'll take your mom in."

"Oh, okay." Her mother shot Jayne an uncertain look.

"Thank you." Jayne unbuckled her mother, and Barbara helped her get out of the car and slammed the door.

Barbara hooked arms with Miss Natalie and smiled at Jayne. "Why don't you come back in two hours? We'd like to sit and visit a bit after the Bible study." She turned to Miss Natalie. "How does that sound?"

Miss Natalie took a step toward the car, as if she had changed her mind. "Oh, I don't know. I didn't bring anything." Miss Natalie tended to do that. Got hyperfocused on something and couldn't let it go. Right now it was her lack of baked goods.

"Well, I brought plenty. You can bring something next time, okay?" Barbara stroked her mother's hand reassuringly.

God bless Barbara.

Miss Natalie nodded. "I told Jayne we should have stopped by the bakery."

Jayne regretted not taking five minutes to stop at the bakery, because she saw now how much comfort it would have brought her mother.

Barbara raised a perfectly manicured eyebrow. "Wait until you taste my brownies. I added caramel and chocolate chips."

Miss Natalie smiled uncertainly. They started to turn, when Barbara paused and leaned on the frame of the open window. Her mother walked ahead and lingered by the community-center door without going in. "How are you, dear? I was so sorry to hear about Melinda. Such a tragic accident."

"Thank you."

"What did the police say happened?"

Jayne couldn't begrudge the woman's curiosity, but she didn't have to like it. *What did happen?* Danny had called her late last night and brought her up to speed on the chief's quiet investigation. Apparently Quinn had been with Kyle the night of Melinda's accident.

Why hadn't Quinn mentioned that?

Jayne ran her hand over the steering wheel. "A tragic accident."

"Melinda's been in my prayers." Barbara patted the doorframe. "Victoria's blessed to have you. She said as much when I dropped off a casserole."

"Melinda was a good friend."

"I heard her stepdaughter has been around a lot lately. Now with her stepsister gone, she'll probably slide right in."

Jayne's jaw dropped and she quickly snapped it shut. *What a bold thing to say.*

"I had Carol Anne during Vacation Bible School a few summers in a row when she was maybe twelve or thirteen," Barbara said. "She was a strange little girl."

"She has a good heart. She's there for her stepmom and dad."

"I'm sure she is. She's probably already redecorating Melinda's bedroom."

"It's been hard for everyone," Jayne muttered.

"Well, we'll go in before we're late for Bible study."

Jayne waited until they were inside before she slid into a parking spot. She Googled "Carol Anne Green," and multiple sites listed her as living in the Leisure Acres neighborhood. Jayne entered the address in her GPS.

Everyone seemed dismissive of Carol Anne. The poor girl had lost her stepsister. Jayne tapped the steering wheel with her fist. She hadn't been any better. It was too easy to hold Carol Anne at arm's length because she always seemed so resilient. So earnest.

So eager to please.

Jayne knew what that was like.

Hitting the "Start" button on the GPS, Jayne decided she owed Melinda's stepsister more than empty platitudes and good intentions. Jayne understood what it meant to lose a sibling, and the least she could do was reach out.

Jayne glanced down at the little dot on the screen of her navigational system that indicated Leisure Acres was up on her right. She followed the GPS into a neighborhood of single-story homes that had seen better days. An uneasy feeling skittered up her spine as she read the house numbers on the mailboxes.

Number 171, Carol Anne's home, had a rusted-out mailbox and grass in need of mowing. Jayne pulled alongside the curb and put the gear in park. A large section of shingles was missing from the roof, and a screen hung askew from one of the windows.

Jayne's mouth grew dry, and she second-guessed her spontaneous decision to stop unannounced to visit Carol Anne. Some people didn't appreciate that. Jayne wasn't really sure what she hoped to say—she just wanted an opportunity to connect with Melinda's stepsister.

"She's probably already redecorating Melinda's bedroom." Barbara's words floated to mind. Why was she allowing the gossip of one of her mother's church friends to get into her head? Wasn't she bigger than that?

The cool fall breeze swept across her cheeks, soothing the uncertainty that slowed her footsteps up the gravel driveway. Weeds twisted around the flagstone pavers lining the path to the front door. She felt like she was prying into a secret Carol Anne wanted to keep buried.

Jayne paused with her hand on the metal railing of the small stoop. *Last chance to get out of here. Pretend you were never here.*

A rustling sounded at the tinny door. The skewed curtain covering the window on the door pulled back. A flash of an angry face appeared in the window before the interior door flung open, leaving only the ripped screen door between them.

A woman stood in the doorway, a cigarette dangling from her bottom lip. She gave Jayne the once-over, making her wonder if she had the wrong house. "Um, I was looking for Carol Anne Green."

"You're that girl on the news. Murphy, right? Your brother was killed in that sub shop." She pulled the cigarette from her lips and ran the back of her hand across her mouth. "What a crummy way to go. One minute you're ordering a ham and pastrami, the next . . ." The unkempt woman had the good sense to cut it short.

"I'm sorry. I must have the wrong house."

"No, no, you have the right place. I'm Carol Anne's mother."

The apprehension brewing in the pit of her stomach was no less prickly than the supersized weed growing up through the crack in the crumbling porch. "Is Carol Anne home?"

"What's she done?" Curiosity brought her closer to the screen.

Jayne cleared her throat and plastered on a smile. "I'm Jayne Murphy. I'm friends with Carol Anne and her sister, Melinda."

"Stepsister," the woman corrected.

Jayne nodded her agreement. "I wanted to see how she's doing."

The woman leaned heavily against the frame of the door and took a long drag on her cigarette. "She's doing fine. She's always fine. Tough girl. You never stopped by before?" A wracking cough got hold of her.

She kept coughing, her face turning red. She kicked open the screen door and jerked her head, indicating Jayne should come in.

"Can I get you some water?" Without waiting for a reply, Jayne took her arm and ushered her inside; a stale smell hung heavy in the air. Ignoring the state of the house, she continued past piles and piles of stuff to a well-worn chair in front of a TV. The woman's coughing had calmed to an intermittent hack and a popping sound. Jayne went over to the sink filled with dishes and opened a few cupboards before she found a glass. The glass felt gritty.

She ran the water until it went cool. Then she filled the glass and brought it to Mrs. Green, careful not to trip on the random shoes, books, and newspapers littering the floor.

"Mrs. Green."

The woman looked up and her dark eyes narrowed. "I haven't been Mrs. Green for twenty years. Call me Sylvia."

"Sorry." Why Jayne felt contrite, she wasn't exactly sure.

Sylvia collected herself, then slid forward to the edge of her seat, wrapping her hands around the arms of the chair as if she were about to stand but couldn't muster the strength. "Carol's not here. She was supposed to be back to take me to an appointment." Sylvia glanced at her watch. "Not sure what happened to her."

Feeling like she was hovering, Jayne sat on the edge of a chair that was otherwise stacked with newspapers. She rested her elbows on her thighs, clasped her hands, and leaned toward Sylvia. "Can I take you to your appointment? I have to pick up my mother in two hours, but we could figure something out."

Sylvia gave her an incredulous stare. Blinking rapidly, she waved her hand in dismissal. "No, no . . . Carol Anne knows what I need when we go. And she keeps me company during chemo. It's so depressing sitting in there with all those sick people." Sylvia leaned back, grabbed a pack of cigarettes, and tapped one out. She put it between her lips but didn't light it. Then she locked eyes with Jayne and let out a raucous laugh. "Don't look so horrified. I have colon cancer, not lung cancer." She made a fist and tapped her chest. "Everyone dies of something."

"I'm sorry. I'll keep you in my prayers."

Sylvia grew serious for the first time. She put the cigarettes down and bowed her head, letting her long, gnarled fingers—the hands of someone who had seen a lot of manual labor—hang between her knees. After a moment, she raised her head and her voice sounded raspy. "I appreciate it." Then she seemed to snap out of it. "Maybe you can also pray for a housekeeper. I could really use one of those, too."

"Isn't Carol Anne able to help you around here?" Jayne feared she might offend the woman.

"Pfft . . . She's too busy helping Victoria." Sylvia rolled her eyes. "Poor girl doesn't seem to understand where she belongs." She pointed at the floor, as if to say, *Right here.*

"I'm sure she wants to be helpful," Jayne said.

"Helpful. Do you think she's helpful?" The abrasive nature of Sylvia's comments bothered Jayne. A little piece of her heart broke for Carol Anne. *This* had been her home life. No wonder she was so eager to fit in.

The room began to feel close, and the lingering smell of cigarette smoke and sweat clung to the insides of Jayne's nose. A tingling started in her fingertips, and she pressed her fist to her nose and turned away in an effort not to offend Carol Anne's mother.

"Okay . . ." Taking shallow breaths, she scanned the room. If Sylvia didn't live with her able-bodied twenty-six-year-old daughter, Jayne would wonder if she was capable of living on her own. Why wasn't Carol Anne doing more around here to help her mother? Probably because her mother was critical of everything she did, so why bother?

A feeling of dread twined up Jayne's spine. What did living in this type of situation do to a person's psyche? The urge to flee was strong.

"Do you need anything, Sylvia?"

"Carol will be back. She always comes back."

Jayne scanned the piles of magazines and papers and found a pen. She wrote down her phone number and slipped it onto the table. "Here's my phone number if you ever need anything."

Sylvia took a long drag on her cigarette, studying Jayne. "Why would you do that?"

"Why not?" Jayne smiled and stood up. "Carol Anne and I are friends." She hesitated a moment. "I really should go. Please tell her I stopped by."

Sylvia fingered the piece of paper that Jayne had placed on the table next to her chair. "I will."

Something deep inside Jayne told her Carol Anne wouldn't be happy to receive the news that she had stopped by.

TWENTY-NINE

J ayne stared at the clock on the wall and watched the minute hand shift to the top of the hour. *Finally*, the last dance class would be wrapping up for the night and she'd be able to go home and relieve Hannah, who seemed to be enjoying making a few extra dollars and spending time with Miss Natalie, while Jayne was comfortable knowing her mother wouldn't wander away from the house.

Jayne heard coughing coming from the dancers' lounge. Stretching her legs, she got up and walked to the converted sunroom. She found Cindy sitting cross-legged on the couch doing her homework. When Jayne walked in, she looked up and smiled. "Hi, Miss Jayne."

"Oh, I didn't know you were still here."

Cindy shrugged. "My mom's running late. She'll be here before the last class lets out."

Jayne leaned a hip on the arm of the couch. "This is your home away from home, isn't it?"

A slow smile crept across Cindy's face. "It is. I think I've spent more time in this room doing homework than in my bedroom."

Jayne tilted her head, studying her. "Wouldn't you rather be home? In your PJs? Sitting on your bed?"

Cindy jutted out her lower lip and shook her head. "Sometimes, but not always. Most of the time, there are other dancers here with me. We help each other with homework. It's fun."

Being a homebody herself, Jayne had never thought of it that way. An unexpected feeling of satisfaction warmed her insides. Miss Natalie had made this possible for generations of girls. *Jayne* was allowing this to continue. Building girls' confidence. Creating second families. There was so much more to dance than a leap across the stage.

"You doing all right?" The cloak of sadness since Melinda's death seemed to be drawing back.

Cindy pinched the bun on top of her head. "I really miss Miss Melinda, but she's inspired me to follow my dreams."

"You plan on studying dance in college?"

Cindy smoothed her hands over both sides of her head. It was obviously a habit, because every hair was in place. "Maybe I'll pick dance as a minor, but I want to be a math teacher. I want to be able to influence kids like she influenced us." Her lower lip quivered and she turned away. A giggle of embarrassment escaped her lips. "I'm sorry."

Jayne slid in and, sitting down next to Cindy, gently touched her knee. "You don't have to be sorry. It hurts to lose someone you love."

Cindy looked up with watery eyes and nodded. "I have to follow my dreams to honor her memory."

"Following your dreams is a wonderful thing." Her words whispered across her soul. Swallowing hard, Jayne leaned over and grabbed a tissue from the corner table and handed it to her young friend. "I'm sure you'll make us all proud."

Cindy nodded.

Jayne didn't want to leave Cindy just yet, so she asked, "Have you talked to Paige recently? How's she doing at Miss Gigi's studio?"

"Okay, I guess." She shrugged. "Her mom thinks she'll do better there."

"Do you think Miss Gigi runs a better studio?"

Cindy tapped the back of her pen on the open page of the notebook resting in her lap. "She called our house, trying to get me to go to her studio, but I like it here."

Jayne stifled a gasp. *Miss Gigi is actively trying to poach my students?*

"We like having you here, too."

Ugh, the nerve of Miss Gigi.

Cindy's cell phone dinged and she glanced down. "That's my mom. She's in the parking lot."

"You better get going, then. Have a good night." And she would not let Miss Gigi ruin her night.

"I will." She gave Jayne a half smile, gathered her stuff, and, instead of putting it in her bag, carried it all in her arms—a mess of sweatpants, books, and dance shoes. No wonder the lost-and-found bin was overflowing.

After Cindy left, Jayne wandered the first floor of the studio, making sure all the doors and windows were secure. Sometimes the teachers opened them to allow fresh air in and get rid of the odor of sweaty dance shoes, the stink of which could rival a hockey bag any day. She shuddered, remembering the years her brothers had played and how the mudroom smelled rank with the pile of wet equipment.

Miss Quinn popped her head in the doorway of Studio B. "Hey, I'm going to scoot. All my students have been picked up. Want me to wait for you so we can walk out together?"

"I have to finish a little paperwork. Go on ahead." She watched Quinn head to the doorway, then called out to her, "Hey, wait. Do you have a minute?"

Quinn's hand froze on her dance bag, and she slowly turned around with the grace of a dancer. "Yeah . . ." Hesitation flickered on her features before she seemed to catch herself. Clinging to the strap of the bag slung over her shoulder, she jutted out a hip. "What's up?"

"Let's go to my office." Once there, Jayne sat on the edge of the desk.

Quinn's dance bag landed on the floor with a thud, and she slowly sank into a chair, clutching the strap. "Is something wrong?"

"I wanted to check in with you. Melinda's death has been hard on everyone."

Quinn wound the strap of her dance bag around and around her hand, pulling it tight. "We started dance together when we were three." Her voice grew quiet as she reminisced. "I should have come to her memorial, but I got as far as the parking lot and just couldn't. Celebrating her life here at the studio was too painful." She made no mention of Kyle.

"She had more talent in her little finger . . ." Quinn waggled her pinky.

Jayne moved to sit next to Quinn and pulled the teacher's free hand into hers. "You're a beautiful dancer."

"Not as beautiful as Melinda." The anguish in Quinn's eyes was heartbreaking.

Jayne squeezed her hand. "Melinda was a beautiful dancer, too. But you each had unique talents."

Quinn unwound the strap from her hand and let it drop. "I didn't know she was moving to New York City." Her voice cracked over the last word. "If I had known, maybe I wouldn't have felt so jealous toward her. Her shadow is a pretty cold place to be."

Shifting in her chair, Jayne's knees brushed against Quinn's. *I have to play this carefully. Keep Quinn talking.* "I never gave you enough credit."

One of Quinn's eyebrows hitched slightly, either with surprise or disbelief.

"I've watched you in your classes lately. I mean *really* watched you. I needed to figure out our plans. You're great with the dancers. Your choreography is strong. I see you as an integral part of the studio's future."

Quinn's shoulders dropped and she quietly sobbed. "Thank you. That means a lot to me. I should have been confident in myself and not compared myself to Melinda. That was stupid, right?"

"You're not stupid. I think we all have a tendency to compare our-selves." Even as she spoke words of comfort, a tiny alarm bell in the back of her head was clamoring for attention.

Quinn dipped down and picked up her dance bag. "Thank you, Miss Jayne. I really do want to teach more classes. This is what I want to do. This is what I've always wanted to do. Teach here at Murphy's Dance Academy." She stood and lingered in the doorway.

"That's good to know." The small office space grew smaller as a mil-lion thoughts swirled in her mind.

A line of confusion creased Quinn's forehead. "Is there something else?"

"Um . . . yeah . . . Do you know anything about Melinda's accident?"

"What do you mean?" She glanced behind her at the door. Her escape. "I only know what everyone else knows." Her voice sounded strangled.

"*Were* you with Kyle between nine and ten the night of the accident?"

"Umm . . . How did you know?"

"Talk to me, Quinn. What happened?" Despite her trembling jaw, amazingly she didn't garble her words.

"The police officer said no one would know. I didn't want you to hate me." Quinn opened the door and stepped out on the porch.

"Wait. Wait. I don't hate you. *Please,* stay and talk to me."

Shaking her head, Quinn darted down the steps, flung her dance bag inside her car, and climbed in. Jayne chased her as far as the porch and stopped. In the distance, she saw lightning flash. A storm was coming. Her thrumming pulse drowned out the crickets hav-ing their last hurrah in the fields surrounding the studio. Suddenly aware of her vulnerability, she backed into the studio and locked the door.

Between Carol Anne's home life and Quinn's breakdown, Jayne could hardly focus on the paperwork at hand. She resigned herself to calling Danny as soon as she got home and his shift was over.

Sighing, she slid the last few checks for dance tuition into a binder, then bent over and pulled Melinda's tablet out of her tote. She opened the app for messages and stared at them again.

Why was Kyle so determined to hold on to Melinda when he had Quinn?

Why wouldn't Quinn stay and talk to me? Why didn't she admit to being with Kyle that night?

Resting her elbow on the desk, she dragged a hand over her hair. Possessive men defied logic.

Tapping her fingers on the edge of the tablet, she wondered what was *really* going on. *Someone* had sent the anonymous text luring Melinda out onto Lake Road.

Who would have the most to gain by Melinda's death? Kyle, a needy man-child who couldn't accept Melinda's rejection?

Miss Gigi, who was slowly stealing one student after another, destroying everything that Miss Natalie had built?

Or Carol Anne? Barbara's words about Carol Anne redecorating Melinda's room kept bouncing around in her head.

Leaning back in her chair, she stared out toward the empty lobby, recalling Quinn's outburst. *"If I had known, maybe I wouldn't have felt so jealous toward her. Her shadow is a pretty cold place to be."*

Staring at the last few texts on Melinda's tablet, Jayne tried something she'd tried a few times before with no luck. She picked up the handset on the phone and dialed the number that had sent the last text Melinda received right before she crashed.

Her breath sounded in her ears as the call went through, even though she didn't expect anyone to answer. The number was probably long disconnected.

Brrringgg . . . Brrringgg . . .

A few seconds later, Jayne heard a distant ring from inside the dance studio.

She froze and struggled to listen above the *whoosh-whoosh-whoosh* in her ears.

Holding the phone in a white-knuckled grip, she felt like her feet were glued to the floor. Releasing a slow, shaky breath, she lowered the phone to her side but didn't hang up. She carried the portable phone out to the foyer. The ringing was coming from the back dance studio.

Did one of the dancers leave behind her phone?

One of the teachers?

Was the ringing phone just a coincidence?

She glanced over her shoulder at the front door. Miss Quinn was long gone.

A kaleidoscope of all the episodes of *Dateline* and *48 Hours* swirled in her head, making her dizzy. It was much easier to make armchair judgments regarding all the victims who so foolishly went to investigate.

Run. Run. Run.

But the ringing drew her deeper into the studio. *Brrringgg . . . Brrringgg . . .*

Louder. Louder.

Into the student lounge.

Heart pulsing in her throat, she saw a cell phone dancing on the top of the student cubbies. With a trembling hand, she had reached out to pick it up when her eye caught the caller ID: *Murphy's Dance Academy.* She yanked her hand back and clutched it to her chest.

Run. Run. Run.

THIRTY

Get out! Get to the car! Call Danny!

Jayne spun around, ran toward the foyer, and froze. Carol Anne stood in the hallway, blocking her exit.

Pinpricks of terror blanketed her scalp.

"Carol Anne," she finally squeaked out. "I didn't realize you were here. How did you get in?"

"Back door." Carol Anne shrugged. "Your teachers really should lock up after opening the door for fresh air."

"I don't understand." Jayne struggled to keep her voice calm, her gaze drifting to the exit.

"I think you do." The lack of emotion on Carol Anne's face was more terrifying than if she had been pumped up with rage.

"That phone . . . that phone was yours?"

A slow smile split Carol Anne's face, and renewed dread skittered down Jayne's spine. "Things needed to end tonight. *Tonight.* I had no idea you'd dial the number, but when you did I thought it would be fun to put it on the shelf back there. Add a little drama." She narrowed her gaze. "You always liked crime drama, right?"

Carol Anne? Carol Anne sent the text to Melinda? Had she done more than that?

"Did you run Melinda off the road?"

She tilted her head, neither confirming nor denying.

"Carol Anne . . ." Jayne pressed.

Melinda's stepsister pressed her finger to her mouth. "Shhh . . . Sylvia"—she made a face as if her mother's name tasted bad in her mouth, as if she were in her own little world—"told me you were looking for me."

Jayne's thoughts drifted to Sylvia. The dishes piled in the sink. The funky smell. The full ashtray. The wet, popping sound of Sylvia's cough. The death—or sickness—of a parent could set a person off, especially a child who already lacked confidence. A person who was eager to please.

Eager to please.

"Yeah . . . um . . ." Jayne took a step backward and banged her heel against the wall. *Carol Anne must have snuck through the other studio to get past me to the front door.* Drawing in a deep breath, she tried to remain calm. "I wanted to check on you. See how you were doing."

Carol Anne cocked an eyebrow, a curious light in her eyes. "Yeah, I'm sure. In all these years, you've never checked on me."

"I'm your friend."

"No, you're not." She leaned forward, staring at her with dead eyes.

Jayne's brain scrambled to all the possible things she should say, and she knew another lie would be her undoing. "I stopped over because I felt bad. I know how hard it is to lose a sibling." She forced a sympathetic smile. "I thought maybe you'd want to get some coffee? How about now?" Something, anything to get to a public place. "We can chat."

"Stop." Carol Anne reached into her pocket and pulled out a gun; the action happened in slow motion. "Don't try to be nice to me now. You've always treated me like I was in the way. A nuisance. Yet you had the nerve to lie to my mom and claim we were friends. Give her your phone number and offer to help her. *I'm* the only one my mom has. *Me!* You're not going to take her away from me, too." The last remnants of composure shattered, revealing the crazed, angry girl beneath.

A bead of sweat rolled down Jayne's back. Her brain grew fuzzy. The walls closed in.

"You couldn't let things rest." Carol Anne waved the gun. "Come here."

Reluctantly, Jayne stepped closer. Carol Anne grabbed her by the ponytail and yanked her head back. "Take it easy." Jayne bit back her anger since she wasn't the one holding the gun.

Carol Anne forced her toward Studio A, pointed the gun at the newly replaced mirrors, and fired a shot. Shards of glass rained to the ground. "Just in case you doubted I had bullets."

At that moment, Jayne doubted everything.

Jayne braced herself against the wind and rain as Carol Anne forced her out the front door of the dance studio, down the steps, and behind the wheel of Carol Anne's car. A nondescript sedan.

Without car keys, Jayne considered jumping out and running, but based on the vacant look in Carol Anne's eye, she didn't doubt the girl would plug her in the back. *If* she actually knew how to aim. Jayne wasn't about to take any chances.

The thought of her mother having to face the loss of another child made Jayne a compliant kidnapping victim. All her police-academy training up to then kept her strangely calm.

Keep Carol Anne calm, too.

Jayne stared straight ahead and watched Carol Anne run around the car and climb into the passenger seat. "Put on your seat belt," Carol Anne said. "It's a stormy night. Would hate to get into an accident." A hint of glee edged her tone.

Jayne tugged on the belt and drew it across her. She glanced down at the gun pointed at her midsection, then up into Carol Anne's eyes. "Are you afraid I'll get hurt?"

Carol Anne scoffed and put her own seat belt on with one hand. Jayne's stomach pitched at the idea of her accidentally firing a shot.

"Do you know how to handle a gun?"

Carol Anne lifted the weapon and trained it on Jayne's forehead. Jayne stared at her coolly.

Carol Anne was crazy enough to kill. Jayne could see it in her eyes.

"I'll make you a deal," Jayne said. "Put the gun down. At least turn it away from me, and I'll drive wherever you want."

"You're not in a position to make deals." Her lips peeled away from her teeth in a surly smile. "You'll drive anywhere I want."

Carol Anne leaned over and jammed the key into the ignition. "Let's go."

"Move that gun away from me." Jayne stared at Carol Anne, a challenge.

Carol Anne's shoulder sagged and she rested the gun in her lap, but she still held it at the ready.

Jayne turned the key in the ignition and the car sputtered to life. Even before Carol Anne started giving her directions, she knew where they were headed.

It took seven minutes to reach Lake Road and another two minutes until they came upon the roadside memorial to Melinda. Teddy bears, deflated balloons, and a cross with "Melinda" written on it. Only a few candles, partially sheltered from the wind and rain, remained flickering.

"Park here."

The gravel crunched under the tires as Jayne pulled alongside the guardrail. The damaged rail where Melinda had gone into the lake below had been replaced.

Jayne stared at the dark waters. "Did you run Melinda off the road?" she asked again.

"Yeah, it didn't take much. She was such a cautious driver." Her tone suggested she considered that a character flaw. "I sent her a text. We'll never know if she actually looked at it, but I drove into her lane seconds later. She overcompensated." Carol Anne relayed the events as if from some YouTube video she had watched on repeat.

"Why?" Jayne cut a sideways glance to Carol Anne, who didn't take her eyes off the water.

"I never meant to kill her. I figured she'd break her leg. Her back. End her dancing career." Carol Anne grunted. "I was so *sick* of hearing how perfect Melinda was. Of her plans to take her dreams to New York City. I was so sick of it. *Melinda* this. *Melinda* that." Jayne glanced over as Carol Anne fisted her free hand and held the gun in the other. She lifted both and pummeled her head. Jayne winced, expecting a wild shot to fire.

"Please stop, Carol Anne," she pleaded. "You didn't mean to hurt Melinda. The police believe it was an accident. No one's investigating. Everything will be okay."

Carol Anne stilled and lowered her hands. Shifting in her seat, she gave Jayne a wild, wide-eyed stare. An image of Bette Davis from Jayne's first experience with horror movies flashed in her mind and sent terror zinging through her. *Everything is* not *going to be okay.*

"You won't let it rest. *You.*"

"No one has to know."

"Don't you see?" Carol Anne continued. "Melinda's death was fate. She was meant to die and I was meant to take her place."

When did trying to fit in—trying to relate—drift into the deranged? Into the I'd-do-anything-to-insert-myself-in-your-family territory?

Carol Anne's nose scrunched, disgusted. "*You* tried to take her place. *My* place. The money my dad gave you for the studio should have been mine. Oh, it felt so great to smash those mirrors . . . *I* should have comforted Victoria over a glass of wine . . . I was outside in the car, watching, waiting to be invited in . . ." She lifted the gun; her hand was trembling now. "You got in the way."

"I didn't mean . . ."

"Shut up," Carol Anne roared. "That idiot Kyle almost made it too easy. If anyone didn't believe Melinda died in an accident, all arrows pointed to him. I saw that creeper photo he took outside her bedroom window shortly after he sent it."

"How?" All the pieces were beginning to click into place.

"Melinda never logged out of anything. I was able to check her e-mail on the home computer at my dad's house. I'd read her e-mails, then mark them as unread. Can you believe she never opened that one? She never cared about anyone but herself." Carol Anne scratched her forehead roughly as if trying to scrape something out of her brain. "I hardly had to do anything. Kyle would have self-destructed on his own if left to his own devices. He tried to send it from a fake account, but I *knew* it was from him. Once you saw that photo taken from outside her room . . . it was meant to be. My dad would love me for once. When I knew you had the tablet, I was counting on you finding it. Pointing the finger at Kyle." She nervously tapped the barrel of the gun. "But Kyle's family loves him. They'd protect him at all costs. Soon, I realized the real problem was you. You and this stupid studio. My dad and Victoria would do anything for you. *You're family,*" she said, mimicking her father. "*You're* not family. *I'm* family."

Suddenly Carol Anne's shoulders slumped as she stared at the road-side memorial. "Look at that. Everyone still loves Melinda."

"You have people who love you." Even before she finished the sentence, Jayne knew she had made a misstep.

Carol Anne scoffed. "Yeah, right. I couldn't get my father to pay attention to me if I was the last person on earth." Her voice broke over a sob. "I'm his last surviving daughter and I'm still not good enough."

Jayne swallowed back her rioting emotions. "Your mom needs you."

"Sylvia doesn't need anything except her TV and her cigarettes." Something almost imperceptible changed in her tone.

"You've been so brave dealing with your mom's illness. She needs you." Jayne tried to sound encouraging. "And . . . *and* . . . look how you helped my mom. If it weren't for you, she might have wandered all night."

Carol Anne laughed dismissively. "You're a fool. Who do you think got your mom to leave that house the night of the Silver Alert?"

The walls of the car grew closer as Jayne's vision narrowed on Carol Anne's face.

"I made her leave the house, then I brought her back, as if I had found her. I knew she wouldn't remember. Or if she did, you'd all think she was confused."

"Why would you do that?" Jayne was unable to keep the disgust from her tone.

"I wanted you to like me." Carol Anne bowed her head a moment, then lifted it with renewed determination.

"We did—"

"I wanted you to *need* me. But instead, you invited Goth Girl into your home." Snot dripped from her nose. She dragged the back of her gun hand under it and sniffed loudly. "Why aren't I good enough?"

"You are. You are."

"Stop lying to me." Carol Anne pounded her fist on the ledge of the door.

Biting back a yelp, Jayne glanced up at Mr. King's house. A single light burned in his three-season sunroom. She wondered if he was engrossed in a best seller or if he was watching their car, if he'd call the police just as he had done the night of Melinda's accident. But Jayne feared that nothing about this looked suspicious.

Just a grieving friend stopping at a roadside memorial.

"What are you going to do now?" she finally worked up the nerve to ask.

"Get out."

Jayne pulled on the door handle, but Carol Anne dug her long fingers into her wrist. "Wait."

Jayne snapped her head around and gave her a *What?* look.

"Walk around to the guardrail. If you try to run, I'll shoot you."

Jayne was losing patience. "Do you think you'll hit me?" When a dark look fluttered in the depths of Carol Anne's eyes where true evil lurked, Jayne reconsidered her plucky response. "I'll do what you say. Please don't hurt me."

Jayne pushed open the door. The windswept rain pelted her face. She pushed her hair out of her eyes and squinted up at Mr. King's house. A man was outlined in the window. She wanted to wave to him, run to him, but she didn't want to put that poor man in danger.

Jayne's head yanked back. Hard. Carol Anne had her ponytail firmly in her grasp. "Hey, take it easy," Jayne barked. Her head ached as the roots separated from her scalp.

Still holding her by the hair, Carol Anne shoved Jayne around to the other side between the car and the guardrail, next to the memorial. She forced her to her knees in front of the white cross with the name "Melinda" scratched on it. The cool rain peppered her face, in contrast to the fiery heat welling up inside her.

Carol Anne bent over and whispered in her ear, "You made her not like me."

Jayne tried to shake her head but couldn't. "I didn't. I was only around more because we were neighbors."

"I was her *sister*." Carol Anne grew hysterical. "Her *sister*! You stole my family." Carol Anne yanked on Jayne's hair and made her stand up. "Let's see who poor Mommy and Daddy find to replace you."

Carol Anne's high-pitched voice made Jayne flinch. Made her realize the situation had escalated to the point of no return.

"All those sorry people can build you a memorial right here, next to Melinda's." Her voice grew low, sinister. "And maybe they'll build me one, too."

The sound of tires on wet pavement made Jayne's racing heart spike with hope, hope that was quickly dashed as the car raced past.

Jayne had to handle this herself. Her fate was always in her own hands, despite all the outside forces on her—the forces that dictated she do the right thing.

Adrenaline made her dizzy. Could she talk Carol Anne out of this? *Not likely.*

Jayne did the next best thing. She held her breath, pivoted around, and took Carol Anne's knee out. A horrible screech ripped from Carol Anne's throat as she dropped to her knees. The gun flew out of her hands and over the guardrail and disappeared into the darkness.

Jayne jumped on Carol Anne's back and wrenched her arm up behind her, shoving her cheek into the pavement. Her screams cut through Jayne as she tightened her grip and prayed for help.

THIRTY-ONE

Two men argued over a parking spot in the busy diner lot. Danny flipped up the collar of his coat against the rain and encouraged the men to take it down a notch or risk being brought in for disorderly conduct.

More like being idiots, but he couldn't charge anyone for that.

His cell phone chirped and he glanced down at it, mostly because he was tired of dealing with stupid people.

Danny squinted at the caller ID. It was a local number. He took the call. "Officer Danny Nolan."

"Yes, Officer, this is George King on Lake Road."

Danny couldn't deny his annoyance, amplified by the two men in front of him. His father was right. Some people liked the attention they got from calling the police and making nuisance reports.

"How can I help you, Mr. King?" Danny turned his back to the wind.

"There's a sedan parked down here by the makeshift memorial they made for that girl. You know what I'm talking about? Reminds me of the car I saw the night of the accident."

"The memorial? For Melinda Green? Yes."

"Well, two people got out of the car and one of them looked a lot like that lady friend you had out here with you. It's hard to tell from here, but it looked like they were having a bit of a tussle."

Danny's adrenaline spiked. "Is she there now?"

He heard a rustling over the phone. "The car's still there. I can't see your friend. Want me to go check?"

"No, stay where you are. I'll be right there."

Danny turned to the two men. "Get back in your cars and go home. If I get another report about either of you, I'm taking you in."

He could feel their eyes on him as he jogged to his vehicle. Turning on the lights and sirens, he peeled out toward Lake Road.

He found himself saying a prayer, something he hadn't done since he'd pleaded for Patrick to stay with him before his partner's blood and his life slipped out of him. But prayers hadn't done him any good that night.

Danny hadn't been there in time to save Patrick.

He had to get there in time to save Jayne.

"People love you, Carol Anne," Jayne said as she straddled the woman, praying help would arrive soon. Carol Anne fought against the weight on her back, but Jayne didn't dare get up for fear the woman in her adrenaline-soaked state would rage against her and send them both hurtling into the lake below.

Jayne bemoaned the fact that they were behind Carol Anne's car. From the road, there was a good chance that no one could see them.

After a few futile bucks, Carol Anne seemed to relax, but Jayne didn't dare loosen her grip, wrenching the woman's arm tighter behind her back.

"A person shouldn't have to work so hard to be loved." Carol Anne's words floated away on a gust of wind.

Jayne wiped her cheek across her shoulder, trying to get her hair out of her eyes. Her knees ached from where little bits of gravel dug into her flesh.

Dear Lord, please help me out here.

"Carol Anne, if I get up, are you going to relax? Stop fighting me?"

Carol Anne's body posture tensed momentarily, then relaxed, defeated.

"Carol Anne?" Jayne shouted above the wind and rain. She leaned closer and heard a quiet whimpering.

Holding Carol Anne's arm high and tight against her back, Jayne yanked Melinda's stepsister to her feet. As she pressed the woman against the car, she heard a siren in the distance. Squinting down the street, she saw the lights of a patrol car approaching fast.

Thank you, Lord.

"Stay put," Jayne said to Carol Anne in case she got any ideas.

It seemed like an eternity for the patrol car to stop and the door to open. Jayne let out a long breath when Danny emerged. With his hand hovering near his duty belt, he ran over to her. "You okay?"

"I am now."

Carol Anne remained slumped against the hood of the car.

Danny slid in next to Jayne and handcuffed Carol Anne, then forced her to straighten. Holding her tightly by the elbow, he glanced at Jayne. "What happened?"

"She kidnapped me at gunpoint. She was the one who lured Melinda down here and ran her off the road."

Carol Anne hung her head and said nothing.

As Danny led Carol Anne to the back of his patrol car, Jayne glanced up at the house on the hill. George King lifted his hand and waved it high over his head. Jayne lifted hers in return, now understanding how Danny had gotten here so quickly.

"Come on." Danny guided her with a solid hand to the small of her back. "Let's get you out of this weather. I'll send someone to get the car."

After securing Carol Anne into the back of his patrol car, he walked Jayne around to the front passenger side. He leaned in to open the door when Jayne flung her arms around him and buried her face into his warm neck. "Thank you."

"I'd never let anything happen to you." Leaning back and looking into her eyes, he swept a wet strand of hair from her face. Planting a kiss on her forehead, he lingered for a long moment. "Let's get you warmed up."

Jayne smiled and climbed into the car. Behind her, Carol Anne quietly wept. Staring past her own wet-dog reflection, Jayne took in the well-tended memorial to her dear friend. Someday soon, Melinda's friends would grow tired of remembering. Tired of the sadness. Yet years from now, when they traveled this road with their spouses—maybe with their children—they'd remember their friend who had crashed through the guardrail. It was up to Jayne to let them know the truth. Melinda hadn't died because she was a foolish girl who'd decided to text and drive. Or because the weather and an unfamiliar road had been a fatal combination.

No, Melinda had been run off the road by a jealous stepsister.

There'd be no explaining that.

THIRTY-TWO

"Thanks for coming." Jayne slipped past Danny while he held the heavy wood door open for her. "I know church's not exactly your thing."

"Maybe it should be."

"That surprises me." Jayne turned around to face him. Members of her family lingered inside the church vestibule talking to Father John, who had offered the day's Mass in memory of Patrick. A few days had passed since Carol Anne's arrest, and law enforcement and lawyers were trying to sort it all out. Carol Anne's need to vent was definitely helping the prosecution.

"Should it be a surprise?" Danny gave her a shy smile. "I've watched you, over these past few weeks, deal with one issue after another with grace and determination."

"Are you serious? I've been flying by the seat of my pants."

The warmth in Danny's brown eyes filled a space in her heart that had been empty—neglected—for a long time now. "That's how you might have felt, but that's not how it looked. I'm beginning to think I need to start going to church. Practice my faith."

Jayne raised an eyebrow. "You know what they say about practice." She laughed, then grew serious. "I think it's easy to practice your faith when everything is going great. It's another thing when your world is falling apart. I realized that when my father died. I was so mad at God. My mom reminded me to look to my faith. It took a little time—and I still have to work at it—but because of it, I've kept my sanity."

"I could use a little bit of sanity."

The church door swung open, and Miss Quinn appeared with her jacket in her hands and a meek smile on her face.

"Quinn," Jayne said. Her hand flew to her cross pendant. "How are you?"

"Fine." She shifted her jacket from one hand to the other. "I'm fine." Her eyes flicked to Danny, then back to Jayne. "We haven't had a chance to talk since . . . since the other night. I'm so sorry I didn't wait for you. If I had been there, maybe Carol Anne wouldn't have—"

"It's not your fault. Don't give it another thought." Jayne smiled, trying to telegraph her sincerity. "But I *am* sorry how we left things."

"Me, too." Quinn sidestepped the door as voices from inside grew louder. "I saw the announcement in the bulletin for the Mass for your brother. I wanted to show my support. You and your mom mean the world to me."

"You mean a lot to us, too, Quinn."

Quinn fumbled with her jacket before growing still. "I ran out the other night because I was ashamed and I didn't know what to say. I'm not seeing Kyle anymore." She winced, as if she couldn't believe that she ever had. "I deserve better."

"Yes. Yes, you do. Please, don't worry about all this other stuff. We've all been under a lot of stress." Jayne reached out and touched Quinn's arm. "We love having you at the studio and so do the girls."

"Thank you. That means so much to me." Drawing her shoulders up, Quinn descended the two steps with a lightness that had been missing earlier. She flicked her hand as a good-bye and strode off toward the parking lot.

Jayne reached out with the intention of simply squeezing Danny's hand for reassurance, but he captured it and laced her fingers with his. Her gaze traveled down the length of his arm to their joined hands, then back up to his face. Her cheeks heated, despite the cool autumn day.

Finn came through the door first, holding Miss Natalie's arm. He smiled down at his little sister. "I'll see that Mom gets home. Why don't you drive with Danny?"

"Um, okay." She paused, cleared her throat, and tried again, minus the high-pitched squeak. "We'll stop and pick up the cake. See you at the house." Today would have been Patrick's twenty-eighth birthday.

Jayne and Danny walked hand in hand down the steps of the church and across the cement that served as a gathering area. Little feet sounded behind them and Jayne spun around. Her niece, Ava, bolted toward her with open arms. Jayne let go of Danny's hand, then crouched down to pull Ava into an embrace.

"Hey there, peanut. You need to wait up for your mom."

Ava wrapped her arms around Jayne's neck and squeezed. Jayne's heart filled with love. Cara ran over and held out her hand. "Come on, Ava. We'll see Aunt Jayne at the house."

"You're coming?" Inexplicable tears filled Jayne's eyes.

Cara smiled and nodded. "Ava loves her aunt and uncles." She glanced over her shoulder. "We'll drive over with Uncle Sean."

Jayne watched Sean place his hand on the small of Cara's back and lead them to his car. She leaned in close to Danny. "Do you think?"

Danny nudged Jayne toward his car. "It wouldn't be a bad thing."

"I know, but wouldn't it be weird? Cara's Patrick's widow."

"And I'm Patrick's best friend."

Jayne paused before climbing into her side of the car. Once they were both inside, she stretched across the console and cupped Danny's cheek. Before she had a chance to say anything, he leaned over and kissed her on the lips. Soft. Warm. Gentle. Her entire world shrank into that one moment.

Jayne wrapped her hands around his neck and pulled him closer—until the honking of a horn pulled them apart. They both glanced over to see Finn, Melissa, and Miss Natalie driving slowly past.

Smiling, she tilted her head against Danny's shoulder, reveling in the feel of his strong arms wrapped around her. She'd never hear the end of this one. But it was worth it. Oh, so worth it.

Jayne cut the last of the kimmelweck rolls and had set them out on a tray on the large kitchen table when her cell phone buzzed on the counter. She was going to ignore it, until she noticed Ricky's caller ID.

"Hello?"

"Hi, Jayne, it's Ricky. I'm at my desk doing some research on burner phones"—he rushed right into his spiel—"and there are a few ways—"

"Hold up," Jayne cut in, struggling to hear over the chatter of her family. "We figured out who owned the phone."

"Oh." Ricky's dejected tone floated across the line on that single word.

"I do appreciate your getting back to me, though."

"I was tied up with a few projects or I would have got back to you sooner."

"Really, it's no problem." She turned her back to her family in order to hear better. "Would you mind if I called you in the future if I had other tech questions?"

"Um, yeah, sure . . . Okay, well . . . Sounds kinda loud over there. I'll let you go."

"My family is over. And Ricky . . . thanks a lot."

"No problem."

Jayne ended the call and tossed her phone down. "Dinner's ready."

"Where should I put the au jus?" Danny carried over the gravy boat filled with juice from the roast beef.

Jayne leaned in close so no one else would overhear. "I could get used to having you around." A smile curved the corners of her mouth as she glanced over at Finn reclining in the family room, taking it easy after Mass. Some traditions were hard to change.

"What do we have here?" Sean strolled in, clapped Danny's shoulder, and gave Jayne a knowing smile.

She gestured toward him with her chin. "How about you?" Cara helped Ava off with her shoes at the front door. "You told me Cara was dating someone. It was *you*. You were feeling me out."

"Would it be so bad?"

Jayne shook her head and kissed her brother's cheek. "Not at all." She squeezed his hand. "Love you, Big Brother."

"I love you, too." Sean glanced over his shoulder at his brother and mother in the other room. "I know we don't say it enough, but we really appreciate everything you do for Mom. And for us." He dragged a hand over his hair. "I'm going to try to be better. Help you out more."

"Gee, if this is Cara's influence? Go, Cara."

"I guess it took a lot of things to open my eyes." Sean playfully nudged his little sister's arm.

"Uncle Sean, can we go out on the swing set?" Ava ran into the room and tugged on his shirt.

Sean spun around. "We need to wash up and have dinner first." He scooped up Patrick's daughter and planted a kiss on her cheek. "Looks like we got here just in time for dinner. I hope Grammy made her potato salad."

"Of course I did." Miss Natalie looked up from pouring pretzels into a basket. She walked over and kissed her granddaughter's cheek.

"Hi, sweetie. You look so pretty." Ava reached out and wrapped her arms around Grammy's neck. Holding her granddaughter tight, Natalie asked, "Is Hannah stopping by today?"

"I invited her." Jayne's mother loved Hannah's company, and the young woman seemed to genuinely enjoy spending time there.

"Good, good. I was teaching her how to knit."

Only her mother could get someone Jayne had once referred to as Goth Girl to pick up knitting needles. And it did Jayne's heart good to know her mother had resumed one of her old hobbies, recently fallen by the wayside. Jayne suspected there was a lot of teaching going on both ways, based on the knitting magazines she found on the coffee table.

Jayne took a step back and scanned all the faces, and a contentedness expanded inside the once-hollow part of her heart. She was truly blessed.

The phone rang, the sound barely audible above the happy chatter that filled the room. Jayne considered letting the call go to voice mail—who called the landline anyway?—when something compelled her to answer it. Thankfully, her brother had purchased a portable phone for the kitchen, the first step in modernizing the dated space.

"Hello." She pressed the phone to her ear and covered her other ear to hear above the noise.

"Jayne?" The woman's soft voice sounded familiar, but she couldn't place it.

"Hold on, please." Jayne went into the formal living room at the front of the house, since the voices had now reached an impossible-to-hear-anyone-on-the-phone decibel level.

"Yes, this is Jayne." She plopped down on the couch and rubbed her forehead.

"Hello, this is Tiffany. Tiffany Wentworth." She paused a minute, then added, "Paige's mom."

"Yes, yes . . ." Jayne's brain scrambled to put all the pieces together. Of course she knew who Tiffany Wentworth was; Jayne just struggled to understand why she had called her at home on a Sunday. "How are you, Mrs. Wentworth?"

"Fine, fine." A ragged breath sounded across the line. "Not really. I need to ask you something. Well, two things . . ."

Jayne had never heard Mrs. Wentworth be so wishy-washy. She had always been a fierce advocate for her daughter. Determined. Decisive.

The front doorbell rang, and Jayne glanced toward the kitchen. No one was going to get that. "I'm sorry, Mrs. Wentworth, can you hold on two seconds?"

"Of course." Her voice sounded high pitched.

Pressing the phone to her chest, Jayne strode to the front door, fully expecting to tell an unwanted solicitor she wasn't in the market for new windows or a new religion.

She opened the door and found Hannah standing there dressed in blue jeans and a pretty pink T-shirt. A hand-knit purple infinity scarf capped the ensemble. Based on Hannah's smirk, Jayne had failed miserably at hiding her surprise. She opened her mouth to comment on how pretty—how un-Goth-like—Hannah looked when her young guest held up her hand, silencing her.

"Miss Natalie made it for me. It would have been rude not to wear it." Her eyes glistened behind black, blunt-cut bangs.

"Of course, you wouldn't want to disappoint Miss Natalie."

"Nope."

"The color is pretty on you."

Hannah fingered the scarf shyly and smiled. "Thanks."

Pointing at the phone, Jayne whispered, "I have to take this. Go on in. I'll be there shortly."

Jayne watched Hannah join her family and then returned to the call. "I'm sorry, Mrs. Wentworth. How can I help you?"

"Paige is miserable at Miss Gigi's studio," Mrs. Wentworth said in a rush, as if she had been holding her breath. "Would it be too late for her to come back to Murphy's Dance Academy? She'll work hard. Catch up. It's asking a lot, but she misses her friends. I overlooked that one important component. I lost sight of that."

Drumming her fingers on her thighs to temper her excitement, she paced in front of the living-room window. "Paige is a hard worker. We'd love to have her back."

"Oh, thank you. She'll be so happy. She was mad at me when I pulled her out of your studio. I let my competitive side get the best of me, but I know Miss Natalie runs a top-notch studio . . . Well, I'll stop rambling."

"Jayne, you coming in for dinner?" Finn called from the kitchen. He and Melissa were probably in a hurry to go house hunting that afternoon. Their wedding date was drawing closer.

Covering the mouthpiece of the phone, Jayne hollered, "Give me a minute."

"Oh, you're busy, I'll let you go," Mrs. Wentworth said apologetically.

"No, please, is there something else?" Jayne held her breath, fearing Mrs. Wentworth would immediately revert to her old self and request that her daughter be given the key roles in the dances she had abandoned a few weeks earlier.

Mrs. Wentworth cleared her throat. "I heard you were the reason Carol Anne was arrested for Melinda's death."

"Well . . ." Jayne immediately grew uncomfortable. She didn't want the darkness of recent events to overshadow the brightness of today.

"Paige told me you were thinking about doing some PI work."

"She misunderstood. I was telling her to follow her dreams."

"Oh, I thought with your background . . . well . . . That's too bad, because I need some help."

"With . . ." Jayne stopped pacing and lowered herself onto the edge of the couch.

"My husband . . . Harrison is having an affair, and I need proof before I file for divorce. Otherwise, with our prenup, Paige and I will be left with nothing. Paige will have to quit dance."

Jayne rubbed her free hand up and down her arm.

"There are PIs in Tranquility. Experienced ones."

"Harrison is a well-respected lawyer. He's utilized most of those PIs. I can't risk word getting back to him."

Jayne swallowed hard. "Can I think about it?"

"Oh, would you?" Hope sounded across the line. "I would really appreciate it."

"Can I get back to you in a few days?"

"Yes, please. Thank you. And Jayne, Paige will be thrilled to be back at your dance studio."

"We'll be thrilled to have her."

Jayne pressed "End" and turned around. Danny stood in the doorway, resting a shoulder against the wall and holding the box for a Monopoly game. With a gleam in his eye, he pushed off the wall and said, "I wasn't eavesdropping. Just got here." He tilted his head, studying her, then gestured to the box in his hand. "I saw this on the shelf in the family room. Maybe after dinner, we could play that game you never got to play."

Jayne stood, took the game box out of his hand, and placed it on the coffee table. "You remembered."

He raised his chin, indicating it was no big deal. "I call the race car."

She glanced from his solid jawline to the box. A million memories from her childhood flooded her. "I'll take the Scottie dog." Closing the distance between them, she placed the palm of her hand on his solid chest. A tingling awareness coiled deep inside. "You're not going to run off after I get the bank set up, are you?" She leaned closer and pressed a kiss to his lips. A challenge.

He slipped his hand around her back and tugged her closer, the move so sudden it made her gasp. He smiled, his lips against hers. "I'm not going anywhere."

"Good." Jayne slid her hand around his neck and whispered in his ear, "Because I'm going to whip you at Monopoly."

She kissed him again, this time lingering a bit before pulling away and patting his cheek playfully. "I think we're going to have fun." Raising her eyebrows, she spun around and strolled toward the kitchen. The heat of Danny's gaze bore into her backside.

Danny partially laughed, partially groaned. "Me, too, Baby Jayne. Me, too."

ACKNOWLEDGMENTS

A special thanks to Scott, my biggest supporter. I truly appreciate that you roll out of bed every morning at the crack of dawn to head to the office so that I can roll out of bed, grab my laptop, and be at mine. Love you, forever and always.

And to Scotty, Alex, Kelsey, and Leah, thanks for believing Mom actually works for a living, when some days you find me in my office streaming Netflix or Amazon Prime. It's all in the name of inspiration, I promise. And I really can do two things at once. I'm raising four of you, aren't I? Love and kisses.

Thank you to my super agent, Nalini Akolekar, for encouraging me to submit to Waterfall Press. You gave me the encouragement I needed to finally submit this "dance-book idea" that had been bouncing around my brain for years.

Thank you to my editor, Erin Mooney, for taking a chance on the book of my heart. And to Colleen Wagner for her keen editorial insight. This book is much stronger because of the strong editorial staff at Waterfall.

Thanks to all my dance-mom friends, former and current. I don't want to list you by name for fear I'll forget to mention someone. You know who you are. You make dance competitions and recitals so much fun. I'm blessed to call you friends, and our daughters are also blessed to have each other. As far as the stereotypical "dance mom" as perpetuated on reality TV, I'm happy to say I've never encountered one, but what fun would fiction be without a villain or two? All characters in this book are fictional and products of my imagination. Any resemblance to dance moms in my real life is purely coincidental. I swear.

Thanks to all the dance teachers my daughters have had over the years. Through your dedication, talent, and love of dance, you have given my daughters the gifts of grace, poise, and confidence. The ability to perform onstage with confidence is awe inspiring to this writer who makes her living behind a laptop. And thank you to Miss Erin Alongi, who advised me on the opening dance scene. Any errors I've made are my own.

Thanks to Nichole C., "Richie Hollywood," Tracy A., and the law-enforcement experts at SilverHartWriters.com, for answering my random law-enforcement questions. Any errors I've made are my own.

A special thank you to Margie Lawson, whose online workshops and in-person Immersion Master Class have allowed me to take my writing to the next level. (Waving to my wonderful writing friends from Atlanta 2013 Immersion Master Class.)

To my sister, Annie St. George, who's willing to answer the most random questions, including the types of caskets on the market. Love you.

Thanks to all my writing friends: Rachel Dylan, Jessica Topper, Amanda Usen, Barb Hughes, and Stephanie Haefner, just to name a few. Thanks for listening to me complain. Encouraging me. Making writing conferences *so* much fun. And most of all, thanks for being you. Only another writer can truly understand this crazy business.

I know firsthand the ravages of Alzheimer's disease and the toll it takes on both the patient and their caregivers. Miss Natalie, a character in *Pointe and Shoot*, is in the beginning to mid stages of this horrible disease. I didn't want to portray Miss Natalie as a burden to bear, but rather as an integral part of a loving family who comes together to do what it takes to ensure the care and safety of their much-loved mom. I hope I have achieved that. To all the caregivers out there, I wish you patience, peace, and comfort. And I pray that a cure is found soon.

I felt there were several "God winks" when it came to the writing and sale of this book. For that, I thank my big sister, Lisa, who always looked out for me. Her short life has been a constant reminder that nothing is promised. So live well, laugh often, and love much.